DEATH AT THE BLACK BULL

"Move over, Walt Longmire. There's a new sheriff in town. Virgil Dalton is the kind of character that comes along maybe once a decade—a classic Western hero and so much more. When you're done with Frank Hayes' stellar debut, *Death at the Black Bull*, you'll smell the sagebrush in the air and have to clean the dust off your boots. An absolute must-read for fans of Craig Johnson and Tony Hillerman."

—Reed Farrel Coleman,
Shamus Award–winning author of *The Hollow Girl*

"This is one of the most impressive debut crime novels I've ever read. There's such depth and humanity in the characters, such tension in the story itself, and the sense of place is as good as it gets. I know I'll be reading every book in this series!"

—Steve Hamilton,
Edgar® Award–winning author of *Let It Burn*

DEATH AT THE BLACK BULL

FRANK HAYES

BERKLEY PRIME CRIME, NEW YORK

THE BERKLEY PUBLISHING GROUP
Published by the Penguin Group
Penguin Group (USA) LLC
375 Hudson Street, New York, New York 10014

USA • Canada • UK • Ireland • Australia • New Zealand • India • South Africa • China

penguin.com

A Penguin Random House Company

This book is an original publication of The Berkley Publishing Group.

Berkley Prime Crime Books are published by The Berkley Publishing Group.
BERKLEY® PRIME CRIME and the PRIME CRIME logo are trademarks of
Penguin Group (USA) LLC.

Library of Congress Cataloging-in-Publication Data

Hayes, Frank, 1940–
Death at the Black Bull / Frank Hayes.—Berkley Prime Crime trade paperback edition.
    pages cm.—(A Sheriff Virgil Dalton mystery)
    ISBN 978-0-425-27429-3 (paperback)
    1. Truck drivers—Crimes against—Fiction.   2. Sheriffs—Fiction.
3. Murder—Investigation—Fiction.   4. Southwestern States—Fiction.   I. Title.
    PS3608.A924D43 2014
    813'.6—dc23
    2014021485

PUBLISHING HISTORY
Berkley Prime Crime trade paperback edition / October 2014

PRINTED IN THE UNITED STATES OF AMERICA

10   9   8   7   6   5   4   3   2   1

Interior text design by Tiffany Estreicher.

To my family, without whom any success would be meaningless,
but especially to my wife, who one day on a beach on Cape Cod gave me
a spiral notebook, a pen, and a note on the first page,
which set me on a path that brought me to this place. I love you all.

ACKNOWLEDGMENTS

To all the people who helped me find my way. From Corlies (Cork) Smith to Bill Appel and everyone in between . . . Kevin, Marlane, Verneece, Douglas, and all the others who encouraged and criticized in a good way. Most of all Bill Keller and Steve Hamilton who have been rock solid in pushing me toward my final goal.

1

He sat on the tail of the old pickup, watching the dark as it crowded the western sky. Red flares, tinted with gold, like a thousand times before. Over the years, a rugged trail had been worn into the hill where his truck was perched. Scrubland stretched in every direction. Below him, partly hidden by the old cottonwood tree, rested the clapboard house where he had spent most of his life. In the dim light he didn't have to acknowledge the peeling of the paint or the slight sag in the middle of the roof. Beyond the house stood the two barns, same vintage as the house.

The barns formed a right angle and the far sides of a large corral. A horse named Jack stood quietly alongside the fence, occasionally swishing his tail to chase away a nighttime fly or to stir the warm night air. His tail was the only movement in the landscape. No leaf moved. No breeze blew. The earth held its breath in expectation. Virgil felt this as he sat on the dented bed of the truck. He was not a man to waste time on idle thought, or to muse on what might have been, but he did have an innate sense of premonition. When he had ignored such thoughts, or passed them off as coincidence, they had always come back to haunt him, so he had learned to live with them. Never comfortably. Always reluctantly.

He looked past the barns to the long driveway twisting through the cottonwoods to the county road. With the sun going down, the shadows had crept over the land. A first star appeared in the night sky. He shifted his weight, making the tailgate swing and hit the frame of the truck with a metallic clank. An owl hooted. Virgil half smiled at the rebuke.

"Point taken," he said. "Much better without the noise."

He turned back and this time he could see a pair of headlights a good mile out on the road.

"Looks like company." He hopped off the truck. By the time the car turned into the driveway he was leaning against the corral fence. Jack had joined him.

The SUV with the red dome light pulled to a stop alongside the pickup. When the door opened, the man who stepped out was a good twenty years younger than Virgil and wearing a uniform. He glanced around, then crossed the driveway. Virgil still leaned against the fence. Jack was nibbling at his sleeve.

"Don't you feed that horse?"

"More than I feed myself, but it's never enough."

"Yeah, I guess." The man in the uniform smiled. "Nice night." He looked toward the last of the light on the horizon.

"I guess you didn't drive all the way out here to tell me something I already know. What's going on, Jimmy?"

"Well, Sheriff . . ." The deputy hesitated. "We got a call about Buddy Hinton. Charlie's boy. Seems he's gone missing."

"How long?"

"How long?" Jimmy repeated.

"How long has he been missing? Who reported it? When? Fill in the gaps, Jimmy."

"Charlie called it in. It seems he went out last night after supper. Said he was going to meet up for a coupla beers with Wade and some of the boys. Charlie figured maybe Bud got a snootful and that's why he never made it back home. But when he didn't show today, Mrs. Hinton started prodding him, so he called it in."

"Okay, we'll give him till morning. If there's no sign, we'll give it a look."

Jimmy nodded in response. Virgil stepped away from the fence. Jack gave a soft nicker.

"Okay, hang on," Virgil said. "I ain't forgot."

He walked over to the nearest barn door and stepped inside. He returned with a couple of flakes of hay and tossed them over the corral fence. They landed on the far side of the water trough. Jack gave a little louder call and moved toward the hay.

"C'mon, Jimmy. I'll buy you some supper before you go back to work. Don't expect much. Just leftover meat loaf."

"Sheriff, you don't have to do that. I can get some chili at Margie's place."

"And if you do, you'll be stinking up the office all night. Least the meat loaf ain't toxic. C'mon." Virgil walked across the driveway with Jimmy following. Small clouds of dust stirred at their feet.

"Sure could use some rain," Jimmy said.

"Couldn't hurt."

At the door, Virgil locked a boot in the boot pull then did the same with the other. He paired them together just inside the front door. Jimmy started to do the same.

"Don't bother. I'm in for the night. You got miles to go before you sleep."

He looked to see if Jimmy got the reference. Apparently he didn't.

"It might not have the same impact as Margie's chili but it's a lot cheaper," Virgil said as Jimmy was wiping his plate with a piece of bread. "By the way, did you check on whether or not Buddy hooked up with Wade and the boys?"

"Yes, I surely did, Sheriff. Follow up. I try to remember all the things you tell me."

"That's good, Jimmy." Virgil looked on as Jimmy finished wiping his plate.

"That sure was good meat loaf." Jimmy was looking at the baking dish sitting on top of the stove.

"Sorry, Jimmy. That's all there is. Wasn't expecting company. Here, have this last piece of cake with your coffee. Maybe that'll hold you for an hour or two. So . . ."

"So what, Sheriff?"

"What did you find out about Buddy?"

"Oh, that. Yes, sir. He did meet up. According to Wade, he left them about one or two in the a.m."

"Did Wade say if he was going home?"

Jimmy paused as he took a bite out of the cake. "No. He didn't say nothing about that."

"It might have been a good question to ask him, Jimmy."

"Yeah. I guess maybe you're right. Well, maybe tomorrow morning if Buddy hasn't shown up you should ask him about that, Sheriff."

Virgil looked at Jimmy shoving the last piece of cake in his mouth and smiled. Then he stood up.

"Good idea, Jimmy. I'll have to remember that. You'd better get back to town now before any other folks go missing."

"Yes, sir." Jimmy stood to go. Then he hesitated.

"What is it, Officer?"

Jimmy smiled. Virgil knew Jimmy liked the title.

"There was something else. Oh, yes. A call from Hayward Ranch. They want you to come out. I think Mrs. Hayward wants to see you."

"Okay, Jimmy. I'll take care of it."

Virgil stood on the porch and watched as the patrol car went down the driveway, a cloud of dust trailing its path. When it was out of sight, he looked into the night. A few clouds still showed on the horizon but he didn't think they held much promise. The air was dry. A bare hush of a breeze stirred a few leaves on the cottonwood. A couple of peepers could be heard from the creek on the other side of the barn. The broken flight of a few bats from the barn could be made out, but that was pretty much it. He was alone. He pulled up the chair by the wall outside the front door. He sat so that he could rest his stocking feet on the porch railing, the chair tilted at a slight angle.

He thought of Jimmy. He had been one of those kids that nobody outside of his family wanted, least of all to be hired as a deputy. Virgil was not unaware of Jimmy's limitations, but he liked him. Always had. His father was a drunk who died young. His mother tried hard, but was one of those people for whom life was too much. So Jimmy pretty much raised himself. From where Virgil stood, he hadn't done a half-bad job. He didn't end up into drugs or trouble when a lot of kids who had a lot more did. The turning point seemed to be when Virgil picked him up off the ground after some kids beat him up in back of Talbot's hardware store. From then on it seemed like Jimmy was always around. Virgil would occasionally buy him a taco or give him a ride when he saw him walking along the road, usually on his way to the trailer he shared with his mother and younger sister down by the river. He started coming into the office and Virgil began to give him odd jobs. Rosie, the dispatcher, started giving him clothes that her kids had outgrown. Being his family had become a joint project. Even Dave, Rosie's husband and Virgil's longtime deputy, warmed to Jimmy. By the time it became necessary to take on another deputy Virgil had made his mind up. When the mayor and council balked at the idea, he was ready. He had long since come to the conclusion that Jimmy was not simpleminded or a half-wit like many described him. Virgil knew Jimmy just hadn't been exposed to what most kids get growing up in a normal family environment. So when he took him on two years ago, he knew it was going to be a work in progress.

As he sat mulling over Jimmy's report, he thought about Buddy Hinton, Wade Travis, and the rest of the boys. They were not unknown to him in his official capacity, and Virgil had a gut feeling where this was going to lead. Which led him back to Hayward Ranch and the summons from Audrey Hayward. He sat in the dark a long time, trying to enjoy the night and the quiet, but he was uneasy about what the morning light would bring.

2

The sun rose from the earth in white heat. Virgil squinted in its light even though it was not yet seven. He stood on the porch, his second cup of coffee in his hand, contemplating his immediate future. A movement caught his eye. He saw the slight figure of a man emerge from one of the barns. He knew Cesar had started his day even earlier than he had. While he sipped his black coffee, he watched the man's quiet movements as he went in and out of the paired barns. At last he emerged, carrying a small basket. Virgil watched and waited.

"Doesn't look like a full basket."

"Too hot . . ." Virgil stepped aside as the man walked past, then followed him into the kitchen, swallowing the remnants of his coffee. Cesar went directly to the refrigerator. After he placed five or six eggs in a bowl on a shelf inside, he closed the door, placed the basket on the counter, and poured the last of the coffee in a mug. Virgil watched as he took his first swallow.

"I'm probably gone all day. Don't bother checking the stock

tanks. When I get home this evening, I'll do it. Jack could use the exercise. It'll be cooler then."

Cesar didn't reply.

"Buddy Hinton's gone missing . . . I gotta look into it."

Again Cesar said nothing.

"You want to tell me anything?" He looked at the man he had known all his life. The dark, weathered face showed little change; only in the black eyes was there a hint.

"Maybe, a girl . . . a picker at Hayward Ranch. There's a bunch there already getting things ready and helping with the cattle even though harvest is a long way off . . ."

"Okay . . . I'll check." Virgil stood and walked toward the door. "See you tonight. Take it easy today, old man."

"Old man," Cesar said.

Virgil half smiled and stepped out onto the porch. He got into his car. Jack and three other horses galloped across the field that bordered the county road, heading for the barn as Virgil drove by. It was a scene he'd witnessed as long as he could remember, but it never failed to get his blood racing. He hit the horn, then swerved around a tractor pulling a hay wagon.

The ride into Hayward took less than fifteen minutes. Although it was the county seat, there wasn't a lot to recommend it. The population had hung in for the last decade at about ten thousand. The nonlegals didn't count in that figure, though everyone knew that without them there would be a lot less reason for the majority of the ten thousand to stay. It was the kind of town where a dog could take a nap in the middle of Main Street during the day with little fear of becoming a traffic casualty. Virgil drove around the back and parked in the dirt lot.

"Coffee's got a few more minutes, Virgil." Rosie was not the kind to waste time on formality. She and Dave had been with Virgil ever since he became sheriff. Virgil looked at the clock hanging on the wall over her head. It was just eight thirty.

"Hope you're not looking for overtime, coming in this early."

"As if," Rosie said. "By the way, did Jimmy catch up with you last night?"

"Yes. He told me about Buddy. I'm going to look into it today if he hasn't shown up."

"Well he hasn't. Viola called about ten minutes before you got in. She said they haven't seen him. He never came home. Charlie's been out looking. No trace of him or his pickup. Maybe you should go look for sign."

"Look for sign?"

"Well, I always heard you people could track a duck across water."

"Yeah . . . well that's only if you're FBI."

"FBI?"

"Full-Blooded Indian," he said. "Remember, I'm only a half-breed."

"Does that mean you're only right half the time?"

"Hey, don't forget, you're talking to the guy who can lock you up and throw away the key."

"Yeah. I know. Next, you'll be taking out the handcuffs. You into that bondage thing, Virgil?"

"Not with a married woman, especially one that's got a husband that can shoot like yours. By the way, to get professional for a minute . . . Where is Dave?"

"He slept over last night at the substation. Alex was going to meet him this morning and they were going to look into that report of cattle gone missing over near Redbud."

"Cattle rustling. Guess the Old West is alive and well."

"In this economy, it's probably just somebody trying to cut down on their meat bill."

"You may be right, but we still can't ignore it. Tell Dave if it's like that to call me before he does anything. We don't want some poor guy going to jail for trying to put meat on the table for his kids. You can get me on the radio. I'm heading over to talk to Wade Travis to see if he can point me in the direction Buddy might have gone. Then I'll be going to Hayward Ranch."

He gave a slight wave and started for the door.

"Virgil!" Rosie called.

He stopped with his hand on the knob.

"Be careful," she said. "I got kind of a funny feeling about this."

Virgil nodded then went out the door.

Wade Travis was a little rough around the edges, but he was good at what he did. He was the go-to guy for any kind of automotive repairs in Hayward. He had been trying to put together a NASCAR team, and they'd even had some local success, but the problem was his boys were long on wanting and short on reliable.

Virgil pulled into the station. He got out and filled up his tank, all the while looking for Wade. A teenager in the office pointed him in the right direction. Around back he saw a car up on ramps with a couple of legs protruding from underneath the front end.

"Wade, you got a minute?"

Wade, on a dolly, rolled out from under the car. "Well, if it ain't the law. How did you know it was me under there?"

"I'm a good detective. Besides, the rattler that got you a couple years back left two pretty nice identifying marks on that left leg. It'll help them figure out who you are if they ever find you tangled up in one of those cars after you hit the wall doing a hundred forty."

"A hundred forty? Hell, that's only second gear. So I guess I owe this visit to Buddy."

Virgil nodded.

"Don't know what I can tell you, Sheriff. We got to drinking a little tequila, lost track of time. Buddy went outside . . . maybe to howl at the moon or to work up the courage to swallow the worm. But he never did come back."

"And you didn't look for him?"

"To tell the honest-to-God truth, the shape I was in I'd a probably gone missing myself if I was to go lookin' for Buddy. Besides, he ain't exactly a juvenile."

"Let's try another tack. Do you have any idea where he might have gone?"

Wade squinted in the sun then ran his hand over his three-day beard. "Maybe he decided to take a little trip down to Juárez and find himself a girlfriend from a foreign country."

"That's a long way to go. I understand there's some nice-looking pecan pickers over at Hayward Ranch."

"Yes, Sheriff. Heard the same thing. Gotta be kind of careful there. Some of those boys with them are pretty quick with a knife. Least that's what I've heard. Sorry I can't give you more, Sheriff. But like I told you and Charlie Hinton, if I hear something, I'll give you a call."

Virgil sat in the car, completely unsatisfied. As he reached toward the ignition key the red light on the radio lit up.

"What's up, Rosita?"

"Rosita . . . Haven't heard that for a while. Sounds like maybe you're doing some heavy thinking."

"Kind of goes with the job. What have you got?"

"Alex called in. He and Dave found two cows or what was left of them. Looks like somebody needed meat for the table like you said. They're wondering what to do next."

"Where did they come from?"

"Alex says he thinks they're from the Grafton Ranch, based on where they found them. The brands were cut out."

"Give me a minute, Rosie." Virgil took off his sunglasses and rubbed his eyes. He knew the Grafton Ranch bordered the reservations. He also knew there wasn't a lot of love lost between the two neighbors. He picked up the speaker. "Rosie, tell the boys to hold off for now. I'll get back to them."

"Virgil, Alex said the two steers were not exactly prime. Must have been some poor people outside of Redbud."

"I know, Rosie." There was a long pause. "Okay, tell Dave to indicate in his report that these kills might be a red wolf predator. The feds can reimburse the loss to the Grafton Ranch and we can keep the peace. I know they're trying to reintroduce those wolves, so the feds might not balk at reimbursing. Then tell him and Alex when they are on patrol to keep a lookout for Buddy's pickup.

"Got it. Ten-four."

By the time he got to Hayward Ranch, it was a little after two. It had been a long time since he'd been here. None of his most recent visits had been memorable. He doubted that this one would be any different. As he turned off the road heading to the main house, he had a familiar apprehension. He knew there was no use trying to chalk it up to the refried beans. He'd only be lying to himself. Row after row of pecan trees lined the drive. Their perfect symmetry contrasted with the mixed feelings he had whenever he came to this place. For a fleeting second, he saw an image of himself running through the rows, a young girl in hot pursuit, a smile on his face. Quick as it came, the reverie passed. Like a flashback of someone else's life . . .

But no, he knew it was his and he would never forget it.

3

At the center of Hayward Ranch, a house they called Crow's Nest stood on a knoll, looking down on a half-breed sheriff. As he drove up to it, he wondered who was more misplaced.

There wasn't another house in the county or probably the state like it. A huge Queen Anne–style Victorian, capped by a widow's walk, it should have been perched on some craggy rock face on a lonely New England coast. Instead, it looked down on a sea of pecan trees. The history behind its coming to be in this place was of course something that he, Virgil Dalton, sheriff of Hayward, had heard long ago from a girl named Rusty.

A newly widowed man named Hayward from those far New England shores, a man who had amassed a fortune in the triangle trade, had taken his two sons, Caleb and Micah, out onto the ocean for the first time. A storm hit. Waves pounded the sides of the ship. Snapped like matchsticks, the mainmast and then the mizzen both crashed to the deck. The ship was driven into the rocks.

The two boys clung to each other, watching as one after another man disappeared from topside into the sea. The father, a captain no longer, held on to the two as long as he could, until he, too, was torn away. Micah and Caleb Hayward, locked together as Siamese twins, awaited their fate. A wave snatched them with the beam their father had tied them to. It bore them from wave to wave until at last they felt the ground beneath their feet.

They left that place to never again return, to never again feel the sea spray on their faces. In coming to this dry place, so many miles away, they built their future and this house, so named Crow's Nest, to always remind them of why they came and what they left. In the years since, the Hayward Ranch had grown far beyond its original boundaries. Pecans, cattle, even an entire trucking operation outside of Redbud on the opposite end of the county, where most of the business end of the ranch was managed, gave witness to the descendants of the original Micah and Caleb.

"Hello, Sheriff." The voice came from a chair on the porch as Virgil climbed the stairs.

"Hello, Micah." The names had managed to survive the passage of time long after their original owners.

"What can I do for you?"

"Actually, I got a call that you wanted to see me."

"That wasn't me. It was probably Mother but I have no idea what it was about. She doesn't always confide in me."

Virgil didn't miss the sarcasm in his voice. Despite his history with Audrey, he had a certain affection and empathy for Micah. Micah had never been able to escape his mother's control. Maybe if his older brother, Caleb, had survived Vietnam, things would have been different. After Caleb's death, he never had a chance. His life had been determined.

Or maybe if Rusty . . . The image that popped into Virgil's head cut as sharp as a surgeon's scalpel. He gripped the railing hard.

"I'll see if Mother's ready to see you. Come on up and have a seat." Micah disappeared inside the massive front door.

Virgil stepped up onto the porch but did not sit. He looked out over the acres of trees and the collection of barns and outbuildings which housed the machinery that helped to sustain the family fortune. Beyond the barns he saw the farm roads which branched off the driveway and divided the orchard into equal parts. They wound for close to a mile before crossing the top of a distant hill. Virgil knew that one of them led to a collection of bunkhouses which housed the migrant population that was used to harvest the abundant crop. The population grew this time of year, but there was always a nucleus of farmhands.

"Virgil, she's ready to see you."

He turned at the sound of the voice, then followed Micah into the house.

"In the study." Micah pointed to the opened door at the end of the hall just to the left of the central stairs that led up to the second floor. "I don't think my presence is desired so I'll leave you. By the way, Virgil, it was good seeing you." He turned away then stopped. "I wish . . ." He hesitated. "I wish things had been different."

The two looked at each other. Virgil gave a slight nod, then Micah turned away and walked through the door on the other side of the stairs. Virgil took a breath then walked into the study.

He hadn't been in the room for many years, but he realized that it was virtually unchanged from the room of his memory. There was little about Audrey Hayward's office that suggested family, but then it was only in Rusty's room that he had ever felt at ease. He stopped himself before the thought led him down another path he didn't want to go down.

"Have a seat." Audrey Hayward's voice was without emotion. No greeting accompanied it.

"I'll stand," Virgil said.

"Suit yourself."

For the first time, their eyes met. She sat back in the chair, her back to the window, a short stack of papers on the desk in front of her. She pushed them to the side, than took off her glasses and laid them on top.

"Yes, I guess you will." Her hair was whiter than he remembered, with just a hint of the russet color that she had passed on to her only daughter. There was little of the softness in her face that Rusty always had. Virgil wondered if there had ever been softness in those eyes.

"You never did take direction."

He bridled at the comment but showed nothing.

"I understand that there are people who would like to see you as district attorney. Politically correct, I assume, you being indigenous and educated. A law degree, too . . ." She paused as if waiting for a denial. "Anyhow, Micah is thinking about the state senate."

"Does he know this yet?"

He saw the tightness come into her face.

"Anyhow . . . this idea for you. I don't think it's a good one. It seems to me . . ."

Virgil raised his hand. "I am not your son. Whatever I decide to do or not to do will be my decision."

She didn't respond.

"If that is all, I'll be on my way."

She finally stood up, her hands resting on her desk. "I should have known there would be no reasoning with you. I curse the day you ever set foot in this house."

"So do I, but for a much different reason."

When Virgil stepped off the porch a few moments later, the heat rose in layers, making a shimmering impressionist watercolor of the landscape. There were no sharp lines, everything softened and blurred. High overhead in the cloudless sky a hawk circled, looking for its next meal. A couple of men came out of the nearest barn. Micah was with them. They stood for a minute talking. By the time Virgil had gotten to his car, Micah had stepped away and was walking back up to the house.

"How did your visit with Mother go?" he asked with a trace of a smile.

"Pretty much the way I reckoned it would."

"Yes . . . well . . ."

Virgil accidentally brushed the car door with his hand. "Damn!"

"Careful. You get branded here, you're in for life just like me."

"I'll try to remember that." Virgil opened the car door, then took a step back from the rush of contained heat. "By the way, Mike . . ." It had been years since he had called him by the name. "Does Buddy Hinton work on the place here?"

"No. He's down in Redbud at the trucking operation. Works on the trucks and drives . . . long hauls. I don't get down there as often as I should. Why do you ask?"

"Well, he's gone missing. Or so it seems."

"Did you check with Cal? He's pretty much running that part of the business these days. He's caught on real quick since he came home and I'm not just saying that 'cause he's my son. Even my mother says he and Virginia give her hope for the future."

"I haven't checked with him yet, but thanks for the update." Virgil tipped his hand to his Stetson then got into the car.

When he got onto the paved road, he called Rosie. "I'm heading down to Redbud. Then I'll stop at Hintons' on the way back."

"Good idea, Virgil. Viola called again. She's pretty upset."

"I'll be back around five. Jimmy's coming in around four, I believe. See you then if you're still there."

The ride to Redbud took a little more than half an hour. It was due west of Hayward so he was driving into the sun. By the time he got to Redbud, he was working on a pretty good headache. Redbud was little more than a wide spot in the road and the boundary at the western edge of the county, nevertheless it was a good spot for Hayward Trucking since it was so close to the interchange at the interstate. Because of the operation, in the last ten years there had been a minor population boom. At the only light in town, a gas station had opened with a mini-mart, and across the street a fast-food restaurant. Lately, there had been talk that a large motel was going to be built.

Virgil made a right at the one light, crossed the railroad tracks, and headed down the gravel road that dead-ended at Hayward Trucking. He had been there only once before and was surprised at how much it had grown. He saw at least ten semis parked perpendicular to the chain-link that encompassed the facility. Another couple were backed up to the loading dock. A few of the men were eating ice cream and standing next to an ice cream truck. He parked outside the separate office, which sat alongside a huge warehouse.

There was a receptionist sitting at a desk just inside the front door. Virgil didn't recognize her, but he did recognize a couple of people on the other side of the glass partition separating her from the inner office. They were busy at their computers, entering data from stacks of invoices or bills of lading.

"Can I help you?" The girl looked to be in her early twenties and eager.

"Yes. I'd like to see Caleb Hayward if possible."

"I'm sorry. He's not here right now and I doubt if he'll be back much before five. Is there anything I can help you with?"

"It's about one of your employees . . . Buddy Hinton."

"Buddy Hinton," she said. "I don't recognize that name. I've only been here a few weeks."

"You might know him as Charles Hinton Jr., but that's okay. I think I see someone who can help me."

Virgil stepped to the glass and knocked loudly. All the people inside immediately looked up. He gestured toward one of them. The man started walking quickly toward the door that led into the reception area. "This fella will be good enough," he said to the girl at the desk.

"Hey, Virgil," the man said as he came through the door.

"Step outside for a minute, Carlos." Virgil retreated through the door he had just entered. Carlos followed.

"There a problem?"

"Not for you, Carlos. I need some info on Buddy Hinton. He still works here, right?"

"Well, I guess so. I'm not sure. Haven't seen him in a while. He usually does long hauls, but I heard there was some kind of dustup. I'm in the office usually, so the most I see Buddy is when we play ball together. Once the season's over, not so much. I'm married, a couple of kids. My lifestyle's a little different from Buddy's. If I run into him down at the Black Bull, we'll have a beer together, but that's about it."

"Do you know who he had the dustup with?"

"Sorry, Sheriff. This is a pretty big place. Stuff happens."

"Didn't realize this operation had grown so much."

"Yeah, this place is always hopping. We ship all over."

"But pecan harvest isn't for another couple of months."

"We're pretty much year-round now. We have the two-week shutdown coming up, but even then there's a crew here taking care of what's left of last year's inventory before the new harvest. Things are a little slower but not much."

"So you have no idea what the problem was."

"Not really. I just heard he was upset about something. One of the guys said it had to do with a transit problem, but I don't know."

"Okay, Carlos. Thanks. Say hello back home. By the way, if you hear anything that you think I might like to know, call."

"Will do, Sheriff."

Virgil watched as Carlos walked back inside. As far as Buddy Hinton was concerned, at this point he was digging a dry well. He hated to go to the Hintons' empty-handed, but it didn't look like he had much choice. A few minutes later he was back on the road. The sun was now at his back, but he still had the headache.

Jimmy Tillman was ready to go to work. He tossed the ball a few more times to his twelve-year-old sister, Abby, then he hopped on his bike. He worked hard to make sure her life as a twelve-year-old was much better than his had been.

"Jimmy, can I have a ride on your bike?"

"Not now, Abby. Gotta go to work."

He saw the disappointment on her face.

"Tomorrow maybe," he said. "We'll even stop and get a slushy and fish off the bridge."

He didn't wait to see the transformation, just gave a wave. It didn't bother him that the town council wouldn't let him take a cruiser home. He liked the exercise because he knew once he started making his rounds he'd be sitting most of his shift. Besides, Virgil had told him he was going to see to it at the next meeting that the policy changed. Twenty minutes later, he was walking through the back door of the sheriff's office.

"Hey, Jimmy, you're early. I just got off the horn with Virgil. He was just leaving Redbud."

"Anything happening? About Buddy, I mean?"

"Nothing yet. No trace. It's starting to get worrisome."

"Maybe since I'm early I'll go have a look-see."

"That's fine. I'll be here for another hour."

Jimmy knew he had a lot to learn, and he was paying attention, especially to Virgil. There had been men in his life, of course. His dad for a little while, but it was hard to remember him sober. Then there was Grandpa. He was always good to Jimmy and glad to see him when he stopped over, but Jimmy did that less and less since Grandpa's latest woman. She was meaner than a snake and Jimmy couldn't figure out why Grandpa would want any part of her. But then he'd come to understand there was a lot about people that was a complete mystery to him. That was, with the exception of Virgil. To

Jimmy's way of thinking, there was Virgil, then all the others. He would walk barefoot over broken glass for a mile if Virgil asked him. It was as if his life was going nowhere before Virgil came along. Now he couldn't think of his life as being anything without him.

Once in his car, he headed out of town, crossing the bridge that he and Abby would probably fish from the next day. He rode pretty much aimlessly around town, stopping at occasional places where he thought Buddy might be. He ended up at the Black Bull. It had been the local watering hole on and off for the last thirty years and the last place where anyone had seen Buddy Hinton.

Jimmy got out of his car and stood in the parking lot. There was no sign of life yet. His was the only car in front. He saw some staff cars around back. It would be at least another hour before the first beer of the day would be poured. Jimmy wandered around, not quite sure what he was looking for, although the thought struck him that everyone was convinced that Buddy had taken off from here for parts unknown. He wondered if maybe that wasn't the case.

He walked around the back of the roadhouse. There were a couple of Dumpsters, a lot of broken glass, and not much else. The sun bounced off the shards of glass all over the lot and even on the hillsides that marked the boundary of the flatland on which the building stood. Obviously, Buddy had only been one in a long string to come out and howl at the moon. Some had obviously climbed to the top of the ridge in back during their lunar sojourn—maybe not alone and maybe leaning on each other—looking for a little privacy.

Jimmy noticed for the first time there was a snakelike cut between the sloping hills. He walked toward it. Where it disappeared around one of the slopes, he saw a tire track. Probably, he thought, somebody too drunk to walk tried getting to the top with their four-wheel drive. He reckoned the hardpan at the beginning of the climb wouldn't show a tread but the softer sand midway up would. The upward swath, he realized, was wide enough for a vehicle, but why anyone would chance it just for a little sweet-talking when there were a lot more accessible places was beyond him. Barren desert for miles, it led nowhere. It would be a miserable place to get stuck. He continued the climb, sweat freely running down his back. The rough path snaked for a quarter mile or so, then started a gradual straight-up climb onto the ridge.

There was no more sign of tire tread, but the ground was so hard and baked that was not surprising. The sun beat down on him, evaporating the sweat before it got a chance to mark his shirt. He walked along the top of the ridge, looking down on the barren landscape that stretched to the horizon. Cottonwoods, cholla, and tumbleweed filled the flatland and in the deep draws that creviced the earth.

Then a brighter flash of reflected light caught his eye. He scrambled along the ridge in order to be able to look into the crevasse. The reflected light hit his eyes at such a sharp angle that he had to shield them with both hands when he finally stood over the draw. There, down fifty feet below him, he saw what he realized had brought him to this place. It was Buddy Hinton's truck.

4

"So, you're sure that's Buddy's truck."

"Yessir, Virgil. I checked. Went down there myself. A 150, blue with the white stripe down the sides just like Buddy drives."

"You went down there?" Virgil looked down over the edge of the ravine as he spoke. "Jimmy, you could have broken your neck. What were you thinking? Should have waited till somebody got here. Hell, if that had happened, I'd have been short-handed."

"I had to check," Jimmy said. "See if Buddy was down there. He coulda been lying there hurt for two days. I just couldn't wait."

"I know, Jimmy. Woulda done the same thing myself. It's just that I don't want to lose one of my top men."

A sideways glance told Virgil his pat on the back had been received.

"Good detective work," Virgil said, "but you know there's a

lot of 150s around here. How do we know for sure this is Buddy's? I bet there's more than a couple with those white stripes."

"It definitely is," Jimmy said proudly. "When I came back up, I ran the plates."

"Follow-up," Virgil said, smiling. "That's what it's all about." He looked out over the wide expanse. Shadows were lengthening. He knew the truck would probably have to sit there until the next morning. It was already past six.

"What are we gonna do, Virgil?"

"There's not much we can do. It's getting late."

"I know, but what about Buddy?"

"Well, we know he's not down there. From what you described I don't think he ever was. So we just have to keep on looking."

"Whaddya think happened to him?"

Virgil looked down at the truck one last time then stepped back from the rim.

"I don't think it looks too good for Buddy," Virgil said. "It's not likely he drove that truck off this ridge for no good reason. So I figure someone else did it. That leaves me with only one conclusion. That person alone knows what became of Buddy."

Jimmy headed back to town. Virgil stood in the Black Bull parking lot watching him until he was out on the county road. A couple of cars had pulled in carrying some workmen with an early thirst. One or two hesitated when they saw Virgil's car but he waved to them to let them know that they could go on in. He absentmindedly kicked a stone with his foot while he digested what he'd just learned. He was happy with Jimmy's success and handling of everything. Now he was wrestling with his next step, his visit to the Hintons'. At least he had something to tell them now, even if it wasn't what they wanted to hear. And there was no way he could say it that would make it less fearful.

He tried to ignore it, but that feeling that had been gnawing at him more and more was getting stronger. This whole thing was going to end badly.

For Buddy, it probably already had.

5

It was almost eight when Virgil started for home. He was thinking about Viola and Charlie Hinton. He wished he had more for them. They were the kind of people you wanted to do for. About as close to normal as you could get in this crazy world. He'd told them about the truck and how they'd get it out of that ravine the next day and look it over real carefully. It wasn't much to offer, but it was something.

They didn't say much. Viola insisted he have a glass of iced tea. He'd accepted and sat awhile, trying to talk of unrelated things. It was as if they were choosing not to speculate, but Virgil knew. This was the one piece of information he'd given them that would maybe start preparing them for the worst. He'd seen it in their eyes. The only spoken hint was when he got to his car to leave. Viola and Charlie had walked across the yard with him.

"Well, folks," he said as he opened the car door, "I wish I had more for you."

"Thank you, Sheriff, for what you gave us. It ain't much, but it's something. Buddy sure did like that truck."

Charlie looked at Viola when he spoke. She nodded. That's when Virgil knew they were getting ready.

It had been a long day. He shut off the AC and rolled down all the windows. The warm breeze felt good. The shadows had overtaken the hillsides, and everything else was bathed in a soft glow. He was looking forward to a ride into the high country to check on the stock tanks. It was probably unnecessary, but it made him feel like he hadn't completely abandoned the day-to-day that had to be done on his place. Ever since he'd become sheriff, he'd been forced to let Cesar and a couple of hired hands pretty much run things. It struck him how much his life had changed, yet stayed the same. If anyone had told him right after college that this was going to be his future, he would have questioned their sanity. Hayward was the last place he expected to end up. He'd seen one tumbleweed too many. There were places to go and things to do. Or so he thought.

He remembered sitting in a bar one late afternoon in Bisbee, on his way home from school. It was a nice town, about the size of Hayward but a few rungs up the ladder in chic. He'd never been there before and he was thirsty and hungry, so he'd stopped. The cold beer tasted good. It was cool and pretty quiet. He'd been thinking a lot about his future and law school.

"One on the house," the bartender said, breaking his reverie.

"Thanks," Virgil said. "Nice town."

"Yeah, it is. See the Hole?"

"The Hole?"

"On your way into town. It's probably the main thing we're famous for."

Virgil remembered the huge crater he'd passed on his way in. "Yes, that's some hole," he said.

For the next five minutes the bartender talked about what a tourist attraction it was, how people marveled when they saw it. The five minutes sitting with that cold beer, listening to that bartender, had been a moment of clarity for him. Not to denigrate the good people of Bisbee, but he wanted to live in a place that was known for more than just a hole in the ground. That was his epiphany when he left the bar. Convinced, he went home.

Then he fell in love with Rusty.

All these years later, here he was in Hayward. And there wasn't even a hole.

"Why do you have Jack in the stall?"

"Picked up a stone, got a little bruise. A day or two. Just a little rest. He'll be fine."

Virgil reached over the stall door and stroked the horse.

"Guess you're going to wait for another day, pal." He grabbed a halter and a lead rope off a hook next to Jack's stall. Then he walked from the barn out into the corral. A few minutes later, he was back, leading a young bay mare. Cesar looked up as he threw a last flake of hay to Jack.

"That hay smells good," Virgil said. "Got some nice color, too. Wonder if we're gonna get a second cutting?"

"Pretty dry. Not if this heat keeps up. You still going? Getting late."

"Yeah. I need to get out. Besides, I been out in the dark before."

"I'm just saying be careful. She's not Jack."

Virgil looked at the horse calmly standing next to him, tail swishing slowly in the evening air.

"Still water runs deep," Cesar said, as if reading Virgil's mind.

"She'll be fine. Look at her, doesn't have a mean thought in her head."

Cesar shrugged and shook his head.

"What?"

"Thought the same thing about my second wife, till she slid a knife between my ribs."

"Yeah, but you probably gave her plenty of reason. I'm just gonna sweet-talk this little gal right through the ride."

While he bantered with Cesar, Virgil finished saddling. He kneed the horse firmly in the abdomen, then drew the cinch a couple of notches tighter.

"Sucked in some air, didn't she? She's not too anxious for a ride up into them hills in the dark."

"There's a full moon. It won't be total dark for another hour. She's just letting me know you been slow at your work. Ain't been using her enough. I'm gone all day, and you, Pete, and Joe spend a lot of time leaning on fence posts talking about your past and future amorous adventures."

"Pedro and José ain't hardly had any amorous adventures worth talking about."

"So you're the only one worth listening to. Cesar, the great lover. Boy, conversation around here must be a lot duller than I thought."

Cesar mumbled something Virgil couldn't make out.

"What did you say? Must be all the noise in here. Couldn't hear you."

Virgil waited for a response as he flipped the reins over the mare's head, getting ready to lead her from the quiet barn. This time Cesar spoke in the loudest voice Virgil had heard in a long time.

"Wouldn't hurt you none to have one of those amorous adventures. That little mare is getting more action than you. That belly of hers is filled with a little more than air."

Virgil stopped her after she took a step. His eyes locked with Cesar's for an instant.

"Okay, you win," Virgil said. "But it does have something to do with opportunity."

"Maybe that and maybe a little work, too."

"I'm done with this conversation. You're a regular Ann Landers, ain't you?" He waved and walked the mare down the runway toward the opened barn door. He barely caught Cesar's smile.

The air felt good. Just a hint of a breeze as he stepped from the barn. The sun had slipped below the horizon and the persistent heat had finally relented. He slid his foot into the stirrup, then lifted smoothly into the saddle. Pressing his knees lightly into her sides, he moved her forward. When he did it a second time, she crow-hopped a little and snorted. Virgil slapped the loose end of the reins against her neck, dug in his heels a little harder against her sides. She snorted once more, then moved out into a trot. He repeated his action until she went into an easy canter.

He rode for a little over a half a mile until he reached the ridge where he had sat the night before against the bed of his pickup. He stopped. It had always been his favorite spot on the ranch. From here, he could see the ever-flowing creek which had made this land more valuable than most, as it meandered out of the hills, wandered down behind the barns, filled a small pool, went under a bridge on the driveway, ran a bit, filled another pond, then ran under the county road to the land on the other side. As far as he could see in any direction, the land was his, bought and paid for. It was what enabled him to live a life he loved, but it was not the way he had wanted it.

His father had worked hard, constantly adding to the land that had originally been homesteaded by his great-grandfather, but to get the deeded land he finally got, he almost lost it all. There were a couple of bad years, livestock prices down and people eager to see him go under so they could get his prime land with its ever-flowing creek. Among them was Audrey Hayward's father-in-law. What had helped out in the hard times was his sheriff's salary. Just about the time Virgil and Rusty discovered each other, Virgil's mother and father were killed on the brand-new interstate. Insurance money had paid off and saved the ranch once and for all. The bitter irony was that Virgil's future had been secured by the loss of his parents. There were now over fifty thousand acres of deeded land and another thirty thousand leased through the Bureau of Land Management.

He heard the hoot of an owl and wondered if it was the same one that had chastised him the previous night. The mare's ears were forward. Virgil leaned over and stroked her neck.

"Guess we better get to those stock tanks." He nudged her away from the overlook and headed for the backcountry. Although the creek flowed through a large portion of the acreage with the BLM leased land, it was necessary to have the stock tanks to make sure, especially in the summer months, that the cattle were well watered. Sometimes in a bad year even the creek could be brought down to a trickle. This had been a fairly good year overall. That made this jaunt more of a choice than a necessity.

By the time he got to the second-to-last stock tank, the nocturnals were starting to scurry around in the underbrush. An armadillo crossed in front of the young mare, but she didn't even flinch. He caught sight of a coyote and heard another. These were the night sounds of the prairie that he'd grown up with and loved. The smell of sage crushed underfoot mixed with the stored daytime heat rising into the nighttime sky, filling the air with a different perfume.

The last stock tank was on the other side of the county road. By the time he got to that one, having ridden in a loop, he would be closest to home. Everything to this point had been in working order. Around or near the tanks he had seen his cattle, most with calves at their side. They all looked in good condition. Resting in the gullies and washes during the heat of the day, they moved to the tanks in the dusk, then spread out throughout the grassland to graze during the night. It looked like a good year for the ranch.

It was only when he was in sight of the last tank that anything seemed out of place. The moon had risen full, flooding the brushland in silver. The mare had no trouble picking her way. When the creek was running full, the land on this side of the county road was always more lush and better pasture. When there was an abundance of rain, the water tank was virtually unnecessary. At this point in midsummer the rains had been spotty, not drought conditions but dry enough that the cattle would water at the tank rather than forage in the rocky and reduced streambed. Virgil saw them in clusters, shadows bunching up, starting to move into almost a herd formation. It puzzled him. He hadn't by now really expected to see any of them in the vicinity of the tank. He figured by the time he got to this last tank, they would have all watered and spread out to graze. He moved toward a couple of them near the tank but they spooked as he got close. Then the mare did an unexpected sidestep and a crow hop. Virgil caught himself, the pommel of the saddle digging into his groin. He slipped a stirrup but quickly got it back.

"What the hell!"

The mare snorted. The cattle nearest the tank bolted back to the perceived safety of the herd. His puzzlement grew as he allowed the mare to step away, trailing the cattle.

There was a little prominence a quarter mile back. He turned the mare and rode to it quickly. She did not have to be urged. He pulled her to a stop at the top. From here, he had a pretty good view in all directions. Deep shadows untouched by moonlight marked the ravines and washes where he knew danger could lurk. But he saw no sign. He reached down into his saddlebag and pulled out his cell phone. Cesar answered the barn phone on the fourth ring. Virgil described to him what he saw and how the cattle were acting.

"Could be a cat. Maybe a lobo wolf."

"Yeah, that's what I was thinking. Strange, but they're acting almost thirsty. I can see a few that took a chance with the bad footing down in the creek, but even from here I can see the stock tank is brim full."

"Maybe a cat hiding near the tank in the shadows, waiting for them to come near."

"Could be," Virgil said, not quite convinced himself. "Well anyway, I'd better sleep out just in case. See you in the morning."

"Be careful that cat don't sneak up on you while you're dreaming about your last amorous adventure."

"Don't let it keep you up, old man. Hell, I can't even remember that far back. I'll snuggle with my rifle."

"That's a pretty sad picture," Cesar said. "See you in the morning. I'll have breakfast ready."

Virgil closed the phone and put it back in his saddlebag. Before he got off the mare, he stood in the stirrups a couple of times, scanning the landscape, seeing nothing unusual. But the herd stayed huddled, seventy-some-odd head with their calves bunched together.

Finally he slipped his thirty-thirty from the scabbard and dismounted. From the back of the saddle he untied a bedroll and dropped it on the ground alongside the rifle. Then he led the bay over to a cottonwood where he tied her. He didn't bother with a fire. He smoothed out the ground in a flat area not far from the horse and spread a blanket. Then he went back to the mare, unsaddled her, and set the saddle at one end of the blanket. It would not be the first time he had used a saddle as a pillow. He took a cloth from the saddlebag and a medium-sized leather pouch which doubled as a nose bag. For the next ten minutes he grained the mare with the few scoopfuls he had thrown in before he had left the barn. While she ate, he took the cloth and rubbed her down. He was pleased to see she was only truly wet in the saddle area. As he dried her, the moisture rose in the night air.

When she was rubbed down and finished eating, he untied her and led her carefully down to the branch for a drink. It was obvious she wanted no part of the stock tank. While she drank, he chewed on an energy bar. Then they carefully climbed the grade, where he tied her again to the cottonwood and sat down on the blanket.

The night was so bright that when he lay back, he felt like he was looking at the whole universe. A soft wind occasionally dusted the little knoll. He heard the far-off call of a coyote. His eyes were getting heavy and even though he hated to acknowledge it, his lower back was aching from his nighttime ride. It was a solemn reminder of how long it had been since he had climbed onto a horse. One last time, he rose up on his elbow to listen and scan the area. Nothing but the night and a flooded moonscape. The mare was a silhouette against the night sky, her head dropping slightly as she shifted her weight. His last thought was of the long-ago nights when he had done this as a child with his father. The ground had seemed softer then.

First light brought Virgil to his feet. He stood, a little bent over, trying to throw off the stiffness. There were just enough morning chills to bring on a shiver. A cup of hot coffee would have been welcome, but that would have to wait. He walked over to check on the mare, who was still standing with a droopy head and shifting weight so she balanced on three feet, her left rear hoof slightly cocked and just resting on the ground. She was so deep in her trance that Virgil didn't bother her. Instead, he walked over to a nearby bush and relieved himself. Then he walked over to the edge of the little knoll to check on the cattle. Most had settled in and around the creek bed where some were eagerly drinking. Even from this distance he could see the flow was way down and they had to be real careful to reach the water. He saw no sign of a cat or other predator and knew that no predation had occurred, for he surely would have awakened. On the other side of the creek, more than a quarter mile away, stood the unused water tank.

He decided to have a closer look. Picking his way down the hillside and across the creek, he hit the flat ground. It was only a ten-minute walk to the tank. His throat was dry. The cool water would be welcome. Many times during his childhood, alone and with friends, he had shed his clothes and plunged into the cool depths. This morning he'd settle for a face wash and a cold drink.

He finally reached the tank and grabbed the metal side, already warming in the morning sun. He reached over to splash the cool water on his face. Then his knuckles tightened on the rim.

He could feel the retch rising like a tide in the back of his throat. An involuntary gag choked him as his eyes fixed on a swollen, bloated carcass that floated in the tank.

He had just found out why the cattle wouldn't come to drink.

But even more important, he had just found Buddy Hinton.

6

Hayward Memorial was a regional hospital serving a population of about a hundred thousand people, spread over three counties. Besides Hayward Ranch and Trucking, it was the area's largest single employer. Virgil knew that if you lived within fifty miles of Hayward, chances were you worked either for one or the other. He was all right with that, except that it felt like a company town and he knew for a special few there was a sense of entitlement that went along with that. He had experienced that the first time he incurred Audrey Hayward's wrath.

He drove around to the back of the hospital and parked in front of an unmarked door. It was a little after eleven. He pressed the buzzer outside the door and waited, his hand on the knob. As soon as he heard the expected clicks, he pulled the door open and stepped inside. He walked down a short hallway, then turned left. He stopped at the second door on his right. He hesitated a moment, sucked in a deep breath, then opened the door.

Viola and Bud senior were seated in the small room. Virgil saw how much they had aged in a day. As often as he had been part of this scenario, he had never gotten used to it. Usually, it was for victims of the road, occasionally drownings, rarely homicides, but they generally had one common denominator: they were all young. Buddy Hinton's viewing would be about as bad as it gets. He knew this going in. The Hintons stood up when he entered.

"You both don't have to come."

"He belonged to both of us," Viola said.

"Yes, but I know how hard . . . I mean, I only need one of you for the identification."

"It's all right, Sheriff. We kinda prepared ourselves for this. We saw Buddy into this world together. We'll see him out, too."

Bud senior put his arm around his wife.

"We're ready."

"Give me a minute," Virgil said. He left the room, then came back a short while later. The Hintons followed Virgil into an even smaller room. There were a couple of chairs facing a large viewing window, which was curtained.

"Why don't you just have a seat? I'll let the attendant know you're ready. He'll draw the curtain. Buddy will be lying on a gurney. Only his face will be visible. I'm afraid because of the heat and the water his face is somewhat swollen, but I've been told that will lessen over the next twenty-four hours. All you have to do is nod. That'll be enough for me."

As Virgil left the room, he couldn't help noticing how Viola was reaching out to her husband, like she was supporting him even more than she was looking for support herself. A minute later, Virgil returned and stood alongside them. The curtain finally began to draw open. Virgil looked at Viola, then her husband. Their eyes were fixed on the gurney. On the exposed face.

"That's our Bud Light," she said.

Virgil cocked his head.

"It's just a nickname he got early on," she said, "instead of Bud junior."

Her husband didn't move. He didn't say a word.

Virgil nodded to the attendant, then he slowly drew the curtain closed.

"Thank you," he said.

Viola nodded. "Come on, Dad," she said to her husband. "Time to go. We got things to do." She tugged at her husband's arm until he turned his face from the closed curtain. Then she led him from the room.

Virgil saw them out of the building and stood in the open doorway watching until their pickup pulled out of the parking lot. Then he went back inside. A few minutes later, he was sitting in the medical examiner's office.

"It's a little early, Virgil. I can't give you much. Toxicology will probably be a week or more. Cause of death at this point, a blow to the head. This is strictly preliminary, of course. There was water in the lungs. My thoughts are he was probably struck unconscious, dumped in the stock tank, and then ultimately drowned. I'm afraid unless something different comes back from the tox screen, that's about it. I might also add, there's little or no retrievable DNA. The water pretty much took care of that."

"Thanks, Doc. I appreciate you taking care of this right away. I know you have a lot on your plate."

"No, something like this goes right to the top of the pile. Just wish I had more for you. If he'd been found out in the brush or even been buried, I'd probably have had something, but . . ."

"I understand. I don't know whether it's because it's been so dry and the hardpan is too tough to dig in, or if this was the plan all along, but the result is, my job got a little harder."

"If I learn anything different, I'll call. One thing we know, Virgil. This wasn't done by some transient. Whoever did this knew that stock tank was there."

"Doesn't exactly make for a good night's sleep, does it? Knowing that the person who pushed Buddy into that water may be sitting next to you in Margie's place, drinking a cup of coffee. Thanks again, Doc."

It was a little after two when Virgil got back to the office. Rosie had gone out for a bit. Her husband, Dave, was minding the store.

"How are the Hintons holding up?"

"About as well as you'd expect."

"Good people. Viola was in my class in high school. Married Bud right after. Glad they got that daughter with the new baby. Maybe help them down the line to put this behind them."

"I don't know that you ever put something like this behind you, Dave."

"Yeah, I guess. A lot of crazies out there."

Virgil sat down and picked up some paperwork. Then he looked at Dave.

"Guess that's why we're here doing this job," he said. "To

take care of the crazies. Maybe without the crazies we wouldn't even know what normal is."

Audrey Hayward looked out the window of her upstairs bedroom, pleased with what she saw. It wasn't the scenery. It was what it represented. Her view went way beyond the thousands of acres dotted with pecan trees and herds of Black Angus, even beyond Hayward Trucking. She had worked hard to enjoy this view.

The fleeting reminiscence over, she was about to turn from the window when she saw a car pulling into the long driveway. She recognized the official vehicle as it came closer. Her son Micah and two of the ranch hands had just gotten out of a pickup by one of the barns, and now Micah walked over to the car. Whoever was inside never got out, just rolled down the window. She watched as the window went back up and Micah stepped back. He stood as the car turned around. He continued to watch until the car had driven the entire length of the driveway, dust clouds rising in its wake, until it reached the main road. Only then did Micah turn away and start heading for the house.

By the time Audrey came downstairs, he was on the phone.

"Yes. Well, do the right thing and send a spray of flowers to the funeral home. No, send two, one from the family and one from the employees. Okay."

Micah hung up the phone and turned to see his mother standing in the doorway.

"One of our drivers was found dead," he said to her. "Buddy Hinton. That was Virgil's deputy outside."

"Why didn't they just call?"

"I don't know. I guess because it was one of ours. Maybe Virgil thought a personal notification would be more appropriate. He also said he wanted to see Cal. I told him he was probably down in Redbud."

"Why is he bothering Caleb with this? People die. Even if he worked for the trucking company."

Micah looked at his mother. "A little sensitivity would be nice."

"Just like your father," she said. "Remember, it's a business. Cal knows that. That's why we've done so well these last few years. An employee dies, we send flowers. Why should he have to get any more involved?"

"Buddy Hinton was a nice guy. His father works for us and he's been with us since he got out of high school. Besides, he didn't just die, Mother."

"What do you mean?"

"Virgil found his body floating in a stock tank. He was murdered."

7

When Jimmy pulled into the parking lot behind the sheriff's office, he saw Virgil standing in the far corner looking at Buddy Hinton's truck. He parked the patrol car near the back entrance, then walked across the dirt lot.

"Hey."

Virgil didn't respond.

"Whatcha doing?"

Virgil glanced at Jimmy, but still didn't say anything.

"Why'd somebody do Buddy like that?" Jimmy said.

"There's always a reason," Virgil said. "We find that out, we may find out who did Buddy."

"But Buddy never hurt no one. It don't make sense. Maybe it was a serial killer. Just random."

"You been watching too many of those *CSI* shows, Jimmy. This wasn't random."

"How do you know that, Virgil? I mean, Buddy was well liked. He didn't have no enemies."

"Well, for one thing, he left this truck behind and rode off with his killer. That tells me at least two things. One, that he knew his killer and two, that this was planned. Whoever killed him lured him away and was no stranger to these parts. He knew where that stock tank was and figured that Buddy wouldn't be found until the water and heat did its job. Then he knew to drive Buddy's truck into that ravine to slow our search even more. Actually, that tells me something else, too."

"What's that?"

"That this killer must've reckoned he had a lot to lose if he let Buddy go on living."

"Well, what are we going to do now?" Jimmy said. "Where do we start?"

Virgil hesitated for a second. He looked down at a small tumbleweed at his foot, gave it a light kick and watched it roll off toward the middle of the lot with the help of a breeze.

"I think maybe the best place to start is back at the beginning. Remember, when we started we were looking for Buddy. Now everything's changed."

"What d'ya mean?"

"Well, now we're looking for his killer."

Virgil tried to clear his mind on the way back to the ranch. He was tired and he had a headache. Not the kind of tired that comes at the end of a day baling hay in ninety-degree heat or stringing wire for half a mile on posts that you dug with a manual posthole digger. This was the kind of tired that keeps you up nights, robs your sleep. That has your mind going in ten directions at once. And worst of all, won't quit. No off switch at all.

It had been building all day. His recent conversation with Jimmy had just crystallized it. He'd been sheriff for over a dozen years. This was not his first homicide. But this one was different.

Hayward had its share of murders, of course. They might be in a bar or parking lot, where someone ends up pooling blood from a knife stuck between his ribs, or lying among shards of glass with his head split open. There were also the domestic killings. A woman beaten once too often who is afraid for her kids and finds the strength to put a round or two into a husband she'd married with high hopes.

Then there were the rare occasions when a partner goes over the edge because of the humiliation of faithlessness. A momentary picture of Wendell Tibbs came into Virgil's mind as Tibbs stood over the bloodied bodies of his wife and the rodeo cowboy she'd been sleeping with. Virgil pleaded with him to no avail to put the gun down, and then stood helplessly as Wendell, with tears running down his cheeks, put the last bullet into his brain.

These were the casualties of broken people with broken lives, or flameouts from a combustible moment of rage, but they had a commonality that Virgil understood. Buddy Hinton was different. His death was planned, and executed. Whoever did this to Buddy had a reason. That was what had Virgil's mind working overtime. If they had a good enough reason to kill Buddy, it might not end there.

8

Cesar was sitting on the last hay bale that had come up the conveyor. He was done for the day. Pedro and José had just left in their pickup. Brothers and good workers, they had worked on the ranch for the last ten years. He liked to tease them since they became legal, calling them Pete and Joe. They didn't seem to mind. In fact, he thought they might secretly like it. Of course, what they didn't know was that Cesar had been illegal for over fifty years. Virgil's father had fished him out of the river way back when, and ever since he had called this place home.

Now Cesar sat on the bale, looking out of the hay door at the close of a hard day. He was feeling it. He would never admit it and no one, except maybe Virgil, could tell, but the years were beginning to show. It was probably close to a hundred degrees in the top of that barn and hay chaff was floating in the air, making breathing a challenge. So he needed to sit a bit before climbing down the ladder. He was looking forward to a cool shower to wash the chaff that had gotten down his back and mixed with the moisture of a long day. Uncomfortable as it was, in a way it made him feel good. It was the mark of a job accomplished and part of the cycle of life for him.

He stood up.

A mile or so in the distance, he saw the glare bouncing off a car windshield. He hoped the car was Virgil's. He loved him as much as he had loved his father before him, maybe more. He had been here before he was born, and had been with him every step of the way as he grew up. After Virgil's father and mother had been killed, he became the father Virgil still needed. The bond between the two was strong and unspoken, but always there.

Virgil expelled a deep breath as the group of ranch buildings came into view. He looked to his left at the cluster of horses standing idly, swishing their flyswatters in the shade of a tree by the ever-running creek. He saw the little mare from his recent fateful ride and remembered the soreness in the lower part of his back. As he drew nearer, he could see the figure standing in the open hay door of the barn closest to the road. He knew who it was long before he got close enough to see the man's face. The same man who had been there his whole life. A smile crossed his lips. For the moment, the dull headache that had been building subsided and his mind cleared.

As he pulled into the driveway, he saw that the figure had disappeared. The hay door was closed and all he wanted to think about was the cold beer they would soon share as they sat on the front porch later that evening in the twilight. The only disturbance the distant *yip, yip* of a coyote on his nightly hunt or the soft nicker of Jack calling to him for a little attention.

Jimmy and his young sister, Abby, stood on the bridge watching the bobbers at the end of their lines float in the water below.

"Not much happening," she said.

Jimmy looked at her and smiled. He was glad he had made good on his promise. Hayward was a pretty small town, no place to hide, and if you were a kid without much of a pedigree, it was even harder.

"That's okay," he said. "I like just standing here in the quiet."

Fading sunlight slanted through the trees on the riverbank and danced on the water. There wasn't even a hint of a breeze, and no car had crossed the bridge in the last fifteen minutes.

"You know if you just hold your breath for a minute," he said, "you can hear your heart beating."

Abby inhaled deeply while Jimmy watched her face turn a bright shade. At the end of her minute, she let out her breath.

"Gee, Jimmy. You're smart."

He smiled again.

"Jimmy, what happened to Buddy Hinton?"

"I don't know."

"C'mon, Jimmy. Tell me something."

"Why do you want to know? How do you even know about Buddy?"

"Kids were talking in the schoolyard during camp today. They asked me about it because they knew my brother was a deputy sheriff. I want to be able to tell them something. It's kind of important."

"Have kids been picking on you? Just tell me."

"No." Abby's response was immediate. "They don't do that, no more. Haven't for a long time, ever since you became Sheriff Dalton's deputy."

"Oh, so that's it. You want to impress some boy."

Abby didn't respond right away. She looked down at the water as the float on the end of her line suddenly slipped below the surface and the tip of the rod bent in an arc.

"Ya got something there, kid. Work the line slowly, don't jerk it. Make sure he's hooked first."

For the next couple of minutes, they were both engrossed in the drama of the catch. Finally, with Jimmy's guidance, Abby started to reel in the fish.

"Wow, Abby! You got yourself some big catfish. There's tomorrow night's supper. You did good." Jimmy started to work the hook out of the catfish's mouth.

"Jimmy, it's not about the boys."

"What d'ya mean, Ab?" He saw the serious look on her face, so he dropped the fish in a bucket at his feet and gave her his full attention.

"Well, you know how kids used to make fun 'cause we lived in a trailer and our clothes were . . . Well, you know."

Jimmy nodded at the painful memories he had worked so hard to forget.

"I know it was much worse for you than it was for me," she said. "But people don't do that no more because of you. Kids now treat me pretty nice and when Virgil, I mean the sheriff, picked me up last week on my way to school and dropped me off and all the kids saw when he waved to me and called me Abby, I could tell they were looking at me different and it felt nice. I think some even think I'm special."

"You are special, Ab."

"I know to you, but I never been to other people. It's a good feeling. So, if you were to tell me something about Buddy that they didn't know, well, it would kinda help me."

Jimmy looked out over the stretch of river beneath them. The sun was pretty much gone. The light no longer danced on the surface. The water looked almost black.

"Buddy was found by Virgil floating in a stock tank. He didn't look too good because the water and the hot sun took its toll. You can tell that 'cause I know it will eventually come out, but I don't want you pestering me for more. This is an ongoing investigation and we've got to be real careful with the information we have. We don't want anybody to get a hint we're onto them. Let's get home now, so I can run down something I've just thought of."

"Boy, Jimmy, you sound just like a detective. Wait till the kids hear about this."

Not too far away, sitting with his feet on the railing of his porch, with a cold beer in his hand, Virgil was also enjoying the quiet. The nighttime smell of flowers and trees in full bloom mixed with barnyard smells of hay, manure, and hard work.

Cesar came out of the kitchen, the screen door slapping shut in back of him.

"Got almost all the hay. Left that field across the road for last. If we were to lose it to the weather, it wouldn't be much of a loss. It's pretty poor."

Virgil looked at Cesar, surprised to hear that much from him in one stream.

"Guess it's time to turn that ground over," Virgil said. "Cover it with rye, then plow it under and reseed."

"That's what I was thinking." Each took a sip from his bottle while he contemplated the idea.

"They putting Buddy in the ground tomorrow?" Cesar said.

"No. They don't dig holes on Sundays."

"Any progress?"

"Not much. I think we've got to take a step back and look at this thing from the beginning. That's what I just told Jimmy. Guess I'll head off tomorrow where we found the truck and see if I can come up with something."

"Maybe."

"What do you mean, maybe?"

Cesar took another sip from his bottle before he answered. "Seems to me that's the end. Down the bottom of that ravine is not the beginning."

Virgil turned that over in his mind. Then he pushed back from the railing, put his feet on the floor, and stood up.

"Outta the mouths of babes," Virgil said.

"Guess you're talking about me."

"You got it. You just ruined my night."

"How so?"

"You were right. I gotta begin at the real beginning. And now's the best time to do it. Saturday night at the Black Bull, instead of sitting here with you watching moss grow up that cottonwood."

Fifteen minutes later, Virgil pulled out of his driveway, heading to the Black Bull to walk in Buddy Hinton's last footsteps.

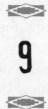

9

It was a little after ten when Virgil pulled into the parking lot of the Black Bull. Early for a Saturday night, but looking around at the packed lot he knew he wouldn't die of loneliness once he got inside. His pickup rolled to a stop at the end of a long line of pickups. Virgil couldn't help noting that his truck was one of the oldest and one of the least attractive. He never competed with the good ole boys who saw horsepower or condition as a measure of their masculinity. In reality, he had never really fit in with that group and on this night, in any event, he was hoping for as much anonymity as possible. That's why he was here in his civvies and driving his old beater.

He pulled down the brim of the sweat-stained Stetson as he walked toward the front door, which was intermittently lit by the flashing oversized bull on the roof. The bull was still short one ear, which had been shot off ten years or so before, by a woman who was aiming at her husband after she'd found him giving mouth-to-mouth to an unknown young lady in the parking lot. Virgil remembered her comment after the incident that she was sorry about the bull, but she had stepped in a hole in the dark and had missed her mark.

Virgil had some history with the place from his late adolescence, but for the last decade or so it was mostly in his official capacity that he came here. The place had changed hands three or four times, but it always thrived. This was more a testament to a lack of competition and the enduring thirst of the locals than any marketing savvy on the part of the series of owners.

The crunch of stone under his boot coupled with the light from the one-eared bull on the roof brought a momentary reflection of his not-too-misspent youth.

"Careful there, Sheriff. You don't want to trip on that step."

Virgil glanced in the direction of the voice. Sitting on one of the rails that lined the porch, on the end of a lit cigarette, was Wade Travis. So much for anonymity.

"Thanks for the warning, Wade." By the time Virgil reached the top step and his boot made contact with the wood floor of the porch, Wade had slipped off the railing and was waiting for him.

"Little bit off the beaten path aren't you, Sheriff? Or is this a line-of-duty visit?"

"No, Wade. Unofficial. Just thought I'd step out for a beer or two."

"Just like a regular fella. Whaddya know. Enjoy yourself."

He stepped away and lit another cigarette as Virgil reached for the door.

"Just make sure when you leave, Sheriff, that you're able to walk that line. You know we don't tolerate drinking and driving in this county."

"Glad you reminded me, Wade. Hope you do the same."

"Don't you worry about me, Sheriff. I got a little designated driver just inside there. She takes good care of me."

Virgil nodded, pulled on the door, then stepped inside.

The place looked pretty much like he remembered. The building actually had some history to it. It had been built in the early 1800s as a trading post and a way station along an old stagecoach route. Time had given it a certain cachet, so even though it was kind of remote from the center of town, the last roadhouse owner decided to incorporate as much of the original building as he could into his modernization. He actually went out of his way to construct the new as close as he could to the old. For his efforts, in the final act of construction, one of the ponderosa pine logs that hadn't been firmly set fell on him, knocking him senseless. Virgil heard he spent the next two years sitting on the front porch in a rocking chair trying to remember his first name.

The interior was laid out basically as one huge room divided in two by one of the largest horseshoe bars in the state. To the left of the door, tables lined the log walls around a black mechanical bull. On the opposite side of the horseshoe bar the large open area was filled with tables. In the center stood the original fireplace, while at the rear of the room there was an open dance area with a raised platform for a band. Virgil hesitated for a second or two, then took a seat at a small table.

"Well, cowboy . . . What can I get you?"

Virgil looked up to see a dark-haired woman and a smile.

"Guess I got you before you even got a boot in the stirrup."

"You could say," Virgil said. "Maybe a nice cold bottle of Sierra if you got it."

"Can do. Only one minor problem."

"What's that?"

"Well, on the weekends if we get people that just want to drink, we'd kinda like them to sit at the bar or at one of the tables over there by the bull. We try to keep this side for people who want to eat something. It's mostly a little crowd-control thing. People eating and listening to music or dancing tend to not get as rowdy as the people on the other side of the bar."

"Makes sense. Well, I can always eat. How about you bring me a burger and a mess of fries to go along with that Sierra. Then I'll just sit quiet and listen to the music."

"Perfect. Be back before the band starts up. They're on a break now."

Virgil looked after her as she walked away. True to her word, she came back as the music trio was filing in from the back door.

"Don't think I've ever seen you in here before," she said as she set the plate in front of Virgil.

"It's been a while. I don't get out much."

"Wife got you on a short leash?"

"No wife, just busy."

"Well, I'm Ruby. If you need anything more, just give a wave."

"Okay. By the way, I'm Virgil."

"Nice to meet you, Virgil."

She turned and walked away. Virgil sat for a moment, the untasted beer in his hand, wondering why he'd just offered his name to the waitress.

For the next half hour, Virgil ate while he listened to the music. From the table he'd chosen, he had a good vantage point for most of the room. He could even see an occasional fool trying to be a ten-second hero, spinning around on top of the bull. One who tried and failed was lurching toward the men's room, ready to give up as much as he had drunk.

He could see why the place was popular. The atmosphere was nice. The burger was as good as he'd ever had and the music was a nice mix. A blend of country and modern, which surprised Virgil. He sat over a second beer, noting the steady stream of new customers. He saw more than a few locals that he'd interacted with over the years, both positively and negatively. Buddy Hinton would have been pretty comfortable here, he decided.

As he put the last of the beer to his lips, he saw the door open and Carlos Castillo walk in with two other men. Virgil didn't know the men, but he thought he recognized one of them from the trucking office where he'd last talked to Carlos. He was kind of surprised to see Carlos quickly look away after their eyes met, then head directly to the bar.

"You ready for another?"

"I just might."

He saw the seat at the bar next to Carlos become vacant.

"Maybe I'll give up this table," he said. "I see quite a few couples coming to dance. Give you a chance to make a little more money than you'll get from me. This place always this busy?"

"Always on weekends."

"What about on weekdays?"

"Well, we have our regulars. Then of course there's always every other Thursday."

"Why every other Thursday?"

"Payday at Hayward Trucking. That's our biggest two days of every month."

After she left, Virgil put the empty glass down, then wove his way around the tables until he reached the empty barstool next to Carlos. Carlos was talking to the man on his left and didn't notice Virgil. Virgil waited for a break in their conversation and for Carlos to put his glass to his lips.

"Hey, Carlos," he said. "We don't run into one another in months then twice in a couple of days. Go figure."

Carlos glanced quickly around the room before returning his attention to Virgil.

"Yeah. Like they say, it's a small world."

He drained the last of the beer, said something to the man to his left, and stood up. "Well, I gotta get home before the wife starts looking for a replacement. See ya, Sheriff."

Before Virgil could say anything else, Carlos was gone. Virgil hesitated just a moment, then headed after Carlos. He caught up with him just as Carlos closed the door of his pickup.

"Carlos."

The look on Carlos's face told him his instincts were not wrong.

"I gotta get down the road," Carlos said.

"Talk to me, Carlos."

Carlos glanced anxiously around the parking lot.

"Let's just say it's been suggested that we not talk to the law," Carlos said. "Virgil, you know I got a wife, three kids, and a mother-in-law who won't quit. I can't jeopardize everything, not in this economy."

Virgil stood in the small dust cloud, watching Carlos's taillights until they disappeared in the dark. When he turned, he was jolted to see Jimmy standing next to him. Then he saw the patrol car parked on the perimeter of the lot.

"Jeez, you must be part Indian to sneak up on me like that."

"Could be. I know my family tree ain't exactly filled with aristocrats. But I didn't want to intrude on your conversation, Virgil."

"What's up, Officer?"

"Well, me and Abby were fishing off the bridge when I got to thinking about what you said, about going back to the beginning. So when I came on duty, while it was still light, I thought I'd come out here and have a look around to see if we missed anything."

"Not a bad idea. So I guess you must have found something if you came looking for me."

"Well during patrol I stopped by the ranch first. The old man told me I'd find you here, so when I got out this way again I decided to stop by."

"Old man's got a name, Jimmy. Remember, he's as good as you or me and better than most by a long shot. Don't forget I'm half-blood myself."

Jimmy squirmed a little inside, caught in his prejudice. Because of Virgil's influence, he'd worked hard to overcome the legacy that he'd grown up with. In his eyes Virgil stood in a separate place from all other men. When he got even the hint of a rebuke from Virgil, it cut right to the core. He cleared his throat.

"Well, Cesar told me you'd be here. Actually, he said this was as close to a night out for you as you'd had in a long time."

"Okay. So what have you got?"

"Just this."

Jimmy held out a small, brightly colored, sturdy bag with a Hayward Ranch logo and a picture of a pecan tree underneath.

"I found this down at the bottom of the ravine. I guess it's not much, seeing as how Buddy worked for Hayward Trucking, but I remember how you said sometimes you're looking at evidence and you don't even realize it."

Virgil took the bag from Jimmy's outstretched hand.

"Good, Jimmy. I'll hold on to this. You better get back out on the road. Be careful. Remember, it's Saturday night."

"I will."

He started to walk toward the cruiser, then stopped.

"Oh, Sheriff," he said, smiling. "Cesar said one more thing. He hoped you'd get lucky."

Virgil waved Jimmy on. He was tempted to get in his truck and go home, but didn't want to listen to the "old man," so he headed back into the roadhouse. He reclaimed his seat at the end of the bar. The house lights had softened and the lyrics of a George Strait song were coming from a girl with a guitar on the platform at the end of the room.

"I thought I'd seen the last of you."

Virgil swung around in his seat to see his former waitress behind the bar.

"Well, I figured I was old enough to stay out late and listen to some music over a beer."

She walked to the tap and brought back a beer. She set it on the bar.

"You wearing two hats tonight?" Virgil said.

"Oh, I'm usually behind the bar, but tonight one of the waitresses was late so I jumped in."

"The place looks good. The music is nice." Virgil's words sounded a little forced to his own ear. "It's Ruby, right?"

"Ruby it is," she said. "But I don't take my love to town. Excuse me."

He watched her walk down the bar to another customer, leaving him to mull over her song reference. Virgil sat there in the dull light, listening to the music and remembering. He ran his hands over the bar, feeling the slight indentations. Then he started looking more closely. Sure enough, there it was, and he was back to a long-ago night in an instant. When the bar had been installed some twenty years before, the owner had invited the patrons to carve their names, initials, or a comment on its surface. At the end of the month he had the carvings sealed over, shellacked, and laminated. He said it'd be a record for posterity and he hoped it might cut down on the writings on the bathroom walls.

In the right-angle corner of the bar, as fresh as the day he carved them, were the names Rusty and Virgil set like an equation, numerator over denominator, an equals sign and the number one. He ran his hand over the carvings again and again, remembering until it hurt.

Time slipped away. The music and the beer took its toll. Then he heard the signal. He hadn't noticed the woman behind the bar watching him.

"Last call, folks."

Ruby put a last beer in front of Virgil, which he knew he would not finish. It had been a long time since he was buzzed. He tipped his hat and made his way toward the door. The night air was fragrant. Even the distant perfume from a striped visitor smelled good. He leaned against his truck, looking at a night sky that couldn't hold another star. He was drowning in remembrance. It was so real he felt like he could reach out in the dark and draw Rusty close like he had on so many long-ago nights like this. A memory so strong it hurt.

He did not know how long he'd been standing there when he heard the voice. He glanced toward the building, dark now except for the light from the bull on his perch. A few last cars were pulling out of the lot. Then he saw Ruby walking toward one of the remaining cars. A man was pulling at her. She stopped and Virgil heard the "No" in a strong voice. The he saw the man grab her by her shoulders. Virgil quickly made his way across the lot. He reached out and put his hand on one of the man's forearms.

"Hey, fella, take it easy. The lady just wants to get in her car and go home. She's had a long night."

Virgil never saw the man's other hand until it was an inch from his jaw, tightened into a fist. The stars vanished from the sky. Everything went black.

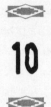

10

Virgil had trouble reconciling the brightness with the night sky. His focus was off, his vision blurred, and the pain in his head was searing.

"Oh, you're back with us." The voice sounded far away, but in the midst of the brightness there was a shadow dividing the light. It leaned over and touched him. He tried to speak, but the words wouldn't come.

"Here, drink this." He felt the straw between his lips. The cool liquid felt so good. He greedily worked the straw.

"Take it easy. It's not going away."

When he finally stopped, he heard the word "thanks" escape his lips. He then felt a cool cloth on his face, which felt almost as satisfying as the cool drink. When that was taken away, his vision started to clear.

"Where . . . ?"

"You're in Hayward Memorial. Now that you're awake, the

doctor will be in shortly. Just take a few minutes to get oriented. By the way, I'm Karen."

The woman left him trying to piece together the events that caused him to end up here. It actually hurt to think. He felt as if the pounding in his head would cause it to explode. A moment later, Karen was back with a needle in her hand.

"A little something for the pain."

Virgil barely felt the needle in his arm.

"This will work pretty quickly," she said as she rubbed the site of the injection again with a sterile swab.

"Thanks." Within moments, he felt the ebbing relief that the needle had offered. By the time the doctor walked in, he felt almost euphoric. A soft wave had smothered the pain and he felt like he was drifting in a languid sea.

"Hello, Virgil." The voice was irritating, calling him away from a place that he was reluctant to leave. "Are you feeling better?"

Virgil nodded. The doctor leaned over and Virgil felt cold metal on his chest.

"Heart's nice and regular." He took the stethoscope off. "I'm just going to check your eyes." He bent down closer this time and Virgil saw the probe coming closer. The doctor looked in both eyes and then asked Virgil to close one while he looked in the other. He reversed the process. Then he asked Virgil to follow his finger while he moved it from one side to the other. When he was finished, he asked Virgil to tell him how many fingers he held up. He repeated this exercise a few times, then sat back on the bed.

"Good. Who am I, Virgil?"

"If you don't know who you are, maybe I should get a different doctor, Sam."

The man smiled. "Glad that blow didn't knock out your

sense of humor. Do you know what happened that brought you here?"

"Yeah. I forgot to duck."

The doctor smiled again.

"That's about it. So you remember everything that happened last night?"

"Last night . . . last night." He looked toward the window and saw the sunlit day outside. "Wow, that must have been some punch."

"I'm sure you've taken harder, but this one was special."

"I guess I owe some guy a little payback."

"Actually, the next time you see him, instead of payback you might want to buy him a drink. He probably saved your life." The doctor paused. "How long have you been getting the headaches, Virgil?"

"Awhile."

"When was the last?"

"Driving out to Redbud the other day. Thought it was from staring into the sun."

"That could trigger it. Bright light, eye strain, a number of things. Are they coming with more frequency?"

"Maybe. Want to tell me what you are fishing for, Sam?"

"Well, Virgil, the tests we've run indicate you have a brain aneurysm. You know what that is?"

"I've got a good idea, but I'm pretty sure you'll tell me anyway."

"Basically, it's a weakness in the membrane covering a blood vessel at a certain point. It starts to balloon out from the pressure of blood flow. Untreated, eventually it will burst, quite often resulting in death."

"Nice of you to sugarcoat it, Sam."

"I know you, Virgil. Remember, I was in the locker room that Friday night, a hundred years ago, when you told Coach Fraser if he showed up drunk one more time you were walking off the field. I'm giving it to you as straight as you gave it to him."

"How long have I had it?"

"You were probably born with the weakness. It just took this long to manifest itself."

"We're talking operation here."

"As soon as possible. It's oozing now. We don't want to wait. If it bursts, the curtain comes down."

"Nice metaphor, Sam."

They talked a little while longer. Sam told Virgil that he had called the sheriff's office and that he'd spoken with Cesar at the ranch.

"I appreciate that," Virgil said as Sam stood to leave. "By the way, when do you want to operate?"

"I was thinking in about three hours."

"Three hours?"

"Virgil, I told you this thing is leaking. We can't afford to waste any time. I'm just waiting to hear back from Dr. Patel."

"Who is he?"

"He's the guy who will do the job."

"I thought you would, Sam."

"No, Virgil. I'll assist but I'm not a neurosurgeon. Dr. Patel is very highly qualified. Without a doubt, if it was me lying there in that bed, he's the man I would want."

"Okay, if you say so. Don't give a guy hardly any time to catch his breath."

"Quit complaining. You got two or three hours." Sam gave a half wave as he left the room.

Virgil lay quietly looking at the sunlight streaming through the window. His mind drifted back inevitably to the night his parents left his life and how his world had changed in an instant. He closed his eyes. He put his hand to his forehead and squeezed, as if to stop the thoughts.

When he opened his eyes again, standing at the foot of the bed was Cesar, the same man who had been at his side the last time he had felt so alone.

"When I said you should get out more, this wasn't what I had in mind." While the weathered face creased into a smile, the fixed clear eyes told another story.

Virgil regarded the man standing at the foot of the bed. He wore a clean, light blue chambray shirt. The slicked-back hair still showing no hint of gray despite his years holding a Stetson that had never seen a sweat stain and was only brought out on special occasions.

"Boy, you clean up real good. You going to a wake or something?"

Cesar didn't answer right away. "I'm not planning to but then I guess that's up to you."

"Well forget about it, old man. You might as well put all that effort you spent in another direction. I'm walking out of this place."

"I kinda figured that, so I reckon I'll stop by Margie's place for some supper after I leave here and then see if I can get lucky."

"Tell Margie that dinner's on me."

"I was planning to."

It was Virgil's turn to smile. He reached out his free hand. Cesar came alongside the bed and gripped it firmly.

"Do what they tell you, boy, and I'll see you tomorrow." As if reading Virgil's mind, he added, "Remember, a lot of people are thinking about you. You're not alone." He squeezed Virgil's hand then headed toward the door. He heard Virgil clearing his throat and turned to look back at the doorway.

"About the rest of that plan of yours at Margie's," Virgil said. "Don't bite off more than you can chew."

Cesar nodded and left the room.

"I'm kinda hungry," Virgil said to the nurse. "What's for supper?"

"For you, glucose and water. Your next meal will be some-time tomorrow, so you'll probably be a lot hungrier by then."

She checked his vital signs and the tube running into his arm, then entered the data into a PC on a cart.

"Welcome to the twenty-first century, hospital style," she said as she saw him watching her. Then she left.

His headache was gone now, but he was left with that slight buzz that gave him the feeling of being removed from the world around him. He closed his eyes for a minute or an hour. He couldn't tell. When at last he opened his eyes again, for a moment or two he wasn't quite sure whether he was awake or dreaming. There was a woman standing by the foot of his bed. She was wearing a brightly flowered light summer dress with a wide scooped neck, revealing her shoulders. Her dark hair fell casually against their whiteness.

"Hey, cowboy. How are you doing? I didn't think you'd still be here, but since I pass the hospital on my way to the restaurant I thought I'd check. I figured it was the least I could do for someone defending my honor. Or at least attempting."

"Ruby. Your name is Ruby."

"That's what it says on my driver's license. My father thought I was a gem."

"Well, sorry my attempt to defend your honor failed. Guess my reaction time was off."

"Yeah. Well it's the thought that counts. I just wanted you to know I appreciated the effort."

She hadn't moved from the foot of the bed. "Well, I . . ."

"Did he give you any more trouble?"

"No. He was just the usual pickup cowboy. A little juiced and he wanted a big ending to his night."

"A pickup cowboy?"

"Yeah, that's what one of the girls started calling them. They come in their pickups, wearing their boots and Stetsons. She says the only time most of them were on a horse they were holding on to a pole for dear life."

Virgil couldn't help but laugh.

"What about you?"

"Me?"

"You ever been on a horse?"

"Oh, once or twice."

Jimmy poked his head inside the doorway. "Hey, Sheriff. How are you doing? I got word that you wanted to see me."

"Give me a minute, Jimmy."

Jimmy stepped back into the hallway, out of sight.

"Sheriff," she said. "He called you Sheriff."

"A lot of people in this county do, but you can call me Virgil. I think that would sound better from you."

"Well, I gotta get going . . . to work." She moved toward the doorway.

"I guess. They say it's the curse of the drinking class. But then I guess you know about that."

"You got that right. Thanks again, Virgil."

The doorway was vacant. For a moment, Virgil wondered if being sheriff was a good thing.

"Okay, Jimmy," he said. "Come on in."

He talked to Jimmy for the next few minutes, reassuring him that he would only be out of the picture for a short time. He gave Jimmy some basic information about keeping the office up to speed. He warned Jimmy to stay focused.

"Alex and Dave want to know if they should both man the substation over to Redbud," Jimmy said.

"For the time being tell them yes. If I get hung up here longer than planned, maybe one of them will have to come to the main office. For now, I want the whole county to feel they're covered. Business as usual. If you need extra help in an emergency, call Dif Taylor. He's always looking for some part-time since he retired. Anything extra becomes casino money for him and Edna."

The nurse came into the room, followed by an attendant. "It's time," she said. "We've got to get you ready."

"Just one more thing, Jimmy. Tomorrow, I want you to pay close attention when you go to Buddy's funeral. I'm going to want to know who was there, and anything at all interesting that you can pick up. You're not just a mourner. Keep your eyes and ears open."

"Do I have to go to the cemetery, Virgil? I don't like grave-yards."

"Yes. They're not my favorite place, either. But at least, unlike Buddy, you get to walk away."

11

"**Y**ou know the last guy who came at me with a razor, I shot."

"Well, I hope you're happy with the haircut," the attendant said.

Ten minutes later, he had collected the results of his work in a pile. There were a few gray hairs in the mix.

"Almost done."

"You mean there's actually still some hair on my head?"

"Just some stubble, but it'll be gone in a minute."

He took a straight razor from the nightstand next to the bed, smeared some foam over Virgil's head, and was done in another five minutes. "Just like shaving a peach," he said. "You want to see?"

"I guess."

"He held up a mirror, and Virgil looked at his bald-headed reflection for the first time. He thought it strange to almost not be able to recognize oneself.

"Guess I'll have to get a Harley when I leave here."

"I think you look pretty good."

"Compared to what?"

"Well, I mean you have a nice shape to your head. Not everybody does. I've had some look like aliens, some their head comes to a point. Yours ain't half bad."

"Thanks for the appraisal. Guess I won't have to shoot you after all."

After the attendant left, Virgil lay quietly. The loss of his topknot made him feel a little more vulnerable. Before he got a chance to feel sorry for himself, the nurse Karen came in, smiling when she saw him.

"Well, you look different. Kinda sexy."

"A lot of good that's going to do me now."

"Well, maybe later. That was a pretty nice-looking visitor you had a while ago."

"Oh, I'll tell Jimmy what you said about him. Maybe he'll be interested."

"Jimmy?"

"My nice-looking visitor."

"Oh, him. Yeah, he was kinda cute. Maybe we could double date. Me and the lady. You and Jimmy."

She winked at Virgil. For the first time, he had no comeback.

The next half hour was pretty much a blur. By the time he was introduced to Dr. Patel, the sharp edge of consciousness was gone and much of what the doctor said was lost on him. A few minutes after the doctor left, Virgil felt strong hands lift him onto the gurney that was alongside his bed. A brief ride along a white hallway, where he saw passersby as if from a distance, then he felt those same strong hands slide him onto an operating table. He tried to help with the transition, but his normally strong arms felt like they almost didn't belong to him. He saw people he didn't know moving about the room talking and even laughing. The room was large and so well lit everything seemed crisp and clear. There was no shadow. The doctor leaned over and Virgil heard him say something about being ready to start, then he saw a couple of masked faces come into view, then nothing.

It could have been an hour or a month when he next became aware of the world. The first thing he saw was the same doctor leaning over him, but without the mask. Virgil remembered the name, Patel. Virgil was struck by how young he looked. He had a hard time wrapping his head around the notion that this man, who looked like a high school senior, had just cut into his brain.

"Everything went just as we hoped. You'll be in this step-down unit a little while longer, and if there are no hiccups, you'll be brought back to your room."

Virgil nodded in response.

"I'll see you later."

Virgil nodded again, closing his eyes as the doctor stepped away. Virgil was eager to get back to the dreamless world that had allowed him to lose a day from his life.

"Well, you either lost that fight or the other guy is dead."

Virgil reluctantly opened his eyes to see Rosie sitting by the side of his bed. He looked around and realized he was back in his room. His throat was so dry that when he responded to her his words came out in a whisper.

"I can't hear you, Virgil. Hold on."

She reached for a pitcher on the table next to Virgil's bed.

After pouring a glass of water, she held it to Virgil's lips. He drained the glass, then lay back into his pillow.

"Who's minding the store?"

"Dif Taylor. Jimmy said you told him to give him a call."

"They bury Buddy?"

"Yeah, they're probably at the cemetery now. I went to the service, then I called Dif. I'm on my way back to the office now, but I knew everyone was anxious to see how you made out. That's why I stopped by, to see if the operation was over. How are you feeling?"

"Better after seeing you. You're one of the best-looking women I never dated."

"I'll be sure to tell Dave. Remind him how lucky he is."

"He wouldn't shoot a man in bed, would he?"

"Some men maybe, but not you. He called three times today from Redbud to find out if I'd heard anything. You got a lot of friends, Virgil."

"Nice to know."

"Well, I've got to get back."

She stood up, leaned over the bed, and gave Virgil a kiss. It felt better than the water.

"We've got to stop meeting like this," he said.

Rosita squeezed his hand and left. Virgil could still taste the softness of her lips and he wondered if Dave realized how lucky he was.

A few minutes later, Karen came into the room.

"Well, back among the living."

"Guess so."

"You ready for that burger and fries now?"

"How about a cold beer to go along with it?"

"Sorry, we don't have our liquor license yet. You'll have to settle for coffee, tea, or juice."

"Coffee it is."

When she returned with a tray, Virgil asked for a mirror.

"Maybe you should wait till after you eat. You're not quite the looker who came in here."

Virgil looked in the mirror she handed him. His head was swathed in white and he realized for the first time he was wearing a light, protective head covering over the bandage. Instinctively, he reached up to feel the hard plastic. His face was swollen and mottled, his eyes blackened and blue.

"Was my nose broken by that punch?"

"Oh, no. The black eyes . . . that's all fallout from the operation."

"I look like he operated on me with a sledgehammer."

"Don't worry. In a week to ten days, you'll be another good-looking guy with a crew cut and that lady that was in here yesterday will be all over you."

Virgil didn't say anything for a few seconds. Then he picked up the coffee cup. "We live in hope," he said. Then he put the cup to his lips and started his healing.

Dirt from the pile next to the open hole in the ground swirled as it caught a steady breeze. Jimmy stood slightly apart from the crowd. He'd come with the rest from the church. The place had been packed. Buddy had a lot of friends and so did his folks. More than a few of them Jimmy did not know at all. He wondered if they were just curious because of the manner in which Buddy died. Jimmy remembered his great-grandpa saying death in the extreme brought out the extreme in some people. The old man had witnessed the last public hanging in the town as a child. As he told Jimmy, he never did see such a crowd. People came from miles around. It was like a carnival. There were vendors selling stuff. People from way out in the country came in buckboards loaded with kids and old folks. Some came alone on muleback. They brought blankets and picnic baskets, waiting anxiously for the big event. He said it was a surefire fascination and he never forgot it.

Jimmy saw this fascination in the eyes of the preacher who had never seen such a crowd in his church. He did not lose the opportunity. By the time he finished, there was hardly a dry eye in the place. Even Jimmy, who had not been brought up in a religious tradition, was stirred. He came away from the service thinking that Buddy was a much better person than he'd ever known. He was so turned around in his thinking that he felt guilty remembering the time Buddy was wrestling with Mary Lou Harris and he reached up under her skirt, or the time he got so drunk he dropped his pants while standing in the bed of his pickup on Main Street and tried pissing on passing cars. The Buddy that came from the preacher's mouth couldn't have done any of those things.

By the time they got to the cemetery the crowd had thinned. The sun was high and the day so hot that if it hadn't been so dry, rivers of perspiration would have been pouring down his back. High overhead, a single cloud drifted across the sky. He could see a flutter among the leaves of the cottonwoods that stood on a knoll in the center of the cemetery. There were a few wooden benches scattered underneath the cottonwoods, he supposed, for people who would come to visit. It puzzled him, why people would want to come, sit on a bench under a tree to look down on a graveyard. The idea that Buddy was soon to be one of these people being looked down upon unnerved him. It wasn't that Buddy was his best friend or even a friend, but he had always treated Jimmy decently, seemed so full of life, and Jimmy kind of felt they were alike. But here he was being lowered into the ground, and Jimmy was not comfortable with the idea of bumping into his own mortality.

The final words of the pastor were floating on the breeze when Jimmy remembered his official reason for being here. He looked over the crowd, trying to focus on the people so that he could give Virgil a full account.

The only standout he saw was the woman he had seen at the foot of Virgil's bed the day before in the hospital. As the service ended, some people walked up and laid flowers on the coffin. A couple touched it. Jimmy didn't join them. He was as close as he wanted to get. As the last of them walked away, he stood for a while in the sudden quiet. He noted how much progress the solitary cloud had made, saw a hawk high in the sky riding the thermals, and he thought about what Virgil had said to him. Then he left the graveyard, as Virgil said he would. Buddy stayed.

12

When she had seen him hanging back from the crowd, she had thought of approaching him to find out how her recent defender was making out. She had gotten the feeling he was standing apart for a reason. Her own feelings about being there were tied up with a lot of emotion and regret that she couldn't even explain to herself. On the ride back to the Black Bull, she thought about Virgil. For a second, she hesitated as she passed by the hospital. She thought of going in again. He might not even be there, she thought, and anyway she wasn't ready to make the first move. Knocked out from one punch, she had been surprised that they had even kept him overnight. No. She was sure he was long gone. Besides, if by chance he was there . . .

She stopped her train of thought, asking herself a different question. Why would she be stopping? The hospital was well in her rearview mirror before she decided to leave it unanswered. By the time she reached the outskirts of town, her mind had moved on to the mundane. It was Monday. She thought it might be a little busier than a normal Monday because a lot of regulars were at the funeral, which meant they might plan on doing some reminiscing about Buddy Hinton over a cold one. That'd be all right with her. She liked to stay busy.

Fifteen minutes later, she was in back of the bar going over the dinner specials and checking the stock, when she glanced down the bar to where Virgil had been sitting. She grabbed a bar towel and started wiping off the bar, ending up where he had been. The names and initials that had been carved into the bar many years before meant nothing to her. But she was curious, remembering his interest. The invitation by the owner to legitimately deface the bar had been well received. Names, initials, wishes of good luck, along with some questionable comments crowded the surface, sealed in perpetuity. Then she saw it. Crowded into the right-angle corner, the carved image of a thrown lariat with a loop at its end. Inside the loop were the names Rusty and Virgil. She ran her hand over the image, but it was as smooth as the rest of the bar, covered in the thickness that had sealed it there forever. She thought of Virgil sitting there and in the hospital.

"I guess we all got a history," she said.

13

"**O**kay, Virgil, you're good to go."

The doctor handed Virgil a packet.

"Here's some information for you. Dos and don'ts. Most of it's common sense, but as Mark Twain said, common sense ain't so common anymore. There's all the post-op protocol listed there, and your next appointment. Your prescription will be waiting for you at Hadley's. Remember, nothing crazy. Try to avoid sudden movement or eyestrain, anything that would trigger a headache. And remember, from now on because of those metal clips in your brain, no MRIs of your head. Have you got your appointment with Dr. Patel?"

"Got everything. Thanks, Sam."

"All right. Get back to the ranch and sit under a tree. There's not enough law around here. You're all we got and we don't want to lose you."

Virgil and Sam shook hands and five minutes later Virgil

was sitting outside in a wheelchair with the nurse Karen by his side.

"Here's my ride. Thanks again, Karen. It was an interesting week."

Virgil stood up as Cesar in the pickup came to a stop. He climbed into the truck and then she closed the door.

"Don't forget what I said. Look up that lady when you become a little more presentable."

Virgil gave a wave from the opened window and they drove off.

"You don't look so bad." Cesar said. "Maybe still a little yellow and puffy. And of course there's that ugly scar that looks like you lost a knife fight."

"You're describing somebody not quite ready for public consumption. Thanks for the reality check."

They drove the rest of the way in silence. As they turned onto the dirt driveway, Virgil let out a sigh.

"It's good to be home."

"It always is," Cesar said.

Although it had only been nine or ten days since he had left, it somehow seemed longer than that. When he got out of the truck and stood a little unsteadily, he realized he was wearing the exact same clothes he'd had on when he left that Saturday night for the Black Bull. He looked around for some sign of change, but saw none.

"I'm going inside. Maybe lie down for a little while."

"Good. You look about as steady as a newborn calf. I'll be back in a couple of hours. Get off your feet."

Virgil watched Cesar go, until he disappeared from view on the county road. He took one more look around, but the only change he could come up with was a little more wilt to the cottonwoods. The screen door slapped in back of him as he stepped into the kitchen. His boots sounded hollow on the floor as he walked to the sink for a glass of water, reminding him that he had failed to use the bootjack outside the kitchen door. Then he remembered they weren't his work boots, but his $150 Noconas, his Christmas splurge, which had never seen the inside of a barn and only a stirrup when he rode in the Fourth of July parade.

In his bedroom, he started to peel off his clothes. He was pulling off his slacks when he reached into the pocket and came up with the small, folded-up sack that Jimmy had handed him the night before he went into the Black Bull. The Hayward name and the logo of the pecan tree reminded him of the unfinished business that awaited his return.

Not now, he thought. A sudden, profound tiredness had come upon him. He slipped off his shorts, letting them lie where they dropped, then crawled into bed. He couldn't remember the last time he had been in his bed in the middle of the afternoon. He looked around the room, largely unchanged in his lifetime. The muslin curtains floated out, catching a slight afternoon breeze. As he fell asleep, an image of the cemetery came to him. The hole in the ground where they had put Buddy Hinton.

He awoke hours later to the sound of Cesar's voice calling him to supper. His sleep had been so deep, he realized he was in the exact position he lay in when he had first closed his eyes. Glancing toward the window, he no longer saw bright sunlight but the softer glow of lateral rays. He yelled down to Cesar, put on some clean clothes, then descended the stairs.

"What did you cook, chilis and beans?"

"I cook lotsa different things," Cesar said, smiling.

"Yeah, but somehow even your Italian comes out Mexican."

"I never saw you push a plate away. Anyhow, tonight it's lasagna with fresh Italian bread courtesy of Rosie. Dave dropped it off on his way down to Redbud this morning. And if that ain't good enough, I got a bottle of Chianti to go along with it. Tomorrow night, courtesy of Jimmy's mom, it's going to be fried chicken, corn bread, and I thought I'd do sweet corn."

"Ah, the living is good," Virgil said.

"Yeah. I was thinking, maybe you oughta lose fights on a regular basis from now on."

"I didn't lose the fight. I never got a chance to be in it."

Over the next week Virgil relaxed to the point of boredom. The staples in his head had been removed and everything was coming along nicely. One morning, when he looked in the mirror he felt he'd gotten to the point where he wouldn't scare small children. The mixed colors of yellow and blue were gone and his head was looking less and less like the skin of a peach, although it was far from needing a comb. Sam had told him one more week ought to do it, but the notion of sitting in a chair on the front porch watching the arc of the sun or trying to find something interesting on TV to fill some of his time was nothing he looked forward to. So the next morning at breakfast he made an announcement.

"I'm out of here for the next couple of days. I'm taking a little drive." He set his coffee cup on the saucer, waiting for Cesar's reply.

"Where to?"

"I'm going to visit Clara."

"That's more than a little drive. It's four hours at least to El Paso."

"I know. That's why I think I'll stay over."

Cesar knew there was no way he could talk Virgil out of the trip, and he actually had been kind of surprised that he'd been able to keep him in the corral as long as he had.

"Maybe you should check with Doc Sam, see what he has to say first."

"Already have."

"Well, leave a message on the answering machine when you get there."

"Sure, Mom." He stood, drained his cup, and walked out the door.

14

He paused by the Black Bull on his way out of town. He thought about stopping. Then the moment passed. He shrugged off the notion, but down deep he knew that any reason to stop would have less to do with Buddy and more to do with the woman.

The rest of the trip passed uneventfully. Outside of the slightly changing landscape there was nothing of interest to slow him down. In less than four hours, he was on the outskirts of El Paso. It had been a while, but he found his way to Clara's house without difficulty.

Clara was his father's oldest sister by almost fifteen years. He figured she must have been well into her eighties by now, but she had sounded unchanged when he had spoken with her. It had been more than a while since he had made his last trip, and he was feeling a little guilty when her house came into sight. It was a small adobe ranch in the old style, with massive logs sticking through the walls on the corners. He could picture the kiva that centered the long wall in the living area and the coolness that contradicted its purpose on a hot, summer day. It always amazed him how the thick walls held the desert heat at bay. Carrying his overnight bag, he opened the heavy oak door and yelled Clara's name. When there was no response, he dropped his bag by a mission oak chair with a multicolored serape draped over its back, then passed through a doorway to the kitchen. Not seeing her there, he went out the back door to Clara's garden. There he finally saw her. She was bent over a row of green. A small wicker basket was on her arm, filled with what Virgil took to be either green peppers or tomatillos. She was wearing a light blue cotton dress sprinkled with desert flowers. Wisps of white hair showed from beneath the straw hat she wore. Her clear, strong voice broke the silence.

"That you, Virgil?" She had yet to stand up or turn around.

"Yes, ma'am."

"'Bout ready to give you up for dead, been so long since I laid eyes on you," she said. "Come, help an old lady."

He walked to her side. She reached for his arm then pulled herself up. "I git down easy enough, but when it comes to standing after I've been bent awhile, that's a different story."

They walked from the heat of the garden into the cool of the adobe. Clara took the basket from Virgil and set it on the counter next to the refrigerator.

"Just let me rinse these off. Then I'll get us a glass of lemonade and we can relax for a moment before dinner."

"Anything I can do?"

"No. Just get that bag of yours and set yourself up down the hall. You know the room."

Virgil grabbed his bag and went down the hall to the same room he had slept in on his last visit, and so many times before.

Nothing had changed. Not that he had expected it to. By the time he got back to the kitchen, two tall glasses of lemonade with sprigs of mint sat ready on the table.

"Virgil, grab them and bring them into the living room while I get us a snack."

He set the glasses on the rustic table with the glass top in front of the wood-framed sofa that sat facing the kiva. The cushions were covered in heavy fabric with a Navajo-style print. A few minutes later, Clara came in carrying a tray and put it down in the middle of the table. Virgil and Clara settled in on either side of the sofa. Virgil picked up his glass, took a long drink from it, then set it back down on the table and smiled.

"Still following your old recipe on the lemonade."

"A little tequila adds just a nice comfort at the end of the day. Don't worry, the worm's still in the bottle."

"I'd say there's a mite more than a little tequila in this glass."

"When you get old, Virgil, you have a little more tolerance for most things. For me it seems to be tequila. Besides, I don't think a classy little old lady like me should sit here in the late afternoon doing shots. A glass of lemonade seems more appropriate."

"No, I guess you wouldn't want to give the wrong impression, you being a retired school librarian and all."

"There you go talking stereotypes. You'd be surprised at what school librarians are capable of. Clyde found that out."

"How long's it been?"

"Almost five years now, and I miss him every day. More so at night."

"Yeah, he was pretty near at the top of my list, too."

"I'm not saying he was perfect. He could hear the pop of a cork from a mile away, but couldn't hear me asking him to take out the garbage from the next room. Nevertheless, he kept me from dying a virgin and gave me two good boys when I figured my eggs had already reached their expiration date. No, warts and all, I couldn't have done better. I was so mad at that bull that gored him I put a load of buckshot in that scattergun over there"   she nodded toward the corner—"then I let him have it all. I don't think he barely noticed, but it made me feel good. The parson said I should have fought hard against my anger. Hell, it was the easiest thing I'd ever done."

"That parson you referred to . . . You got born again?" He said it with a wary look in his eye. Clara almost winced.

"You know better than that, Virgil. I had enough trouble getting born the first time. I figure that'll hold me until they're throwing dirt in my face. But like I said, I've become more tolerant in my old age. What about you? You seen the inside of a church since your last visit?"

"No, ma'am. Guess I'll die a sinner."

"Not according to my religion."

"You got one?"

"We all do, whether we call it religion or not. Mine is I try to do the best I can and try not to hurt anybody in the process. Some probably call it the Golden Rule. I never could tolerate Bible-thumpers, but if that's what it takes to get some folks through, then let them have it. I got an idea you're pretty much like me. I don't see you being mean or doing hurt to anyone on purpose."

Before Virgil could respond, Clara drained her glass and stood up.

"Enough of this serious talk on an empty stomach. C'mon,

let's cook up something. I'll put you to good use and if you do a good job, I'll give you another glass of Aunt Clara's lemonade."

"I don't mind saying that's the best meal I've had in a long time. Sure beats hospital food by a mile."

"Well that's no competition. What about Cesar?"

"Oh, he's good. It's just . . . well, I don't know how it happens, but whatever he cooks, even spaghetti, somehow it all comes out Mexican."

Clara smiled as she set a cup of steaming coffee in front of him then a huge slice of peach pie alongside. "He's a good man," she said. "You're lucky to have him, Mexican food and all."

"No argument there." Virgil swallowed a forkful of pie still warm from the oven. "That is good."

Clara sat watching him wolf down the pie.

"I don't know how Clyde stayed so thin, eating like this. Aren't you having any pie?"

"Maybe later. Just like I used to watch Clyde, I'm enjoying watching you. That's enough for me now. Why don't we take our coffee out on the patio?"

Virgil, cup in hand, followed Clara out the door. They settled next to each other in a glider facing the western ridges. Lateral rays from the setting sun slanted across Clara's garden and the fenced-in field beyond. They sat in the quiet a long time, sipping their coffee and savoring the coolness that came with the departing sun. The hoot of an owl making its first nightly foray broke the quiet.

"Somebody else is hungry," Clara said. She looked at Virgil, studying him in profile, taking note of the long half-moon scar still visible through the new growth on his head. She reached out and took his hand in hers. "I was worried about you. Wish I could've gotten up to see you, but I'm a little leery of a drive that far alone."

Virgil squeezed her hand back. Small and delicate, it seemed lost in his. "I'm fine," he said. "How are the boys?"

"Well, Clyde junior and his family are still up in Seattle. Been there twenty years now. His three girls are growing like weeds. I get up once or twice a year. Vernon's still working on oil rigs. Still single. He gets back here between jobs. You missed him by two weeks. What about you, Virgil? You still sleeping alone?"

"Well, I am at present."

"Hope you're working on that. Remember, you can't shoot a rusty gun."

"Clara, you are a caution."

"C'mon, boy, I'm not telling you something you don't know. You can't dwell in the past."

Virgil didn't say anything.

"She was a pretty girl, that Rusty. So was her mother."

"Still is," he said. "Her mother, I mean. Still hates the sight of me. Which I don't really understand. I loved Rusty, every bit of me. Pretty much finished me when she died."

"She don't hate you. She hates what she lost and what she never got to have. You just remind her of that."

The glider rocked slowly beneath them. The smell of sage was strong in the night air. What was left of the sun barely broke the horizon. Shadows blended into dark as the night settled.

"I didn't realize you knew her that well," he said.

"She's not that hard to figure out, Virgil. Audrey married Micah Hayward more for what he represented than for who he was. It didn't take long for the bloom to come off the rose. Of course, she came to meet the man she should have married for all the right reasons, but by that time she had two sons."

She stopped and looked at him.

"That man she really loved, Virgil . . . that was your father. But the affair was doomed from the start. Your father could never break up a family. There was a lot of damage, nevertheless. By the time the smoke cleared, alcohol had become Micah's sole profession. Then, when your father married an Indian, I think Audrey probably took it as the ultimate denial."

The sun had vanished. It was a moonless night. They were barely visible to each other. The quiet crowded around each, alone with their thoughts. They sat that way a long time.

"I kinda forgot about your history in Hayward," Virgil finally said.

"It was a lifetime ago," she said, "but sometimes it seems like yesterday. You're probably too young to have experienced this, but sometimes, when I look back, it almost seems like somebody else's life."

Virgil nodded.

"I was a girl back then," she said. "In Hayward. The town was little more than a wide spot in the road. Main Street was the only paved road and that was only because it was part of the county highway. Mavis Tillson and me were the first librarians."

"I didn't know that. Mavis Tillson . . ."

"You never met Mavis. She drowned in a gully washer, right after a freak storm. That was before you were born. But anyway, Mavis took a particular interest in Audrey whenever she came into the library. Said she was smart as a whip, but didn't have hardly any friends. Guess that's why she spent so much time in the library. Mavis told me Audrey's father was a rodeo cowboy who didn't come back to town once he found out Audrey's mother was fertile. It was an old story. Audrey's mom worked in the school cafeteria. They didn't have much. I thought I'd seen the last of Audrey once she went away to college. Figured she'd put Hayward in her rearview mirror."

"I thought I'd do that, too," Virgil said. "Once upon a time."

"Small towns can be suffocating. There's got to be a good reason for young people to stay. Guess Rusty was yours. For Audrey, I guess it was Micah. And your father."

"That's why she came back from college? To marry Micah?"

"No . . . no. I think she only came back because her mother was dying. But let me tell you, when she came back, every man in town, from sixteen to sixty, took notice. She had become a real beauty. Micah Hayward, in particular, took notice. And he was at the top of the food chain."

"So that's when she decided to stay."

"Well, I heard this from Mavis, whose father was the only undertaker in town. He told her that he had stood next to Audrey the day after her mother died. It was late December, and there was a Blue Norther coming. Audrey was staring down into the hole in which they had just lowered her mother. When Mavis's father asked Audrey where he should send the bill, she told him, without hesitation, to send it to Micah Hayward at the Hayward Ranch. So I guess you could say that when she came back to the town she grew up in, she came back on top, even taking the town's name as her own. She moved into that house they call Crow's Nest and there she stayed."

"Do you miss Hayward?" Virgil asked the question the next morning after breakfast, as he was preparing to leave.

Clara hesitated a few seconds. "Yes. Yes I do. Clyde and I made a life here in El Paso because of his auctioneering business, and it was good. I know I'll die here, but Hayward was my beginning and I think of it often. I'm reminded of it every time I see one of those Hayward trucks heading for the bridge."

"The bridge?"

"To Juárez," Clara said. "They cross from the highway pretty often."

"I wonder why they're going to Juárez . . ."

"Couldn't tell you, Virgil. But they remind me of Hayward, every time I see one."

Twenty minutes later, as Virgil was heading back to Hayward, his mind was crowded with all he had learned. It struck him that even when he'd decided to take a break, he could never really get away from his past or even his present. For now, though, he was left wondering if Buddy Hinton had driven one of those trucks to Juárez.

And if so, why?

15

Rosie didn't look surprised when Virgil walked through the door.

"I didn't figure you'd have enough common sense to stay down for another week."

"I think Sam said when they cut into my brain they removed my common sense."

"I'm surprised they found any. I suppose you want to know what's going on."

"I've been keeping tabs. Sounds like I haven't even been missed."

Rosie nodded toward the closed door that led to the holding cells. They were used for temporary transfer prisoners or the occasional few-day holdovers.

"Well, if it makes you feel any better, Harry Stanton's been asking for you."

"How long has he been back there?"

"Two days."

"What'd he do this time?"

"Threw a rock through Margie's window 'cause she wouldn't let him in the restaurant. Claims his civil rights have been violated."

"I'll go talk to him later."

For the next hour Virgil went over some reports, including some from the substation down in Redbud, and was happy with everything he read. "Maybe I should stay out of here more often," he said. "I'm feeling kind of superfluous."

"Been telling you that all along," Rosie said. "Well, as long as you're here, I guess I can get out for a regular lunch." Rosie stood up from her desk and headed toward the door. "You sure you can handle this?"

"You don't give a guy an inch, do you?"

"An inch, huh? I always did think size was your problem."

Virgil crumpled a sheet of paper and threw the wadded-up ball at her. Rosie opened the door, then turned toward him, a wicked grin on her face.

"Don't forget about Harry. Tell him I'll bring his lunch back from Margie's. If you don't screw up, I might even bring something for you."

Virgil finished with the paperwork a few minutes after she left, then stood up and headed toward the closed door at the end of the room. There were a couple of these guys in every town, he thought, and Harry Stanton was one of Hayward's. Again he fell into that same category of one of those people for whom life was too much. Not a mean bone in his body, but like so many others like him, he never had a chance. Life was never on their side from the get-go. In Harry's case, he'd spent most of his early life in foster care, no family to speak of, and when he aged out, worked at odd jobs and day labor, then drank any money he made. Once in a while, he'd get in some trouble and spend a couple of days inside. In the winter, Virgil usually let him clean up, shovel snow, and then gave him a bed so he wouldn't freeze to death on the streets. He used to do the same for Harry's partner in crime, Squint. He got the nickname because of a facial tic and how he was always blinking. Squint had died six months before after being kicked in the head by a horse down at the livestock auction in Redbud. He and Harry had been working mucking out stalls and doing general cleanup. Luther, who owns the auction, said Squint blinked at the wrong time. In any event, Harry had been a sad figure ever since.

"Okay, Harry, what have you been up to?"

Harry stumbled to his feet, steadying himself by holding on to the upper bunk. Virgil realized for the first time that Harry was an old man. It came as kind of an epiphany. He'd been part of the landscape, like Cesar, for almost as long as Virgil could remember, but Virgil never really looked at him. He was bent in a kind of permanent way. His wrist bones stood out at the end of his shirtsleeves, looking like they could pop out of the shiny thin skin that covered them. His cheeks were sunken under eyes that seemed clouded and he wore an almost perpetual squint. The stubble on his face was gray and his lips were almost blue.

"Hey, Virgil. Heared you was in the hospital. Was worried about you." Harry took a few slow steps until he was face-to-face with Virgil through the bars that separated them. "You all right now? Was surely worried. Someone said you might die. Was really worried. Don't know what I would do if that was to happen. You 'bout the only friend I got left."

Virgil started to respond but a sudden catch in his throat stopped him. He swung open the door to the cell. It was never locked when Harry was inside.

"I'm fine, Harry. Don't worry. I'm not going anywhere just yet." He had stepped inside Harry's cell and grabbed the solitary chair that stood in the corner. "Here, Harry, but what about you? How come you ended up in here in this nice warm weather?"

Virgil could see Harry working his mostly toothless gums between his thin lips, trying for an answer.

"I remember, Virgil. I remember. It was Margie. She wouldn't let me in. Wanted some food and Margie wouldn't let me in. I was mad, Virgil."

"Now hold on, Harry. Margie wouldn't give you food? Doesn't sound like Margie. She's been feeding you for years."

Harry's eyes widened. Virgil could see a spark amid the yellow-tinted pupils. Harry waved one hand and accidentally hit the bars of the cell.

"No, no. Wouldn't let me in the front door like the other people."

"But, Harry, Margie always gives you food around back." An image of Harry sitting on the bottom step at the back of Margie's restaurant popped into Virgil's head. "Those people going in the front door, Harry . . . they're Margie's paying customers." Virgil could see Harry was getting more agitated. "Take it easy, Harry, you're getting yourself all worked up."

"But, Virgil, I had money."

"What do you mean?"

Harry stood up from the chair unsteadily and started fishing through his pockets.

"See?" He held up a twenty-dollar bill in front of Virgil. "I had money just like those other people. Wanted to give it to Margie, for all them other times, but that kid that works there wouldn't let me in. He pushed me down the stairs, Virgil.

Wouldn't listen. Tried to tell him, but he wouldn't listen. I got mad . . . Picked up a stone."

"Okay, Harry. It just sounds like a misunderstanding."

"Sorry, Virgil. I like Margie, almost as much as you. Didn't mean to cause trouble."

"I'll explain it to Margie. It'll be okay."

Virgil could see Harry's breathing was labored.

"Come on, Harry. Sit back down." He walked him to his cot, feeling his thinness through his shirt as he held him. Harry sat down heavily. "I think you should rest now."

"I am a little tired, Virgil."

"Sure you are, old-timer. Why don't you just lay back and think how you're going to spend that twenty dollars."

"Yeah, that's what I'll do. It was nice of Wade to give it to me."

"Wade . . . Are you sure Wade gave it to you? Wade don't seem like the generous type to me. At least not twenty dollars' worth."

"No, it was Wade, Virgil. He give it to me that night outside that nice restaurant when I saw him with Buddy."

"You saw him with Buddy? Buddy Hinton?"

"Yeah. It was Buddy. It was kinda dark but it was Buddy."

"Do you remember what they were doing?"

"Well, they weren't doing much of anything. Jist sitting in that white truck. I noticed them 'cause they was kinda loud. Maybe they was arguing. Wade saw me and he got out and come over to me. I thought I was in trouble . . . And Wade . . . Well, he wasn't always friendly to me, but this time he give me that twenty-dollar bill. Whaddya think of that, Virgil? Ain't that something? Just outta the goodness of his heart. Imagine that."

"That's what I'm trying to do, Harry. Imagine Wade giving out a twenty-dollar bill from the goodness of his heart."

*   *   *

"Rosie, I'm going over to Margie's, maybe make one more stop, then I'll be back. Just for the record, you guys did a great job while I was gone."

"We aim to please, Virgil. Why don't you head home and put your feet up? Call it a day."

"This isn't heavy duty, just a couple of calls. Don't worry." He picked up his hat from the chair next to his desk. "Be back soon." Before she could make another attempt to dissuade him, he was out the door.

Virgil stood next to the opened car door as the heat rushed out, then changed his mind and shut it. Margie's was only a ten-minute walk and he figured the exercise wouldn't hurt. It had to be close to a hundred, he thought. He wasn't surprised when he walked around to the front of the building to see Main Street deserted. It was like one of those movies where a last survivor wanders a desolated landscape looking for another human being. He turned left on Main and headed for Margie's. By the time he was halfway there, he was sorry he hadn't taken the car. Every time he inhaled, he felt like he was in a blast furnace. Margie's sat at the end of the next block and he quickened his pace. When at last he stepped through the front door and the coolness hit him, he actually felt weak in his legs and he grabbed the first seat he could. Before a minute went by, Margie herself had put a glass of water in front of him.

"Virgil, drink this."

He didn't argue, but put the glass to his lips and swallowed.

"You look like you're about to explode. I saw you coming down the street. Where's your car?"

"I thought I'd walk."

"Virgil, it's one hundred and nine degrees out there! Are you crazy? You just got out of the hospital a week or so ago. When they cut open your skull, did they take out your common sense?"

"That's the second time someone's asked that same question."

"Did you see all the other pedestrians out there? Wait'll Rosie hears this."

Virgil held up his hand. "You tell her, my life won't be worth spit. I'll never eat another meal in this place."

"Okay, calm down. What do you want to eat?"

Virgil told her and she left him, after filling his glass again. By the time she returned, he was feeling almost normal.

"Thanks, Margie. I wanted to speak to you about Harry."

"No need." She sat down opposite him as he started eating. She gave a quick look around to make sure everyone else in the place was being taken care of, then turned to look at Virgil. "I spoke to the busboy. He should have just walked Harry around back, but he didn't know, and for some reason Harry seemed adamant about coming in the front door."

Virgil explained the reason to Margie.

"I'll be damned. Harry wanted to give me his twenty dollars. Well, that old man doesn't know it, but he just bought himself a meal a day for the rest of his life."

Virgil smiled. "You're a good woman, Margie."

"Not so bad yourself, Virgil. Hell, you been taking in strays for years, beginning with Jimmy."

"What about the window Harry broke?"

"No big deal. I already traded a free meal to Silas over at the hardware store and he fixed it. I must say the one thing in this whole story that shocks me is Wade giving Harry twenty dollars. I might have to reevaluate my opinion of him."

After Margie left, Virgil finished the last of his lunch.

When he stood up, he was feeling a lot better. As he got ready to leave, Viola Hinton came up to him.

"I hear you need a ride, Sheriff."

Virgil looked over at Margie, who just smiled.

"Why thank you, Viola, that would be nice."

He followed her out the door to her car. She asked how he was feeling and commented on the heat.

"Sorry, I didn't get a chance to say good-bye to Buddy," he said. "How you all doing?"

"We're good." They had just pulled into the parking lot. "By the way, Virgil, I wanted to tell you before that Buddy was seeing one of the workers up at Hayward Ranch. I couldn't tell you in front of Buddy's dad. He didn't know and wouldn't have liked it. He has a problem with . . . Well, he's a good man, but he has a problem with illegals."

"I understand. Thanks for telling me." Virgil got out of the car and waved as Viola pulled away. Then he walked into the office. He was starting to feel good again.

"I have a few questions for Harry," he said to Rosie, "but at least I took care of Harry's problem. Margie even promised to make sure Harry never goes hungry again."

Rosie didn't say anything. There was a heavy look on her face.

"What's wrong?"

"Harry's never going to go hungry again," she said, "because he's dead in that cell back there."

Virgil sat down heavily into his chair. Suddenly, he wasn't feeling so good after all.

16

"Well, if it ain't the law. We gotta stop meeting like this, Sheriff, or people will get the wrong idea."

"Can't speak for you, Wade, but I think that anyone who knows me knows we won't be buying furniture together anytime soon."

Wade had just come out of his office.

"Looks like you're doing well for yourself," Virgil said as he looked around the place. He could see men working on a variety of vehicles in the two large garages adjoining the building. There was also a construction crew working on a larger building in an empty lot next to Wade's office on the other side. "I hear you're all lined up for the racing circuit and that you're preparing to take a huge step up."

"Yeah, well I been lucky."

"What's that going to be?" Virgil asked, pointing to the new construction.

"Showrooms."

"For what?"

"Cars, trucks, motorcycles . . . I got a dealership."

"I am impressed. You truly are coming up in the world."

"Listen, I got an appointment and based on your past visits, I don't figure you came by to hear about my good luck."

"No, not exactly. Shame Buddy didn't have your kind of luck." At the mention of Buddy, Virgil thought he detected a slight tightness of Wade's jaw.

"Yeah, well, like the man said . . . Life ain't fair."

"Well, it sure wasn't for Buddy, but that brings me to the reason for my drop-by. You remember that last night . . . You know, when you said Buddy left the Black Bull. I think as you put it, he went to howl at the moon."

"Yeah, I remember."

"Well, you said you didn't go with him and you had no idea where he went. That's been kind of bothering me. I mean you and Buddy being so close and all. It got to bothering me a little bit more when I found out you and Buddy spent a little time arguing in his truck."

There was no mistaking Wade's reaction this time. "Where did you hear that?"

"Well, it happened kind of accidental-like, when Harry Stanton told me how generous you'd been to him that night and gave him twenty whole dollars out of the goodness of your heart. That was mighty nice of you, Wade. I didn't realize what a friend of the less fortunate you were. So I guess I was wondering if you'd be able to tell me about that?"

"There ain't nothing to tell. That ole bum was there and he just looked kind of pathetic, so I give him a couple of bucks."

"Well, Harry thought you and Buddy were arguing about something. This is when you were outside, which I guess you didn't remember when you first told me you hadn't gone outside with Buddy."

Again, he saw Wade's jaw tighten.

"Yeah I guess I forgot about that, but we wasn't arguing. Just having a conversation."

"Guess maybe I should talk to Harry some more. See if he can tell me a little bit clearer. He's sleeping it off in one of the cells."

"He's there now?"

"Since last night. I'll probably let him go when I get back, after we have another little talk. That is, if you're sure there's nothing else you'd like to add."

Wade looked down at his highly polished boots, stirring a little graveled dirt.

"Well, maybe we did have a little dustup now that I'm thinking about it. Weren't nothing big. Buddy was complaining about his job. Thinking about quitting. I told him he was crazy."

"Why did you care? What difference did it make to you?"

"Well, Buddy had promised to stay down at the terminal in Redbud to coordinate the service contract I have with the Haywards, but he said he didn't want to stay there anymore."

"Did he say why?"

"Nope. I told him he wouldn't be working for the Haywards. Even told him I'd make him a full partner once I got the dealership up and running. He'd take care of the service end, I'd be handling the showroom."

"That was a real generous offer. But you're telling me he never said why he wanted to get away from the Haywards?"

"No. Said it wouldn't be good to talk about it."

"What do you think he meant by that?"

"I don't know. He just said it'd be best if I didn't talk about it to anyone. That's why I didn't tell you right off. He was acting kind of nervous. Then I left him and went back inside the Black Bull. An hour or two later, I realized he must have taken off."

"He never came back inside?"

"If he did, I didn't see him. The place was packed that night."

By the time Virgil pulled into the parking lot in back of the office, the undertaker's van was already there. It was almost three.

"Howdy, Sheriff." The greeting came as he walked through the door.

"Hello, Titus."

"Mr. Simpson sent us over for Harry." Virgil nodded toward the other attendant who had just come into the room.

"That's what I figured."

"He wanted to know what you wanted for him."

Virgil looked at Rosie.

"Any suggestions?"

"Well, I know he did some maintenance work for that Catholic Church. Saint Ann's. I could give them a call."

"I'd appreciate that. I'd kinda like Harry to go out with a little remembrance. Tell them he's down at Simpson's funeral home and if they need anything I'll take care of it."

"Virgil, the town should handle it."

He sat down at his desk, took off his hat, then rubbed the bridge of his nose with his free hand.

"No. I'd rather do it. Titus, make sure you tell that to Mr. Simpson when you get back."

"Okay, Sheriff. Anything you say. Can we go get old Harry now?"

"Sure. I'll meet you at the back door in five minutes."

Virgil stood holding the door open while they wheeled the gurney through. Then they carefully loaded their burden into the back of their van.

"Thank you, Sheriff. Kind of sad to see old Harry end up this way. I guess none of us knows how we're gonna end up."

"Well, Titus, I think the end for Harry was written a long time ago."

He watched as the van pulled out of the parking lot, then closed the back door. He walked to his car, suddenly feeling very tired.

There was no one around when he got back to the ranch, and he was glad. He just didn't feel like interacting with anyone, even Cesar. It was a little after four, so before he went into the house, he walked down to the corral. It had been unusually hot, so he figured the horses were still in, a fact confirmed by Jack long before he reached the barn. In the heat of summer, the horses were let out late in the day and grazed through the night, then were brought in the next morning before the heat started to build. The barn was quiet as he stepped in, with just the sound of the horses moving occasionally in their stalls. A couple of hens moved up and down the aisles pecking at anything that moved, also content to stay inside out of the day's heat. He opened the door at the end of the barn, which led into a corral. As soon as he did, the wind-tunnel effect with the doors opened at either end flooded the air with barn scent. For him it was rich with the past. He had seen Jack foaled in this barn and his dam die here in a subsequent foal's birth. Virgil's mother had put him on his first horse here and spent hours showing him the way to gentle a horse so that every time he climbed aboard it wouldn't be a re-creation of a bronco-busting episode.

He lingered, wrapped in memory until Jack brought him back to the present with his call. Then one by one as he walked the length of the barn, he opened each stall door. The horses moved in hurried procession toward the corral. When they were all out, he watched them gather expectantly at the far end, waiting for the gate to be opened. Virgil looked them over as they bunched together, to see if any one of the nine showed any signs of injury or problems. They ranged from the blood red mahogany of Jack to the old piebald gelding that Cesar fancied with a mix of colors in between. He knew a couple of the mares were close, their swollen bellies evidence of Jack's potency. He carefully moved through them, talking in a soft voice. It would have been safer to slip through the fence and open the gate from the other side, but the thought never occurred to him. Every one of them knew him as he knew them, and even though they bumped and nudged him, he knew there was no danger.

"Take it easy, guys. You're almost there." He slid the bar across between the rails, jumped on the bottom rail with one foot while pushing off with the other, and the gate swung wide. The horses burst through toward the open prairie, some of them giving exuberant bucks as they called to one another. Through the dust cloud that followed in their wake, their distinct forms morphed into one and the sound of their hoofbeats echoed as a single note.

Virgil watched them gallop toward their freedom, feeling

the same exhilaration that he'd felt hundreds of times before. It never grew old. When at last they disappeared over the first low-lying hill, he stepped off the rail and headed back to the barn. For the next hour, moving from stall to stall, he cleaned them and freshened each with new bedding. The physical activity felt good. He knew it would be a pleasant surprise for Cesar. He could picture the smile on the man's face. When he finished, he walked back to the house. After pulling his boots off on the bootjack, he went into the kitchen, got a glass from the cabinet over the sink, and filled it with iced lemonade. He downed it in three gulps while standing over the sink. Ten minutes later, shower water was streaming over his body, taking with it the remnants of his exertion in the barn. When he walked into his bedroom, he couldn't resist the call of the clean sheets and he slid between them, luxuriating in the feel of smoothness against his skin. A sudden tiredness overtook him and his last, conscious memory was of the curtains at the opened window floating on an errant breeze.

Hours later, a flash of heat lightning illuminated the room and revealed Virgil uncovered, still lying motionless. He stirred, still wrapped in an erotic dream he was reluctant to leave. Finally, he dropped his legs over the side of the bed and came to a sitting position. He listened for signs of life in the house, but heard none. Feeling like he had just emerged from a coma, he rose to his feet and moved toward the bathroom. After he relieved himself, he threw cold water into his face to wash the last of the sleep away, then returned to the bedroom, got dressed, and headed downstairs. Darkness had begun to invade the house, so he flicked on the light in the kitchen. There was no sign of Cesar and he recalled some early-morning reference of his about being gone overnight. He knew he spent some time with a woman Virgil had never met.

He opened the refrigerator and stood looking at nothing inside that appealed to him. He grabbed a slice of cheese, pulled off the cellophane wrapper, and ate it. Still unsatisfied, he glanced at the clock on the wall and saw it was going on nine. Margie's would be closed by the time he got there, but he knew of another place that would be open late. He closed the fridge door, went and got his good boots, and went upstairs to change his shirt.

The screen door slapped loudly in back of him as he left the house. He paused for just an instant on the front porch, listening to the night, then walked across the yard and got into his truck. At the end of the driveway, instead of turning right into town, he turned left and headed toward the Black Bull.

17

It was about nine thirty when he walked through the door of the Black Bull. The restaurant area was fairly empty, but the bar side was busy. Not bad for a weekday night, he thought. He took a seat at a small table on the restaurant side. A waitress brought him a menu, but when she told him the special was ribs, he just handed it back to her and asked for the special. While he was sitting over his beer, waiting for his meal to arrive, he looked over the crowd. There was no live music. The televisions in back of the bar were featuring baseball. There were a lot of familiar faces, but nobody had acknowledged his presence. He could make out a Rangers game on one set getting a loud reaction from the bar crowd as someone connected for a home run. The Black Bull itself was standing idly, waiting for the next guy who'd drunk enough courage to give him a go. Virgil scanned the place, looking for a certain someone, but came up empty. Finally, his gaze came to rest on the plate that had been put in front of him.

Twenty minutes later, he sat back from his cleared plate. He hadn't realized how hungry he was.

"Guess you enjoyed it," the waitress said with a smile. "Surprised you didn't eat the plate."

"Yes, ma'am. That was as good as it looked."

"How about some dessert?"

"A man should know his limitations. I'll pass, but some black coffee would work."

"You got it."

He sat over two cups, replaying the day's events in his head, the talk with Wade and Harry Stanton's exit from a world that had paid him little notice. Virgil generally took things in stride, but for some reason Harry's death had brought him to a dark place. Maybe it was the unexpectedness, or the fact that he had recently brushed up against his own mortality.

"Anything else?"

"No, thank you."

She gave him his tab. When she returned with his card, he signed then she turned to walk away.

"Excuse me," he said. "Is the owner here, by any chance?"

"Upstairs." She pointed to a door next to the door that led into the kitchen. Virgil thought that as long as he was here, he might as well see if he could verify some of the things that Wade had said. He crossed the room, opened the door, and climbed a flight of stairs. There was a short hallway that angled to the right, at the end of which was a doorway. A light showed from under the door. He knocked twice, then waited. He heard footsteps on the other side. When the door opened, Ruby was standing there.

"Well hello, Sheriff. I wasn't expecting to see you. What can I do for you?"

"Actually, I was hoping I could see the owner."

"Oh, well, come on in."

Virgil stepped inside. When she closed the door, she lightly brushed him, and he could smell a certain fragrance. It was not an unpleasant sensation. She turned and he followed her past a desk in a small office that had a couple of filing cabinets against a wall. There was a computer on the desk and an opened folder holding a slew of what looked like delivery forms.

"I was just entering some bills into the computer," she said.

She walked through a doorway which was opened at the other end of the office. When Virgil followed her, he stepped into a huge living area that encompassed a modern kitchen at the far end, separated from the rest of the room by a natural wooden bar that spanned almost the width of the room. At the opposite end of the room was a fireplace, which Virgil realized was a perfect match to the one downstairs and positioned in the middle of the wall, so they shared the same flue. Near the kitchen area was a large rustic harvest table, while the rest of the room was given over to comfortable-looking occasional chairs and end tables. Positioned in front of the fireplace was a large sofa covered in a Southwestern print that matched the fabric covering the chairs. Above the fireplace was the mounted head of a huge elk.

"That's some trophy," Virgil said.

"I prefer living animals, but it wasn't my call. In any event, he is magnificent."

Ruby gestured toward one end of the sofa. Virgil sat down and looked around the room.

"Will he be long?" he asked.

"Who?"

"The owner."

"Sheriff, I *am* the owner."

"But I thought you were just a waitress."

"Just a waitress? Sheriff, I'll do you a favor. I won't repeat that comment to the waitstaff downstairs. That way when you leave, your car won't be sitting on four flat tires."

"I'm sorry . . . I didn't mean . . ."

The smile that crossed Ruby's lips showed she was enjoying Virgil's discomfort.

"It's all right," she said. "I was just teasing."

"It's just that I thought when this place was redone some years back . . . I mean, I thought I'd heard that somebody from back East had bought it and then I guess he died and I figured some other fella took it over."

"That man that did the expansion. He was my father. This was his dream. He was in love with his idea of the West. I think he overdosed on John Wayne and Randolph Scott when he was a kid. His favorite movie was *Shane*. I must have seen it a dozen times over the years. I could recite the dialogue verbatim. Anyhow, he bought the place on a whim with the idea of turning it into what it's become today. But he never lived to see it done. I was working in New York when he died. My mother wanted no part of it. It wasn't her dream. By that time I was looking for something different. I felt bad that after all he put into it, it was just going to be tossed away like he was never here, to some random buyer. So I decided to try something new. In a way, I guess I was trying to keep his dream alive. Probably doesn't make much sense to you."

"No. It makes perfect sense. I mean, a person walks the earth. He leaves a mark. His life should mean something." Virgil looked up at the elk. "Every time, you look at him"—he gestured toward the mounted head—"you can imagine what he must have been. The life he had, the battles he fought. You can see it in his eyes and you take note. A man, any man, should have at least that . . . that the people he leaves behind remember and take note."

Virgil looked away for a second, the last image of Harry Stanton suddenly popping into his mind.

"Maybe that's why I talk to him when I'm here alone," she said, smiling. "So, Sheriff, what can I do for you?"

"Well, you can start by calling me Virgil. I'm not always on duty."

"So this is a social call?"

"Well, I did want to ask you something, but it could wait for another time if you're busy. Actually, when I came in to eat downstairs, after I'd finished I was sitting at the table and looking around for a friendly face, but the face I was looking for wasn't there."

"Did you ever find it?"

"Yes, when I knocked on that door."

"I'm glad, Virgil."

She leaned across the sofa and touched his cheek. Then she turned his head slightly and traced the half-moon line of his scar from beginning to end.

"When I saw you in the hospital," she said, "I didn't know about this. I wish you'd have told me. I would have been there, because I think I've been looking for a friendly face also."

He looked into her eyes and saw the warmth there. He was mesmerized by her touch.

"It's been a long time for me," he said. "I mean, I just want you to know . . ."

She moved her finger to his lips and smiled. "Once you've ridden a bike, Virgil, you don't forget."

He reached across the sofa and drew her close. Her scent filled him, his lips found hers, and the touch of her lifted him up from that dark place.

He left the bathroom, heading back to the bed when the silver light streaming through the window stopped him. The moon was starting its descent in the western sky. The world was a silhouette. The rolling terrain black against the gray. He glanced at the still figure wrapped in a tangle of sheets, one smooth leg exposed, the mass of dark hair against the pillow caught in that silver light from the window. For the first time in a long time, Virgil felt a connectedness that had been missing from his life.

He glanced once more at the outline of the ridge in the distance, the same ridge that had reluctantly given up the terrible secret. He knew that deep down, as much as that had become a focus for him, it was not his whole life. Then he slipped under the sheet alongside Ruby, reached out, and felt her stir beneath his touch.

Virgil reached his hand out to empty space, opened one eye, and saw that he was alone. The imprint of her head on the pillow confirmed that it hadn't been a dream. Then he smelled the bacon and sat up. Before he could get his bearings, she ran into the room and leaped into the bed. She pushed him down and gave him a long, soulful kiss. When she felt him stirring beneath her, she rolled over and sat up.

"There's time for that after breakfast. Come on."

"You know what you said about the bicycle? I haven't forgotten."

"I was aware of that several times last night. Come on, we need to keep our strength up."

Reluctantly, Virgil slipped on his shorts then followed her out to the kitchen. He sat at the long bar while she brought the breakfast. Then they attacked it with a ferocity that they later laughed about.

"I can't think of a better way to work up an appetite," he said as he sat over his second cup of coffee.

She reached her hand across and covered his.

"Is that the right time?" he said, looking at her watch.

"Pretty close."

"I better check in before they send out the bloodhounds."

"Are you really that crucial?" she teased while he punched in the number to the office.

"Ma'am, I'm the last line of defense between survival and Armageddon."

He winked as he waited for Rosie.

"I know what time it is," he said into the phone. "I got hung up. And yes, I know I'm not there. That's why I'm calling. Are you okay? You know what I mean." He paused. "Sure, I know. I just wanted to make sure . . . I mean in case you have to reach me. God! Now I know why Dave likes to stay at Redbud. Yeah, I know you and he have quality time when he's home."

Ruby sat quietly listening to the conversation. At last, he folded the phone and put it away.

"What were you saying about the last line of defense? Armageddon? It sounds like the world is still turning without you."

"Yeah, seems like I'm a legend only in my own mind."

"Who was that, anyway?"

"I guess you'd call her the power behind the throne. At least that's what she thinks. Her name is Rosita. Rosie when she's acting human."

"Sounds like you guys have a dynamic relationship."

"Dynamic, good word. I guess that pretty well describes it."

"By the way, what were the questions? Or was that just a ploy to get in my pants?"

"The questions . . ."

"Last night, you said you had some questions for me."

"Oh. They were about Buddy. Buddy Hinton. I heard you went to his funeral."

"Yes. I saw your friend from the hospital there."

"That's Jimmy Tillman, my deputy. He saw you and I just thought it kind of odd. I mean, you being there, but that's when I thought you were a waitress."

"I'm glad you left out the *just*."

"I won't make that mistake again."

"Buddy was pretty much of a regular. A real nice guy. Came in, had a good time, didn't give anybody grief. The kind of customer you wish all your customers were like in this business. Then, because of the way he died, the circumstances, well, I felt like I wanted to go. That's why I was there."

"Do you remember anything special about that last night? When he was here?"

"Like what?"

"Anything different. An argument, any kind of a mix-up involving him or his friend Wade?"

"You mean Wade Travis? The auto repair guy that's into racing?"

"Yes, anything that night you can remember."

Ruby sat back in her chair. "That was a pretty crazy night, as I remember. Whenever it's payday at Hayward, the place is packed. We even cash payroll checks for a lot of them. But I can't say that night was unusual. Nothing sticks out much. Much as I liked Buddy I wasn't crazy about Wade."

"Why do you say that?"

"A couple of things. He thinks he's God's gift for one thing. Kind of arrogant, looking for special treatment . . . thinks he's a player. Not like Buddy at all. But I'm sorry, I just can't remember any incident. I mean they were often together. They probably were that night."

"What about other people? Anybody stand out? Maybe someone new?"

"No. Sorry, Virgil, like I said, it was just so busy."

"Yeah, I understand."

"I don't know if it would help you, but you're welcome to watch the video."

"The video? What do you mean?"

"Virgil, this is the twenty-first century. We've got video, inside and out. That was one of the first things I did when I came here. In this business, it's particularly necessary. I've even got you forgetting to duck, if you're interested."

"No, I'll pass on that. But you have video of that night inside and the parking lot? What about out back?"

"No, not the back. Sorry, I just never thought that would be necessary. Guess I was wrong."

"Could you get it for me?"

"Sure. It will take a little while. It's downstairs with the other discs. I'll have to locate it."

"Great. I'll look at it when I come back tonight."

"You're coming back?"

"What did you think, this was a hit-and-run?"

She didn't answer.

"What's the matter?" he said.

"Maybe we're moving a little too fast. I mean, remember what you said last night. It's been a long time for you. Well, this isn't typical for me, either. I mean, I'm not denying the chemistry, but beyond that . . . I mean, we hardly know each other."

Virgil reached his hand across the table and covered her hand with his.

"You're absolutely right. I don't want to rush this. How about I come back tonight and we just have dinner together and talk. If you can get that disc, I'll take it with me. Then next weekend we'll build in some time together. I don't want you to think I'm one of those pickup cowboys, so this will be a chance to show you. But I gotta admit, it's pretty hard to get the horse back in the barn after the door's been opened."

"That all sounds good," she said, "but I'm a little worried about that open door, too."

Instead of going to the office, he decided to stop off at the ranch first. He saw Pedro in the barn putting the horses in their stalls. The sun was already pretty high and the heat was starting to build. He waved to him, went into the house, and came back out a half hour later having showered and changed.

"Pete, where's Cesar and José?"

"Up in high country working on a well pump."

"I'll probably be back late this afternoon. Tell Cesar."

"Okay."

He was almost in the cruiser when Pedro waved to him. "What is it, Pete?"

"I forget. Someone came looking for you . . . Funny

name . . . I think he say Billy Three Hats. He say he stop by office later."

"Thanks." Virgil gave a wave and started the cruiser toward the county road. His mind was on the videos and what if anything they might tell him, but whatever Billy Three Hats wanted he knew just might take precedence over anything else on his plate.

An hour later he was sitting in his office when Jimmy came in early for his shift. He waved him over.

"What's up, Sheriff?"

"You got to get more of a life, Jimmy. Coming in here over an hour before your shift starts."

"Too hot to fish or do much of anything outside. Figured at least in here or in the car I'd be cool."

"Well, as long as you're here . . . I've been looking at this damn video footage till I'm practically cross-eyed, and seeing nothing. Maybe we need another pair of eyes. I'm going to run them again."

Jimmy pulled one of the other chairs over alongside Virgil's and together they watched the monitor. Just as Ruby had said, the Black Bull was jumping that night. The parking lot filled early and a few cars and trucks were actually parked along the county road. They were pretty much a blur on the extreme range of the video. On his first viewing, Virgil had been able to make out Buddy's white pickup and he could see that there were two figures inside for quite a while, but the images were indistinct. Then he saw them get out and one of them walk over to another man that he took to be Harry Stanton. Then after a bit they walked into the Black Bull. It was only when they stepped inside that Virgil could clearly identify them as Buddy and Wade. The rest of the video inside showed nothing unusual, and a little after midnight Buddy was no longer seen. Wade was still inside, like he had told Virgil, when Buddy left. Buddy's pickup was in the parking lot, but there was no sign of him. If, as Wade said, he went out to howl at the moon, he could have been around back. While he was watering the landscape, he would have been out of camera range.

Jimmy sat and watched the footage with Virgil and saw nothing that Virgil hadn't seen. They had just restarted it when Rosie came in.

"See you boys are still watching movies. Doesn't look like much of a plot to me. Virgil, I'm leaving. I gotta get home and make supper. Jessie, her husband, and the baby are coming over and Dave's coming home from Redbud for some of that quality time we talked about. Alex is going to stay late down there if you need to talk to him."

Virgil had paused the video while Rosie was speaking.

"That's definitely Buddy and Wade like we seen before in Buddy's truck," Jimmy said as he stared at the frozen frame. "They was in there a long time. Whatever they was talking about sure must have been pretty important."

"All right, Rosie," Virgil said. "You take off. If we ever get through this and I'm hungry, I might just stop by."

"You ain't invited."

"Thanks. I can live with rejection, but these reruns aren't helping me out much." He looked again at the frozen image on the monitor.

"Why is that guy standing by the road?" Rosie said.

"What do you mean?"

"Don't you see out there on the road? That man just standing there?"

"Jimmy, run the footage."

Jimmy pressed play. They sat in silence for the next four or five minutes, until Wade and Buddy got out of the truck.

"Look at that," Virgil said. The figure Rosie had pointed out hadn't moved. "That is strange. He seems to be watching the whole time."

Virgil froze the video again and pulled his chair right up to the monitor. The figure on the periphery of the camera's range remained a dark shadow.

"Who is he?"

"Can't tell," Jimmy said. "It's too dark and he's too far away."

The three of them looked intently at the screen.

"Well, all I can see is a belt buckle," Rosie said.

Virgil looked again at the screen. The few lights in the parking lot, along with the light from the full moon reflected off all of the vehicles bumpers and windows and one other thing near the road, the silver buckle on the belt of the unknown silent figure standing there.

18

Virgil had just hung up the phone when Jimmy came through the door.

"What's up?"

"I was heading out on patrol and I didn't know if you'd be here when I got back so I thought . . ."

"You still thinking about what we saw on that video?"

"Yeah and some other things, like maybe it would help some if you would tell me what you're thinking. Then maybe there's something I can do."

"Jimmy, I don't think this is just about Buddy. I think there's more to this."

"I don't understand."

"From the very first, I've had a suspicion this wasn't just about someone not liking Buddy or getting into some kind of a hassle with him and killing him. I think Buddy was fallout, or maybe what they call 'collateral damage.' He got in the way somehow, or became a concern and it was decided the best way to handle him was to get rid of him. I could be wrong, but so far we haven't found anyone who on a personal level had any reason to cause Buddy harm. There had to be some other reason and it had to be serious enough that the only solution was for Buddy to end up in that stock tank. If that's the case, I can't see any reason why it wouldn't happen again. So I guess we'd better find out what that reason was. Look here."

Virgil got up from his seat and walked to the whiteboard opposite his desk. He took the grease pen that he had grabbed from the top of his desk, and under Buddy's name, which was already written there, he wrote three things: family, friends, and work. Then he turned to face Jimmy.

"Something happened in one of these three areas to result in Buddy's death. From everything I've learned, his family was solid, no threat there. His friends, from what we know, were pretty much in his life for most of his life. Nothing had changed drastically in his relationships. They liked Buddy. He was one of them. Outside of a possible romantic relationship, that's about it. That leaves work and that's the one area where we don't have much."

"Well, we got the bag," Jimmy said.

"The bag?"

"The pecan bag I found in Buddy's truck. The one I gave you just before you went into the hospital for your operation. Why do you think he had it?"

"Maybe he just liked pecans and took a bag of them to snack from while he drove."

"No," Jimmy said. "Buddy would never do that."

"Why not?"

"Because Buddy was allergic to nuts. When we were in school one time, he took a bite of peanut brittle Amy Poland offered him and he blew up like a balloon and they had to take him to the hospital. Buddy was real careful after that. He even had to wear a chain around his neck about his condition, or maybe that was about bee stings. Anyway, you could just ask Mrs. Hinton. She'd tell you."

"You know, Jimmy, I dropped the ball on this one. It's good I've got deputies like you for backup. This is something worth looking into, and there's one other thing. I was going to take care of it, but I think you're ready for some serious investigative work."

"Anything you say, Sheriff."

Virgil had to fight back a smile. "Okay, Officer," he said. "It turns out Buddy was paying attention to some girl over at Hayward Ranch, probably one of the pickers. I want you to look into it and see what you can find out. Be careful, and try not to be too obvious. You know what I mean?"

"Absolutely. I'll get on it right away, while I'm making my rounds."

"We'll talk in the morning. You can reach me on my cell if you need to. In any event, I might not be home till late."

Virgil walked to the parking lot with Jimmy and watched him leave. He hesitated before getting into his car, then went back into the office. He went to the gray filing cabinet, pulled out the top drawer, and reached in back of the folders until he felt what he had put there earlier. It was the emptied bag of pecans Jimmy had found in Buddy's truck.

He closed the drawer and spread out the bag on his desk. It was innocuous enough. The logo HAYWARD RANCH on the front, with the standard packaging information and weight. He opened it. It was empty. He did notice a slight stain like a watermark at the bottom. He laid it flat on the desk again, and reread the printed words, this time out loud to the empty office. It was a technique he'd been taught early in his career. The idea being to employ as many of your senses as you could in the process of observation. He had touched the bag, read it and smelled it, now he heard it. But nothing. Nothing until the very last . . . *Packaged in Ciudad Juárez, Mexico.*

"Juárez." He remembered what Clara had told him, about how she thought back on her life in Hayward every time she saw one of those Hayward trucks heading for the bridge into Juárez.

He folded the bag carefully and placed it in the top front drawer of his desk. Then he picked up the phone.

"Dr. Barrett's office," the voice said. "How may I help you?"

"Mimi, this is Virgil Dalton. Is Sam there?"

"Yes, Sheriff, he's getting ready to go to the hospital."

"Tell him I'd like to speak to him."

The silence on the phone lasted only a few seconds.

"What's up, Virgil? You got a problem?"

"Not of the medical kind, Sam. I was wondering if you could help me out with something." He explained to Sam about the bag.

"Well, we've got a pretty good lab, maybe not as high tech as an FBI lab, but pretty much state of the art for a regional hospital. I'd put Charlene Gibbon's analytical skills up against anyone's. Send it over and we'll take a look."

"Great, Sam, I owe you one."

Twenty minutes later, Virgil dropped the bag in a sealed envelope off at Sam's office, feeling a little better about not picking up on it sooner. He was not in the habit of beating up on himself, but he realized that any possible significance the bag might have had was lost in the face of his unanticipated medical emergency. Fortunately, Jimmy had not dropped the ball. He was glad, because this gave him an opportunity to move Jimmy up a notch, to a new level of police work. His thoughts about Jimmy being ready for more than the mundane work of patrol and night watchman were still with him when he pulled into his driveway and saw Billy Three Hats sitting on his front porch.

"Hey, Billy."

"Virgil."

Virgil took the chair alongside Billy and the two sat in silence for a long minute looking at the barns, the corrals, and a red-tailed hawk watching them from a dead branch on a willow alongside the creek.

"How are you feeling?"

"I'm good," Virgil said. He had taken off his hat and put it on his knee.

"That scar looks pretty nasty."

"Yeah, well, when my hair grows all in, they tell me you won't even notice it."

"He's pretty upset that you didn't let him know."

"I figured he would be, but I was hoping he wouldn't find out. I didn't want to worry him. I reckoned I'd just mention it sometime after the fact."

"He finds out everything. Don't know how, but he does."

"Can't get away with much. Remember that trip to Nogales?"

Billy smiled at the recollection. "I still don't know how he found out about that."

"Yeah, well, when we got back, you only had to deal with him. I had him, my mother, and my father. It wasn't fun."

"Yeah, but that trip to Nogales was . . ." Billy stopped and slapped Virgil's knee.

"Yeah, it surely was," Virgil said, their simultaneous laughter breaking the quiet afternoon.

"So, I got the message that 'Billy Three Hats' was looking for me."

"Yeah, well, I wanted you to know it was personal. If I say 'Captain William Lightfoot,' it suddenly becomes official."

"Well, I was kind of expecting it. I've been feeling guilty about not seeing him, but besides my little hospital visit a lot's been going on."

"I've heard. By the way, I appreciate the way you handled that cattle incident over in Redbud. I keep telling everyone on the rez, we don't need to make enemies out of our neighbors."

"Wish a couple of stolen cows were the only thing on my plate."

For the next few minutes Virgil filled Billy in on the ongoing investigation. When he was finished, he stepped inside the kitchen and returned with two cold beers. Billy took a long swallow from his can. The hawk kept looking down on them.

"I remember Buddy Hinton. That's a tough way to end up. He must have been a burr under somebody's saddle."

"That's what I'm thinking."

Virgil watched Billy drain the rest of his beer then stand up and put the empty on the railing.

"Well, I'd better get down the road. Guess I'll be seeing you next on the rez. By the way, talk to him about not driving anymore. He might listen to you. You were always his favorite."

"That's just because I was always distant. You were close by. He only saw me at my best."

"Whatever," Billy said. He walked down the couple of steps then turned. "Hope for you Buddy Hinton isn't just the first."

"Me, too."

Virgil stood on the porch with his beer in his hand. He and the hawk watched Billy disappear down the long driveway. A few minutes later he went inside. After placing the empties in the recycle bin, he went upstairs to change out of his uniform. When he opened his drawer to take out a clean shirt, he looked at the feather that always stood vertically in the small bud vase on his dresser. He glanced at his wristwatch. It wasn't yet five.

"Oh, what the hell."

He went out the door and down the stairs. He put in a quick call to Ruby, begging off for that night. Ten minutes later, he was on the county road. It was a little after five thirty when he turned off the hardtop. The dust trail clouded in back of him. He followed what passed for a road as he started climbing up to the flat tableland. When he reached the top, he saw a small cluster of sheep in a rough fenced corral mostly patched with mesquite. Nearby was a double-wide backed up against some cottonwoods. In front were a couple of lawn chairs, facing out over the lower plains he had just left to reach the top of the mesa. In one was sitting a solitary figure looking toward the western horizon and the lowering sun.

Taking a deep breath, Virgil shut off the engine, stepped out of the cab, and walked toward the seated figure. There was no acknowledgement until he stood in front of him. Then there was a barely perceptible nod. Virgil took in another deep breath.

"Hello, Grandfather," he finally said.

The old man looked through eyes that had seen thousands of sunsets like the one at Virgil's back. His skin was tanned leather and, like the earth around him, worn deep with the furrows of history. He looked up at Virgil and a softness came into his eyes.

"It is good to see you, Virgil. How are you?"

"I'm fine, Grandfather."

"I'm glad. I had heard something different but I did not put too much stock in it, because I knew if there was anything to concern me, my grandson would surely let me know."

Virgil shifted a little in his boots.

"Sit next to me."

Virgil sat down in the lawn chair to the old man's left. Without thinking, he took off his hat and set it on his knee. The sky was a flaming palette of mixed colors, and the lateral sun no longer reached the deep arroyos that crisscrossed the land. Cottonwoods and pinions twisted by age and wind stood bathed in the fading light.

"That is a large wound."

Virgil instinctively reached up and touched the large welt on the side of his head, instantly regretting removing his hat.

"I'm sorry, but I didn't want to worry you."

"I understand, but I have the right to worry. You are my grandson. My daughter is no longer here to worry about you. It is up to me."

"You are right. I will remember that." Virgil knew there was no point arguing. "How are you, Grandfather?"

"I am fine. Much better now."

Virgil had never heard him complain. He looked at him in profile and saw little visible change, but knew beyond the stiffness which comes with age, the weathered skin covered a multitude of injuries.

The sun had slipped below the horizon leaving one more burst of color in its wake.

"Maybe we better get inside while there's still some light to see."

Virgil stood up and reached out. He felt the grip on his arm still strong and he pulled his grandfather to his feet with unexpected ease.

"Getting up is harder than getting down."

Virgil remembered similar words from Clara in her garden.

"Let's get something to eat."

"I brought supper. Your favorite. We just have to pop it in the oven for a few minutes."

A wide smile followed. "With pepperoni?"

"You got it, half with pepperoni and half with sausage and peppers."

"You are a good grandson."

"As long as I keep bringing you pizza." Together, they glanced once more at the western sky then headed for the trailer.

"Well, how was it?"

He didn't really have to ask. He sat back from the table and took a sip from the cold can, enjoying watching his grandfather relish one of the wings he had brought with the pizza.

"They call those wings Mexican Hot. What do you think?"

"Good name. Very hot."

Virgil saw him strip the wing right down to the bone. Then, like Virgil, he took a cold drink.

"Mexican Hot. I'll tell Billy to get me some. You know I used to know a little Mexican."

"This sounds like the beginning of a bad joke."

"No. I'm serious. I spoke Mexican pretty good."

"I never heard you," Virgil said.

"Yes." After his comment the old man sat back, lingering a

little with recollection. "I learned from a little Mexican girl many years ago. Before you were born. She was nice. Made good tortillas."

"Are you telling me that maybe I have some Mexican cousins somewhere?"

"No," he said, a distant look coming into his eyes. "No, she died before that could happen. A rattlesnake found her up on the mesa. She had gone to pick chokecherries. I was too late."

The new day had flooded the trailer with light when Virgil stepped outside with his second cup of coffee. His grandfather soon joined him. A dozen or so ewes with lambs at their side were wandering around, making their way gradually up the ridge and heading toward easier grazing.

"The sheep look good."

"Yes. We are late with the shearing. Maybe at the end of the week. Billy's been busy."

"Yep, wearing a badge can get a little crazy sometimes. I don't suppose being the law on the rez is too much different from being the law in Hayward."

"Billy told me a little of what you've been up to lately. Do you think you're going to find out who put that boy in the tank?"

"I'm working on it."

"Be careful. A person who would do that would do just about anything. It seems to me the world has become a more dangerous place. Even here, on the rez. It used to be just alcohol, but now it's drugs and all that comes with them. Nobody killed to get a drink, but they kill to get drugs. Make sure there is always a friend at your back."

"That's good advice."

Virgil finished the last of what was in his cup, then handed the cup to his grandfather.

"If I can," Virgil said, "I'll try to get back to help you with those sheep."

"Don't worry, Billy and his son will help."

"By the way, maybe you should think about easing up on the driving."

"I guess Billy's been talking to you. I know my eyes are as old as the rest of me. We'll see."

"Billy's just looking out for you. He's here and I'm not. Maybe you could get somebody to drive you when you need to get off this mesa. You shouldn't be all alone up here anyhow."

"I've been thinking about Mrs. Hoya. I met her at the Senior Center last month."

Virgil couldn't hide his smile.

"What, you think I'm too old? A man likes company and someone to keep him warm on a cold night. She is alone and I think she would be nice and soft. She drives everywhere, too, and doesn't talk too much. It would not be a bad idea for you to get someone to keep you warm."

"More good advice. You know I always listen to you, Grandfather. Ever since you gave me the eagle feather from your vision quest because I couldn't make one of my own. Whenever I feel unsure or need a little bit of courage, I remember when you gave me the feather and you told me it would give me some of the strength it had given you. Thank you for all you've taught me."

Virgil reached over and hugged the old man. Then the two walked to Virgil's truck. After he had settled inside and started the engine, he rolled down the window.

"I'll see you soon. Good luck with Mrs. Hoya."

"Thank you." His grandfather leaned forward, resting his hands on the rolled-down window. "I am glad you listen, but you do not need a feather for courage. You are not a little boy anymore. Besides, I should probably tell you now that that feather is not from an eagle I saw. It's from a hawk I found dead on the side of the road. I figured it would sound better to you with that whole vision quest story if you thought it came from an eagle. Your mother got mad at me for telling you that story."

"Son of a bitch," Virgil said, smiling. "All these years I've been getting inspiration from roadkill."

He laughed until his grandfather's laughter mixed with his. Then he gave a wave and drove off the tabletop.

19

In his entire life, Jimmy had never set foot on Hayward Ranch. He had seen it, passed by, and wondered, but had never been inside the main gate. To him it had always represented something far beyond his world. Now here he was driving through the gate in an official capacity, in an official car, wearing a uniform that by itself placed him in a role of authority. The weight of this thought had his stomach in a knot.

He drove slowly toward the main house, past row upon row of pecan trees. The groves which stretched as far as he could see in every direction did nothing to lessen his anxiety.

Reaching the top, he saw that the drive split, a short leg branching to the left and leading to the mammoth house, the much longer stretching toward an extensive complex of barns, corrals, and what he judged to be tenant housing. He could see also that beyond the barns the roadway continued until it disappeared over a distant rise. Without hesitation and with a measure of relief, he turned toward the right and headed toward the barns.

He didn't see the elderly woman on the second floor of the house watching him make his turn.

There was no sign of life around the complex, so he passed by and followed the road until it reached the top of the rise. Once there, he could see more clusters of low-lying single-story buildings, which he assumed were more housing for the seasonal pickers. He drove slowly downhill until he reached the first building. He parked the cruiser alongside, shut off the engine, and got out. He was still feeling a little anxious in the unfamiliar environment but when he got to the front door he knocked loudly to disguise any nervousness. He was about to knock again when the door slowly opened and a woman he took to be in her midforties greeted him.

"*Hola.*"

Jimmy picked up on her slight reaction when she saw the uniform and the car in back of him. "English," he said. "*Por favor.*"

"*Sí.* Come in."

He stepped inside and realized right away that the building was a kind of community dining hall. After introducing himself, he asked where everyone was. She seemed surprised at the question.

"They are at work," she said, sweeping her hand as if gesturing to the fields in every direction. "In the orchards."

"I'm looking for a girl named Sarita. Do you know her?"

It hadn't taken a lot of spadework for Jimmy to find out that was the name of the girl Buddy had been seeing. "Sarita," he said again. "She is one of the workers."

"No, no," the woman said, scanning the room.

Jimmy followed her gaze. It was a large room with at least ten rectangular tables, each comfortably seating eight people. At the far end of the room on either end of the wall were two doors, one marked IN, the other OUT. In the center of the wall was a large cutout serving area through which Jimmy could see kitchen appliances. He thought he heard someone back there, and he was sure one of the doors was moving slightly, as if someone had just looked out. He realized that this woman and whoever was back there were more than likely the cooks and servers for the dining hall. He was also sure that if that was the case, she would know all of the workers. When he glanced back at the woman, he saw that the expression on her face when he had mentioned the girl's name was still there.

"Don't worry," he said, lowering his voice to almost a whisper. "There is nothing to fear. No one will know that we have spoken. Where is Sarita?"

"Gone," she said. "*Se fue.* Her brother and her. Gone."

"How long ago?"

"*Tres semanas,*" she said, so softly he could barely hear her.

"Do you know where they went?"

"*Quién sabe. No más.*" She backed away a couple of steps. Just then a man appeared in one of the doorways, and Jimmy knew from her reaction that the interview was over.

"Thank you," he said, in a voice loud enough for the man in the doorway to hear. "Sorry I don't speak Spanish. I'll go up to the big house. Maybe someone up there will know where Mr. Hayward is. Thanks anyway."

He nodded slightly and stepped back toward the door. As he was getting into the car, he could see the woman through a window. She was talking to the man who had appeared in the doorway, gesturing with her hands as if to indicate she didn't tell Jimmy anything.

He got into the cruiser and turned it around to head back in the direction he had come from, aware all the time that the man from the kitchen stood watching him from the doorway of the building.

"Micah, there was a visitor from the sheriff's office today," Audrey Hayward said. "What's that all about?"

"I assume it has something to do with the ongoing investigation into the death of Buddy Hinton," her son said, "but maybe it's something else entirely."

"Well, that situation has nothing to do with us. And it wouldn't look good if—"

"Wouldn't look good? I don't really think the sheriff is interested in whether or not something looks good concerning us, Mother."

"Well, maybe I should make a call. It might change his attitude if he got a call from a senator."

"I don't think you know Virgil Dalton very well if you think that would make a difference. But then, I guess you made the same mistake with his father."

"Who do you think you're talking to?" Her voice barely concealed her anger. "You're just like your father."

"I'm sure you mean that as a compliment," he said as he turned to leave the room.

"Yes, just like him. Run away. If you want to stay true to form, your next stop will be the liquor cabinet."

Micah's hand was on the doorknob. He was about to leave, as he always did. But he stopped and turned back to his mother.

"Even after all these years," he said, "you're still in denial.

Did you ever think that your constant nagging and disapproval drove him to the liquor cabinet?"

"That was just an excuse for his weakness. Just as it was for that wife of yours. They were both weak. Unable to cope with the real world."

The knuckles on Micah's hand, still gripping the doorknob, turned white.

"People and their problems don't mean much to you, do they, only insofar as your . . . your status is concerned. Marrying Father was just a way for you to elevate yourself. To do what, to get back at the people who had snubbed you?"

"Nobody snubs me now. You have no idea how it was. When my mother was buried, there were two people there, me and the undertaker. She was invisible to everyone in this town. So was I. Well, I'm not invisible now."

"So, that's what's driven you all these years," he said, letting go of the door and approaching her. "That's why you were always at Dad, then Caleb. It was never enough, was it?"

"Your father just didn't have it in him, but Caleb . . ."

"Ah, yes, Caleb. The favored firstborn. The promise of greater things. Then he didn't come back from Vietnam and you were left with a twelve-year-old and Rusty, a five-year-old, and you had to start all over."

"Things would have been different if Caleb had lived."

"Only in your own mind. Caleb wanted no part of your grand plan."

"That's a lie. He would have taken charge."

"He wasn't coming back. He told me the night before he left. He said he was glad to go. To escape. For Father there was no escape except into a bottle. My wife never had a chance in this toxic place."

"I was not the reason she committed suicide. That was you. You should have paid more attention to her."

The rebuke hit home. Micah started to reply, then stopped. They stared across the room at each other. The silence was palpable. Sounds from the farthest reaches of the huge house could be heard. When at last he responded, the tenor of Micah's voice had changed. The anger was gone, replaced by something cold and drained of emotion.

"You're right," he said. "Much of what I've said applies equally to me. I've allowed myself to become someone I hardly know. I stood by, silently watching your manipulation, knowing the damage that was being done, and said nothing. Worse, I even became complicit. With Father and more so with Rusty and now . . ."

He stopped. Then he turned once again to the door. In a voice that could barely be heard, he said, "We reap what we sow." Then he opened the door and left the room.

By the time Jimmy got back to the office after making his usual rounds, it was almost dark. He had noticed a watery mist on the horizon as the sun was setting and wondered if it was a hint of a change in the weather. It was not unusual in this part of the country to have long stretches of dry heat, but he was hoping for a change. The land and the people were beginning to take on that drained look that he'd seen before. He knew that frayed nerves could lead to explosive situations.

He was surprised to see Virgil's pickup in back of the office when he pulled into the parking lot.

"Hey, cowboy." Virgil was sitting at his desk. The small lamp on his desk cast a soft glow on a couple of folders and something Virgil was holding in his hands.

"What are you doing here this late?"

"I came into town for something and I figured I'd stop by and find out how you made out at Hayward Ranch."

"Well, that was pretty much a bust. That girl Sarita and her brother are in the wind. Seems like they took off right about the time you found Buddy floating in that stock tank."

"Any idea where they've got to?"

"None at all. I was lucky to get that much. The señora I spoke to wasn't exactly eager to give out information. Matter of fact, I kinda had a feeling she was scared. I know for a fact that there were a pair of eyes on me till I left. Maybe it was the uniform. Sometimes it works for you, sometimes not."

"Well, you can take one thing for sure, that pair of eyes you felt probably wouldn't have even noticed you if you weren't wearing it."

Jimmy pulled up a chair next to Virgil's desk. "What you got there, Virgil?"

"Just another piece of the puzzle, Jimmy. How close were you to Buddy?"

"On and off. Back in school we played ball together. He was one of the few that had my back. The last year we didn't see that much of one another. He'd gotten pretty involved with Wade and his posse. Most of them gave me a hard time growing up, so we kinda got away from one another. But I always liked Buddy."

"Did Buddy do drugs?"

Jimmy leaned forward in his chair. "Drugs," he said with obvious discomfort. "Well, back in high school, he did a little wacky weed, but . . ."

"Look, Jimmy. I'm not trying to put you on the spot. I know kids in high school experiment with all manner of stuff. If you didn't, you'd be as unusual as tits on a bull. That's not what I'm talking about. I'm talking hard drugs. A habit. Did Buddy fall into that category?"

"No, not Buddy. He was real careful about stuff. Remember what I told you about his allergies? We all did a little pot, but he was real scary after that reaction he had to them peanuts. He told me they was going to give him some kind of shot right in his heart. Scared the shit out of him. I don't see him doing hard drugs and I never heard anything from anybody about that."

"Okay." Virgil sat back in his chair and glanced up at the ceiling. Then he threw what he'd been fingering in his hand onto the desk.

Jimmy saw that it was the small empty pecan pouch that he'd found in Buddy's truck. "Why you asking about drugs, Sheriff?"

"Well, I'm trying to get a handle on why Buddy had this bag. I thought maybe drugs, so I had this bag tested at the hospital. Dr. Sam told me there were no traces that they could find. So if Buddy didn't use that stuff, the question becomes, what was he doing with that bag, since he couldn't tolerate pecans? Where did he get it? Who gave it to him and why did he have it?"

"Maybe he just had it, you know, from work, and it don't mean nothing."

"Maybe," Virgil said as he sat up in his chair. "But two negatives usually make a positive, and I'm betting it means something."

"The doc didn't find anything at all?"

"The only thing was a water stain," Virgil said, "which he said actually weakened the fabric."

"So what are you thinking?"

"I'm thinking that if we're not getting answers from family, friends, or personal relationships, then like I told you, there's only one other place to look: Buddy's job. So it looks like first thing tomorrow, I'm heading down to Hayward Trucking."

Virgil got up from his desk, grabbed his hat, and walked to the door. With his hand on the doorknob, he stopped and turned to look at Jimmy, who had not moved.

"There may be more to Buddy's death than we thought," Virgil said. "Might be smart to be a little more watchful when you're making your rounds."

He nodded to Jimmy and left.

Virgil glanced over at the temperature gauge on the barn. It read 91 degrees and it was just a little past nine in the morning. He had put in a restless night. One of those nights when you just can't turn it off. He attributed it to the fact that looking into Buddy's death had drawn him in more and more. It wasn't that he hadn't been there before. Over twelve years as county sheriff, there had been quite a few restless nights and fitful sleeps, but this had a different feel. A woman picking up a kitchen knife and shoving it through the ribs of an abusive husband who had made the mistake of coming at her once too often, or two guys holding up a convenience store for some quick cash. These were the day-in-day-out kinds of things that rarely ruined a night or had him leaving his bed as tired as when he lay down the night before.

No. This one was different, and now his mind was racing with possibilities and more questions than answers.

He saw some movement over in the barn, so he decided to look in before he headed down to Redbud. The mixed smell of cut hay and manure brought with it a strong sense memory for him. His earliest recollections were of this place. Whenever he was here, time held its breath. He could see his father throwing loose hay into the stalls or saddling a horse. His mother, in the same place doing the same things, maybe braiding the mane of her favorite horse, Star. More often than not when she rode, it was without a saddle. He'd seen her many times lead the mare outside, then spontaneously leap onto her back and flash across the landscape, her straight black hair flying behind her so that it blended with the blackness of the mare until they became indistinguishable.

The mare continued on all these long years since his mother and father had gone. The movement he'd seen in the barn was her and it was with some apprehension that he'd come to look in on her. Cesar called her Misteriosa. She had been born on the ranch and was so much his mother's that after the car accident that took them both she had brooded for months. Cesar said he had seen it before. A mare bonding so strongly that when her foal was taken away as a weanling, she would go into a long period of sullenness, calling continually for the absent foal. But he said he'd never seen it for a person.

Eventually, she came out of it but she was never again like she had been with his mother. She kept her place on the ranch for the next twenty years, dependable and solid, but there was never again the closeness of that bond. Another part of the enigma for Virgil and Cesar was that for all that time she had been barren. She had been checked by the ranch vet, but a cause had never been established. This was the reason for Virgil's apprehension now. After all these years, now in use only as a companion for Virgil's horse, Jack, she had come into foal. Twenty-seven years old and in foal for the first time. It was not unheard of for an aged mare to catch, but those exceptional cases were broodmares that had been bred with regularity throughout their life. Cesar said he had never heard of a case like this, and even the vet said he had never seen an instance like it before. He had also predicted that it was unlikely that either dam or foal would survive.

Virgil's mother had always believed that nothing was random. Further, there was always a deeper meaning. Her philosophy had left its mark on Virgil. In his marrow, he'd known Buddy's death would lead him into deeper waters. Now in the shadowed stillness of the barn, he had the same feeling, that somehow the swollen belly of the aged mare meant something more.

A few more steps brought him to the last box stall at the end of the barn. They had kept the mare close for the last week, once Cesar had seen that her milk bag had filled and her teats had waxed over. Normally, Cesar would have checked on her already, but Virgil knew that he was probably working with José on the busted water pump at the same stock tank where they had found Buddy. As the days stretched into weeks with little or no rain, the stock tanks became more critical as a water source for the cattle. The ever-flowing creek that passed in back of the house and barns was down to a soft murmur. Even the good bottomland grass was starting to show brown.

Virgil placed his forearms on the top rail of the stall while he rested his foot on the bottom. Star was in the far corner of the stall, obscured by the contrast of the streaming band of sunlight which came through the window.

"Hey, old girl," Virgil whispered, squinting to see the mare. The mare gave a soft nicker in return, then she dropped her head and turned slightly, shifting her rump toward Virgil. Another soft nicker and he saw her nudge something in the dark corner. Virgil undid the latch to the stall and stepped slowly inside. The mare gave another call, a little deeper this time, then turned to face Virgil, her eyes meeting his. A slight movement in the bedding at her feet drew his attention.

"Hey, what you got there?" He moved slowly forward through the shaft of light to the other side of the stall, drawing closer to the mare. All the while, the mare never took her eyes off him. He slowly extended his hand until the mare responded. He could feel the velvet softness of her muzzle and her warm breath on his fingers. He came alongside, all the while talking softly and running his hands down her neck to her withers until he could feel her body relax under his touch. Then he bent down to examine the small bundle lying comfortably at her feet. The thrill of touching the warm, soft body was almost electric. He was completely dry and, as close as he could tell in the dim light, alert and strong. He had the sense that he was a couple of hours old and already had probably nursed once or twice. He reached under the mare as he stood and could feel warm milk puddle in his hand. Then he stepped away and left the stall. A few seconds later, he returned with a pitchfork and scooped up the afterbirth he'd seen in the bedding. He filled the water bucket and gave Star an extra grain feeding. By the time he'd finished, the foal had struggled to its feet and followed the mare as she walked across the stall to eat the grain.

"Mom sure would be proud of you, old girl."

When he left the barn a little while later, the restless, sleepless night was behind him. He was ready for the ride down to Redbud and whatever else he had to deal with to find out why Buddy was left in that stock tank.

20

Mrs. Hinton was watering some struggling tomatoes when he pulled up. He thought she looked older. He knew that she and Bud senior had married young and that Buddy's coming had prompted their marriage. She couldn't be much more than forty-five, he thought. The sudden realization that she was not too much older than him gave him pause.

"Hey, Viola." He'd gotten out of the car. She was still bending over the plants with the hose. She raised her hand, shielding her eyes from the morning sun.

"That you, Virgil?"

"Yes, ma'am."

"Ma'am . . . You trying to make me feel older than I look?"

Virgil didn't answer.

"Grief ages a person," she said. "You know, I'm only a few years older than you."

He felt like his mind had just been pickpocketed.

"Bud's not here if you wanted to speak to him." She set the

hose down in the garden and stepped out of the small plot. "Sure could use a little of nature's help. Plants are hurting with this heat."

Again Virgil said nothing.

"So what prompted this visit?"

"Actually, I was on my way down to Redbud when I saw the turnoff and thought I'd stop by to see how you were doing."

"That's nice, Virgil. You're a good man, just like your father. We're doing pretty good, trying to get back to normal. The three younger ones force us to keep living in the world. Guess that's a good thing."

"Curtis going to be a first-string quarterback this year?"

"He surely hopes so. That's where Bud is now, dropping Curtis off at summer camp on his way to work. Hope that coach keeps an eye on that thermometer. When it comes to football, those kids don't have enough sense to pour sand out of a boot. They'd play in hundred-degree heat."

"Don't think you have to worry. Coach will have them do the heavy stuff, sprints and such, first. Then, run a few quick plays before it gets like a frying pan out there. Then he'll back off."

"I forgot. That was a few years after I graduated that you played."

"Yes, same coach. He's a good man."

"Anything new? I mean as far as Buddy . . ." Her voice trailed off.

"Not a whole lot. I'm heading down to Redbud to do a little more digging. We struck out on that girl Buddy was seeing. She's gone from Hayward Ranch. We don't know where she's got to."

Viola reached down, picked up the hose, then laid it in another part of the garden.

"Well, I'd better be getting down the road." Virgil moved back from the row of knee-high sunflowers that Viola had planted on the perimeter of the garden.

"Hold on a minute, Virgil." Viola stepped across two rows of plants until she was standing next to him. "You know I told you about that girl in confidence. Bud's a good man, but he does have a blind spot about . . . Well, like I told you before . . . A mixed couple. That's why he never knew. Buddy only talked to me about her. She sounded nice. Anyway, if you think it might be important, if you're heading down to Redbud, you maybe could ask Carlos about her."

"Carlos?"

"Carlos Castillo. You know him, don't you?"

"Well, yes, I know Carlos. Just saw him a few weeks ago at the Black Bull."

"Well, that's how Buddy met the girl, through Carlos. Carlos and Buddy became good friends when Buddy started working at Hayward Trucking. Carlos got her the work at the ranch. I think they're related somehow, or she was just a friend of a friend from the other side of the river. That part I'm not sure about, but anyway that's how they came to meet. I think her brother worked there, too."

"Thanks, Viola. I appreciate the information and don't worry, it'll remain in confidence."

Back on the road, Virgil rehashed what he'd just found out while reflecting on Carlos's unusual behavior at the Black Bull. It kind of made sense, that if he had some part in the development of the relationship between the girl at Hayward Ranch and Buddy that he'd be trying to distance himself in light of

Buddy's death. But Virgil had a nagging feeling that there might be more to it than that. The feeling followed him all the way down to Redbud.

The receptionist at Hayward was not the young girl from his previous visit and there was no informality in their exchange. He glanced through the common window where he had seen Carlos on his previous visit, but there was no sign of him. The dozen or so people at work there were oblivious to his scrutiny.

"Sheriff Dalton, you can go in now." The receptionist nodded toward the door to the right of her desk. "It's the office at the end of the hall, on the right."

The hallway that eventually brought him to Caleb Hayward's office ran the length of the building. He couldn't help but think that if any of the support staff were called to these inner offices, the intimidation factor would be huge. He stepped through the door into a room with another secretary who turned out to be the young girl that he'd met on his earlier visit.

"You can go right in," she said, smiling. "Caleb's waiting for you. Nice to see you again."

"Is this a promotion for you?"

"Oh, Cal . . . I mean, Mr. Hayward thinks Marilyn gives a more formal look than me. He's right. I'm not the quiet type."

Virgil smiled in return, then walked into Caleb's office, thinking to himself that his conjecture about the intimidation factor had been pretty much blown out of the water by the young girl's easy and relaxed attitude. The fact that she referred to her boss by his first name only underscored this.

The room was large and done in a Western motif. The mounted heads of indigenous animals decorated three walls, while the fourth wall was mostly glass and looked out on a prairie landscape typical of the area. Caleb Hayward sat behind the one contradiction in the room, an ultramodern desk of chrome and glass. The effect was jarring.

Caleb came quickly from in back of his desk, extending his hand.

"Sorry I missed you on your last visit. I'm in and out of the office a lot. Have we ever met?"

"I think many years ago, but you were only four or five at the time. I knew . . . your aunt."

"I don't remember. I barely remember her."

"Isn't that her picture?" Virgil nodded toward a photograph among other family photos that lined the top of a bookcase.

Caleb followed his gaze to the girl astride a horse, her red hair and smiling face behind the glass-enclosed frame.

"No. That's my sister, Virginia. Everyone says there is a really strong resemblance to my aunt. Have a seat, Sheriff. Can I get you anything? I've got some cold drinks in the fridge."

"No. I'm fine." Virgil sat in one of the two leather chairs in front of the desk. He was surprised when Caleb sat in the other. Virgil liked what he saw in the young man, an air of casualness, a lack of pretense. In contradiction to his sister, he bore a strong resemblance to Micah, although he was taller and his hair was almost black. Virgil tried to reconstruct an image of Micah's wife, but the only feature he could pin down was the black hair.

"I gather this is about Buddy Hinton. That was tragic. I liked Buddy."

"Did you know him well? I mean, outside of the company?"

"I played ball with him at the company barbecues a few times and we had a few beers together, but that's about all. My social life is pretty much catch-as-catch-can right now."

"Do you have any idea why he would have ended up like he did?"

"Not a clue. I'm afraid I can't help you much there."

"Were there any problems with anybody in the company that you heard about?"

"Not that I ever heard. I think he was really well liked."

"I had no idea this company had gotten so big. You're a young guy to be in charge of such a huge operation."

"Oh, I just handle the transport. Pickup and delivery. Dad handles all the corporate stuff and development. He's the one in charge. If it wasn't for him, we would still be selling pecans on the open market instead of packaging and producing under our own label. He brought us to the next level."

"How do you mean?"

"Well, we were almost bankrupt when my grandfather died. It was Dad's idea, the processing factory in Mexico."

"You know, maybe I'll have that cold drink after all. Then maybe you could tell me more about that."

21

The sky was endless blue and vacant when he left Hayward Trucking. He could feel the heat radiating off the car. Squinting into the sun, he figured it was closing in on noon. His stomach reaffirmed his assumption. At the intersection leading to the interstate, he pulled into a convenience store. Ten minutes later, he was back on the road and headed toward the Redbud substation. Virgil needed some time to sort out all he had learned from Caleb Hayward. He needed to let it gestate. A stopover at the substation was a perfect distraction. The realization that he hadn't been there in months was brought home when he pulled off the paved road onto the short graveled road that led to the front door.

The substation had been opened a little over three years before in response to the population growth in the area. That was largely due to the completion of the highway interchange and the expansion of Hayward Trucking. Dave, Rosie's husband, and Alex Timms had shared the operation since it was first opened. Alex's father-in-law owned and operated Luther's Livestock Auction. Alex worked part-time for him. Dave had been with the sheriff's office over twenty-five years. He pre-dated Virgil and had actually been hired by Virgil's father. Virgil felt the substation was a perfect fit for Dave. When he became sheriff, he thought Dave might resent him, but Dave quickly let him know he had no aspirations for the job. He was one of those people very content to let ultimate responsibility rest in the hands of someone else. He told Virgil on more than one occasion that he loved the job but hated the paperwork. Now, at the substation, he was in charge, but he had Alex to handle the clerical tasks and he could do what he liked and at his own pace.

Virgil took note of the physical changes Dave had made since the substation had been established. The horseshoe-shaped driveway had been lined with random-sized stones, all painted white. The station itself had been a large construction trailer donated by a local company and painted to match the stones. It stood at the midpoint of the horseshoe. A flagpole had been erected in the green space in the middle of the oval created by the driveway, with a flourish of multicolored flowers at its base. Two steps and a small wooden porch led up to the front door. On either side of the door stood matching flower-pots overflowing with flowers similar to those at the base of the flagpole. The window air conditioner was humming as he reached the front door. The coolness as he stepped inside was welcome. Dave was just signing off with Alex, who was obvi-ously on patrol.

"Hey, boss. What are you doing in this neck of the woods?"

Virgil slid into a chair alongside Dave. "Your wife sent me to check on you. She thinks you're so happy to get down here that maybe there's another woman. She's probably oiling the shotgun as we speak."

Dave gave a quick laugh. "Rosie's more than enough for me. Sometimes she's too much, if you know what I mean."

"Sometimes, she's too much for me, too. I'm not sure whether she's working for me or I'm working for her." Virgil put the bag he was carrying on the desk alongside Dave. "I brought some lunch. Next time you talk to Alex, tell him there's some for him, too."

"Great, my stomach's been growling for the last half hour."

For the next ten minutes, they made some small talk while they ate. Dave filled Virgil in on the status of anything going on that Virgil might need to know.

"You having any luck with Buddy's case?"

"That's actually why I'm down here." Virgil told Dave about his meeting with Caleb.

"I had no idea about the extent of their operation," Virgil said. "Cal told me that they have a processing plant down outside of Juárez. He said they used to sell their annual crop of pecans wholesale to dealers on the open market, but a couple of years ago they opened the factory in Juárez. He said his father believed the more factors of production they controlled, the better off their position would be, so they package their product down there, then do their own distribution through the facility in Redbud."

"Man, that's turned into some operation. Mexico . . . I understand cheap labor and all, but that requires a lot of capital investment. And I heard that when Micah's father died they were in a bad way financially."

"I had heard the same thing, too," Virgil said.

Dave was distracted by a call from Alex. "When you get back here," he said, "Virgil brought lunch. Okay, see you then."

"Any problems?" Virgil asked as Dave switched off.

"Nothing unusual. A couple of steers got out of the stock-yard and started heading for the interstate. Alex called his father-in-law and they got a couple of hands down there and caught them up. Just another Wild West story."

Virgil smiled. "You know, Dave, if you got a job in a big city, it would probably be a lot more interesting."

"I'd rather chase cows than drug dealers."

Virgil finished his soda and stood up. Dave joined him and together they walked out to Virgil's cruiser.

"I like what you've done with the place, Dave."

"You make it sound like I'm an interior decorator. Alex does the flowers. We try to cover up the fact that we're working out of a trailer. Makes us look a little more permanent." He gave the sheriff a wave. "See you, Virgil."

"See ya, Dave."

Virgil hadn't driven a mile before he got a call from Dave. When Virgil returned and pulled back into the driveway, he saw Dave standing outside the trailer. It didn't escape his notice that Dave was wearing his hat. More telling was the fact that his holster wasn't empty.

"Alex just called back in. Sounded like something. Thought, since you were here . . . Come on, we'll take my vehicle."

Virgil turned off the engine and stepped out. Dave was already in his Bronco. Virgil knew it was likely they might be going off road because of Dave's suggestion. He had a heavier suspension and twice the clearance of Virgil's cruiser.

"What's up? Did some more steers go AWOL from Luther's?

Hell, I'd jump a four-foot fence to avoid ending up on some-one's plate."

"Not sure, but Alex sounded a little apprehensive. That's not like him. Like I said, as long as you're close, I thought maybe you'd want to check it out with me."

"Why not? A little change of pace for me."

Virgil watched the passing scenery on the way down to Luther's Livestock Auction. The chance to look at the world as a passenger didn't come too often. It was less than forty miles from Hayward, but the differences in the landscape were dramatic. There was little subtlety in what was one step removed from desert; his vision filled with sharp lines and right angles. Buttes and stone carved into incongruous shapes by thousands of years of weathering breaking up a landscape that could have been found on the moon. Red rock striated with shades of blue broke up the monochromatic brown. Tufts of cholla, scrub pine, and an occasional cottonwood offered the only hint of green. He saw the distant mountains and wondered how a last band of Apaches could have called them home.

"There's Luther's." Dave's words broke the silence.

Virgil looked at the collection of corrals bordering some larger feedlots, most containing cattle that lined both sides of the road. He knew that if he had rolled down the car window long before the pens came into view a strong aroma would have predicted their presence. It was not an unpleasant or unfamiliar smell. They continued on for another quarter mile until they saw Alex standing by his car. He took off his sunglasses and extended his hand when he saw Virgil get out of the Bronco.

"Hey, Sheriff. Didn't know you were coming."

"What's up, Alex?" Virgil looked into the lean, tanned face

of his deputy, noting how much Alex seemed to fit the land he'd just seen. He was spare and square-jawed.

"Well, maybe it's nothing, but when we were catching up them steers, I saw something. Maybe caught a whiff of something, too. Didn't say anything to the boys I was with, but thought maybe it was something worth checking out."

"Okay, let's have a look."

They got into Dave's truck with Alex behind the wheel. They drove for about twenty minutes until Alex finally slowed, then pulled off onto the shoulder. When they were out of the vehicle, Alex motioned for them to follow him. The road curved for a quarter mile into a steady ascent. He had left the car on the straightaway, the safest place before the start of the curve. Alex walked ahead, followed by Virgil, with Dave bringing up the rear. Virgil could hear Dave's breathing.

"Hold up a second, Alex."

Alex stopped and Virgil waited until Dave came alongside.

"You all right, Dave?"

"Just give me a minute. Damn cigarettes." He coughed twice. "I . . . I gotta quit before I end up in one of those anti-smoking commercials."

"We're almost there," Alex said.

"Stay here, Dave. I'll go on with Alex."

Dave didn't protest. He sat on a huge boulder that had probably broken off from the escarpment on the opposite side of the road. It had stopped before dropping down into the ravine.

Virgil turned away and along with Alex they started farther up the grade. They had just rounded the curve when Alex pointed to the sky. Gliding on the thermals, there were a dozen or more buzzards. A few more yards farther on Virgil caught an unmistakable scent. An odor that, once smelled, was never forgotten.

"Could be an animal," Virgil said.

"Could be." Alex's voice lacked conviction.

They walked a little farther until the stench became overpowering. Alex pointed to something fluttering on the branch of a piñon, fifteen or twenty feet down the slope. "That's what I saw after I caught the smell and got out of my car."

"Go back to the Bronco. I'm sure Dave's got a coil of rope in back."

Alex left, and Virgil waited. A few minutes later he was back. Dave was with him.

"This doesn't smell good," Dave said. He tied the rope to a metal road stanchion that bordered the midpoint of the curve in the road. Alex began to rappel down the rope, with Virgil acting as a guide from the top. Virgil followed when Alex hit the bottom. On the way past the piñon, he reached up and snatched the piece of blue fabric. He could see the pattern of small, yellow flowers against the bright blue background. When he reached the bottom, Alex was waiting for him. The smell of death was intense enough to make a strong stomach churn. Alex had taken out a bandanna from his pocket and made a mask. Virgil had no bandanna.

"I don't know, Virgil." It was the first time Alex had called Virgil by his first name. The color had left Alex's face, and Virgil understood.

"Wait here a minute, Alex."

Virgil grabbed a small cottonwood struggling for life in the middle of road debris, riprap stone, and whatever trace of soil it could find and continued his descent another fifteen feet until he reached the base of the arroyo. He could hear the barest trickle of a creek a little farther ahead as he picked his way across rock and road litter tossed from above. A scrape of boots told him Alex was following as he made his way toward a mix of dense foliage. He slipped and fell to one knee, impaling his right hand on a small cactus. As he pulled himself upright, a bright trickle ran down his fingers from the fatty part of his palm. He reached forward to part the dense cover in front of him. The rebellious calls of the scavengers above circling in the blue sky were like a bizarre chorus. There was little give to the scrub plants that had struggled to life, anchoring themselves in the hard earth. He pulled harder with his right hand until he heard the snap of a large branch as it broke under his grip. He reached with his left to another and felt it give. Then suddenly it released its grip on the hard dirt and pulled away. He stumbled back as a round object rolled out from underneath the bush and landed a few feet in front of him.

"Holy shit!" The exclamation came from Alex, who had caught him as he fell backward. Oblivious to the stench that rose from the bushes, they looked down to see the eyes of a man whose head no longer belonged to his body.

Virgil heard the spontaneous retching coming from Alex. He glanced back to see him clutching a cottonwood branch for support as he emptied his stomach. Virgil felt the piece of blue fabric that he had stuffed in his pocket.

He knew it did not belong to a man.

Leaving Alex, he stepped forward into the copse of bramble, scrub pine, and matted grass, pushing low-hanging limbs out of his way as he went. He had only managed a few steps when he found the headless corpse. As he moved to investigate further, a pine branch that he had released from the grip of a wild grape vine slapped his face. The sting startled him. The pungent smell of death impelled him forward. He had taken the torn fabric, blue with the vibrant yellow flowers, from his pocket. He worked it nervously in his hand as he struggled a few steps forward, until it was wadded into a ball.

Alex was a few feet in back of him. Suddenly, a shaft of light fell on a lot more of the blue fabric. Virgil stopped. Despite the heavy stench, he drew in a deep breath while Alex came alongside of him. Then he drew back a low-hanging branch to reveal what he knew would be there.

He felt Alex's hand dig into his shoulder as he steadied himself. The two just stood there for a long minute.

"I never . . ." Alex never finished the sentence.

"I know."

"Why . . . Why would they . . ." Alex struggled for the words. "Decapitate them?"

"I don't know," Virgil said. "Maybe as some kind of warning."

"Who do you think they are?"

"I'm not sure, but I have a feeling they might be the couple Jimmy was trying to find, who are no longer in the wind."

22

It was closing in on six by the time Virgil started back to Hayward. He'd gone to Redbud looking for answers, but was coming back with more questions and two more murders to investigate. He had stayed until they had processed the crime scene. Alex photographed the scene while Dave searched for any trace evidence up on the road. He had called Virgil over to look at some tire impressions in the loose dirt on the shoulder, but the dirt was more like dust and too loose to make a mold. They had Alex take as many close-ups as they could get. They all agreed the impressions looked like truck tires.

"Well that narrows it down to about ninety-eight percent of the population," Dave said.

Within another hour, the coroner had come down from Hayward. This was part of the protocol Virgil had established when he became sheriff. It was not an innovation warmly received by the town council, since it involved extra pay and frequently overtime.

Dave held the coroner in little esteem. "He's as useless as tits on a bull. If it weren't for that one-eyed intern of his, those two bodies at the bottom of that gulch would have been picked clean by them buzzards by the time he got to them."

"Well, I don't know the intern that well, but as far as that assessment of Doc Kincaid is concerned, your opinion wouldn't be colored by the fact that he was your main competition for Rosie, would it?"

"Well, that kid rappelled down that slope with one eye and was at the scene twenty minutes before Kincaid finally reached bottom."

"Imagine that, a one-eyed twenty-seven-year-old former Special Ops guy, who did two tours in Iraq, got down there quicker than a fifty-five-year-old with a stomach bulge you could set a dinner plate on. Guess things like huffing and puffing when you walk up a hill come easier to guys on the shady side of fifty."

Dave had no comeback.

The coroner said he'd call Virgil as soon as he had preliminary results. Virgil was tired. It had been a long day, so after he left the hospital and Doc Kincaid he headed for home. He was looking forward to a quiet night.

Cesar was sitting on the front porch sipping a beer as he pulled up in front of the house. Five minutes later, Virgil was next to him, sipping on his own beer and trying to put the day's events in his rearview mirror. A soft breeze caressed him, and he felt the stress of the day slipping away. He breathed deep the smells of the ranch, trying to displace the other smells. The mixed perfume was more than green grass, cut hay, and manure. It was home.

Cesar brought him up to date.

"That little foal is coming along. Only thing is that Star won't let him take a step without being on top of him."

"Well, she's waited over twenty years for motherhood. Guess being a mom is a little overwhelming after all that time. How's the graze holding up?"

"Don't think there's going to be much of a second cutting less we get some serious water. Even good bottomland gets thirsty."

They sat a long time in quiet listening to the soft murmurs of the earth. Finally, Cesar stood up.

"Guess I'll head into town. Get something in Margie's then maybe . . ."

"Then maybe you'll visit somebody."

"Could be." Cesar gave a half smile and stepped down off the porch. "You know, maybe later you could pick up that phone. Maybe call down to Black Bull. I hear there's a nice lady down there."

"Old man, someday I'm going to find out how you know everything."

"Then you'll be as smart as me." He gave a half wave and headed toward the pickup parked by the corral.

Virgil sat sipping another beer until the sun slipped behind the barn. Finally, he dragged himself to his feet, went inside, and took inventory of the refrigerator. He got some cold chicken and potato salad and fixed himself a plate, then watched what was going on in the rest of the world as he slipped into the recliner in front of the TV. By the time he finished his supper, he realized that his corner of the world was not so unique after all.

He carried his dish to the kitchen and set it in the sink. He glanced at the clock, picked up the phone, punched in some numbers, and waited.

"Black Bull, how can I help you?" A familiar voice.

"Let me think about that."

He knew he was late, and if it weren't for the accuracy of first light hitting him square in the eyes, he'd still be asleep. Quietly, he swung his legs over the side of the bed, then stood, still squinting. The monotonous weather was getting to him. Another cloudless sky. Looking out at the empty landscape, he had the feeling he was facing another long day, but he felt good. At the realization, he glanced over at the still-sleeping figure, his eyes lingering on the smooth, exposed skin that reawakened a fleeting desire. The taste of the night was still on his lips as he headed for the bathroom.

"When am I going to get that riding lesson?" The question greeted him ten minutes later as he returned from the bathroom. He walked to her side of the bed. She hadn't changed position and looked up at him, her eyes still heavy with sleep.

"You mean you want another one?"

With a speed that surprised him, she reached out, grabbed his pillow, and in the same singular motion threw it at him. He caught it in midair and threw it back at her. Wordlessly, he sank down on the bed as she rolled over. He reached down and brushed her breasts with his hand, then kissed the small hollow in her neck. Finally he brought his lips to hers.

"Yuck, morning mouth," she said as they parted.

"Mine or yours?"

"Mine," she said.

"You taste good to me."

She placed her hand on his cheek.

"I gotta go," he said. "I'm already late." He leaned over once again, gave her a quick kiss, and stood. "I'll call later."

"What about breakfast?"

"I'm good. I'll catch something on the fly." He blew a kiss and left. He thought about stopping by the ranch for a quick change of clothes, but decided to put it off until after he met with Dr. Arthur Robert Kincaid, the coroner, whom everyone in town knew as Ark. So many people in small towns seem to carry nicknames, Virgil thought. How had he himself escaped one?

He pulled into the hospital parking lot. His next thought, once inside, was why were morgues always in basements?

There was no sign of the coroner in his office, so Virgil headed down the hall. Before he got as far as the viewing room, a door opened and the intern stepped out.

"Good morning," Virgil said. "Is Ark . . . I mean Doctor Kincaid in there?"

"Sorry, he is running a bit late."

Virgil reached out his hand. "I'm Sheriff Dalton. We never really were introduced."

"Yes, I know," the intern said. "The badge, the shades, and the cowboy hat gave you away. I'm Chet Harris."

They shook hands.

"It's all right," Harris said, as Virgil couldn't help looking at the man's eye patch. "It's a little disconcerting for most people. The patch—"

"Oh, sorry . . . It's just that you don't see . . . I mean . . ." Virgil rarely got caught with his conversational pants down, but the young intern was still smiling and seemed to be enjoying his embarrassment. "Maybe, if you got a parrot."

"Good recovery, Sheriff. Actually, I've tried a couple of prosthetic eyes, but so far haven't found one that doesn't cause irritation. Can I get you a cup of coffee while you're waiting?"

"Thank you, sounds good."

Virgil followed the intern back through the door and they spent the next ten minutes getting acquainted, until Dr. Kincaid finally entered.

"Sorry, Virgil. Had to drop the kids off at summer camp. Hate starting the day late. I feel like I spend the whole day playing catch-up."

"Relax, Ark. As a guy who didn't become a father till he was almost fifty, I cut you plenty of slack. Besides, this has given me a chance to get to know your pirate." He handed Ark a cup. "Coffee?"

"I've got some stuff to do," the intern said. "Nice meeting you, Sheriff. Good suggestion for Halloween." He started to leave the room.

"Hold on a minute, Chet. It can wait. Sit for a moment. This is part of the job description, too."

"Okay, so what have you got for me?" Virgil said.

"This is preliminary, Virgil. I won't have the tox screen and other lab work for a while, but I can tell you a couple of things. First off, they didn't die a natural death."

"C'mon, Ark. I didn't get out of bed for your gallows humor."

"Okay. They were executions. A round in the back of each head. Then the decap."

"Why?" Virgil mused out loud.

"That's your job to find out, Virgil. My guess? Somebody wanted to send a message. A lot of this kind of thing, as you well know, has been showing up south of the river. By the way, that was a dump site, not a kill site. So they were killed somewhere else, then brought there. No IDs on either body, so I can't help you there yet. I'm guessing illegals, but again that's something for you to figure out."

"Okay." Virgil got to his feet. Then he sneezed. He reached his hand into his pocket for a handkerchief, but came out instead with the scrap of blue with the yellow flowers.

"What have you got there?"

"Maybe," Virgil said, turning over the fabric in his hand, "a way to find out who these folks were."

When Virgil got back to the office, Rosie was sitting at her desk, finishing a sandwich.

"You could've gone to Margie's for a half hour," he said.

"Didn't want to leave the office unattended. Especially not now."

"Yeah, I guess the ante has been raised around here."

"Remember what I said that first day, Virgil. I had a bad feeling about this."

"Sometimes it's not good to be right."

She didn't respond.

"Go on home," he said. "I've got this covered. Spend some time with Dave. Keep him busy so he doesn't have time for a smoke."

"He told me about the walk up the hill," she said. "But I told him he's got to *want* to quit. I can't do it for him. All I can do is bury him if he doesn't."

She left soon after. Virgil stayed in the office until Jimmy came in and brought him up to speed. Then Virgil went home, hoping for a quiet night.

It was close to ten the next morning when Virgil got to the office. He was pleased to see no sign of Rosie's car. He had told her to stay later with Dave. Dave was a big guy, barrel-chested with forearms that could crack walnuts, but the walk up that hill to the crime site had forced Virgil to confront the inevitability of time and its consequences. In the midst of everything else, he had to recognize some underlying realities. Dave's health was only one of these. Dave had always been a bigger-than-life guy, but always with the cigarette dangling from his mouth. Virgil knew for the road he was about to travel, he needed all his resources. For him, this investigation had suddenly turned into more than he had expected, more than just a killing in a small town.

The office was more shadow than light when he stepped inside, so for the first few minutes he raised shades and opened windows. He even left the door open to get some fresh air into the office before he had to hermetically seal it again and give it over to the incessant hum of the AC.

He walked through the door at the far end of the office to the connecting annex. The holding cells were empty, an uncommon scenario lately. He remembered his father talking about how the cells would be vacant for so long that before a new occupant went in they would have to go in and clean out scorpions and cobwebs. He said he didn't want his typical stay-over convinced that his hallucinations were real.

Yes, things had definitely changed. There was such a regularity of cell use in the last few years that their regular cleaning had become a line item in the annual budget. It was no longer just the weekend celebrant who spent a night. More and more, occupancy rates had not only gone up but were starting to reflect some big-city problems. The town drunk had been evicted by the drug dealer and his entourage. Domestic disputes had increased, and violent crime had become a fairly consistent part of the equation. As Virgil sat down at his desk in the midst of the growing sunlight that was inching its way across the room, for the first time in his tenure he was wondering if he needed some outside help. He had just taken a sip from his cup, with the quick realization that this wasn't Rosie's coffee, when she came through the door.

"I'm closing this, Virgil, before the critters think this is an invite." She then went about the office undoing Virgil's earlier efforts. The last thing she did was turn on the AC. Virgil knew a protest would be fruitless, so he made none.

"How's Dave?"

"On his way down to Redbud. We went to Margie's for breakfast. It was nice. Felt like we were on vacation. That's about the only time we ever eat breakfast in a restaurant."

"Yeah. I want you to be able to do more of that."

"How you going to make that happen, Virgil?"

"By waking up the mayor and some councilmen to the fact that the times, they are a-changin'. This isn't the cowtown of yesterday. It's getting harder and harder for that yellow dog to take a nap in the middle of Main Street."

"No argument there, but I don't know if they'll want to hear it."

"They'll have to, and for starters, I want you to call Dif Taylor and get him in here on a regular basis at night when Jimmy's on patrol. We need a body in here twenty-four/seven."

"I'll call him today."

"I also want you to give Dave a call. Tell him to swing by Hayward Trucking and pick up Carlos Castillo. Tell him I'll meet them at Carlos's home. And tell him to be fairly obvious when he gets Carlos. I'd kind of like it to be the talk of the water cooler today."

"Why is Dave picking up Carlos?"

"Because I think that girl we found was friendly with Buddy, and Viola told me there was a connection between the girl and Carlos."

Virgil got up from his desk and threw what was left of his coffee in the sink.

"I'll make a fresh pot," she said.

"I'm done, but from now on I'm going to leave a note that all the coffee making should be left to you. This stuff Jimmy makes would take the shine off a hubcap. Anyway, I gotta get going. By the way, remember what I said about Dave struggling a little with his breathing yesterday."

"I told him he's got to get that patch. I don't want to be eating those restaurant breakfasts by myself."

Virgil headed for the door.

"Oh, tell Jimmy I'll stop in on my way back from Redbud. You can reach me on the radio if anything comes up."

Virgil stepped outside into the building heat. He saw Rosie draw the last shade back down. The only sound he heard was the hum of the air conditioner. Even the critters, as Rosie called them, were hugging the shade and staying quiet. He hoped Dave would be waiting for him by the time he got to the Castillo house. If he was right—and he was pretty sure he was—the visit to the Castillo house was not going to be the high point of his day.

23

Consuella Castillo was enjoying the early morning in her backyard. She liked this time of the day most. Carlos had gone to work. Pepe and Maritza had gotten on the small bus that took them to the summer day camp, leaving her alone with Carlito. On days like this, after cleaning up from breakfast, she would sit over a second cup while Carlito was still in the high chair, then take him out to the backyard and let him try out his newly acquired walking skill on the uneven ground. She liked that as often as he would plop down after a few unsteady steps, he would struggle to his feet and try again. Even when he eventually would reach the end of his rope and sat contentedly for longer periods on the grass, she liked that he was continually curious, picking at a clover leaf, a stone, or even a worm, which on one occasion he was about to turn into a second breakfast just as she got to him. Toward the end of their mornings outside, she would put him in the baby swing that hung alongside the other two swings.

Carlos had built an elaborate play area for the children. Carlito was the most vocal in his appreciation. As soon as Connie picked him up and started walking toward the swing, he would start to squeal and become so animated that getting him into the seat, legs through holes and safety bar down, became a challenge. Once settled, it only took a few moments for him to respond to the swaying rhythm while Connie pushed him. Sometimes she would sing to him until his head would start to droop. Then she would carefully wiggle him out of the swing and carry him into his crib and lay him down. He rarely even opened his eyes and sometimes would be in such a deep sleep that she would have to wipe the drool from her shoulder where his head had been resting.

The plotline for this morning had not changed, and after Carlito was safely squirreled away, Connie went back out into the yard to collect her coffee cup from the table on the patio. She hesitated for a moment, cup in hand, glancing at the nicely kept backyard, enjoying the quiet and the flowers she had planted close to the base of the fence that bordered the yard so they could find some relief from the unrelenting sun. She was particularly delighted with the colorful hibiscus which thrived in the angled corners of the fence. A shiver of joy in her home ran through her. Her world was perfect. She and Carlos had achieved the American dream. Life was good, almost too good.

Then she heard a car pull into her driveway. She walked to the side yard and saw Sheriff Virgil Dalton. He was standing alongside his car. Connie had no idea her world was about to change, or how fleeting happiness could be.

Virgil breathed a sigh of relief when he saw Dave's car pull into the driveway just after he got out of his. Consuella had come from the rear of the house to greet him, and he was reluctant to explain the reason for his visit until Carlos got there.

"What's happened? Connie, are the kids okay?" Carlos had gotten out of Dave's car before Dave had shut off the engine. Carlos ran to his wife, who had no answer to his questions. He had asked the same questions of Dave on the short ride from Hayward Trucking, but Dave had managed to evade direct answers by pleading ignorance himself.

"I was in the back. I don't know," Connie said. "I just saw the sheriff's car and I . . ."

"Maybe if we could go inside, I can explain," Virgil said. "This has nothing to do with the children. Carlos, I asked Dave to bring you here rather than the substation because I thought maybe your wife might have some input to my inquiry."

"Let's go inside," Connie said.

Virgil and Dave followed them both into the house. The house was clean to the point that Virgil found it hard to believe that three children actually lived there. Like so many houses in this climate, it was on one level. Virgil could see as they entered the living area that there was a large sunroom at the rear which let the morning light flood the house, then offered a respite from the heat as the afternoon progressed. When he looked closer through the double-sided slider, he could see some toys scattered about. Beyond the sunroom, he saw the nicely landscaped yard with the play area in the far left corner.

In the short time it took for them to settle in the living room, Consuella had produced a carafe of coffee and some mugs and placed them on a coffee table in front of the sofa where Dave and Virgil sat. Virgil began by explaining to both of them that his questions were related to Buddy Hinton's death.

"I don't get it," Carlos said. "What have we got to do with Buddy's death?"

"Directly, nothing. But indirectly . . . Well, that's what I'm here to find out. I know you and Buddy were good friends. Went to school together, worked together."

"Yes, Buddy and I were close. All our lives."

"I know, but when I first tried to talk to you about him . . . That first time in the trucking office, then later at the Black Bull, you seemed very reluctant to say anything."

Carlos looked around at the house. Then his gaze finally came to rest on his wife.

"We have three children," he said. "I've got to be careful."

"I understand, but this was your friend. I'm sure you'd want to help solve his murder if you could. Then there's the other thing."

"What other thing?"

"The girl at Hayward Ranch. The girl Buddy was seeing."

Virgil could see Carlos stiffen a little.

"I know there was a family connection between you and that girl and her brother," Virgil said. "I need to fill in some of the gaps here, because something has happened that has raised this investigation to a new level of seriousness."

"What has happened?" Carlos asked.

"Well, the girl and her brother disappeared pretty soon after we found Buddy, so I never got to ask them anything. Then yesterday we found two bodies. The strange thing is they were found less than ten minutes from here. We're trying to identify them."

"Bodies . . ."

"Yes. A man and a woman."

"And you think . . ."

"I don't want to speculate. Right now we're just trying to

determine identity. Then I can move on to other considerations."

Carlos had moved to stand alongside the chair that Consuella sat in, laying his hand lightly on her shoulder.

"So you want me to come with you to look at these two?"

"That might be necessary later," Virgil said, "but for now . . ." He reached in his pocket and brought out the piece of cloth he'd been carrying since he had taken it from the branch of the scrub pine. Then he pushed aside the coffee mugs and laid it on the table and spread it out.

"Do you . . ." He never finished the question. He heard Connie gasp, then take in a quick breath. Her eyes were riveted on the bright cloth. Then she raised her hand to her mouth, as if to stifle what might come out.

"Tisa . . . Tisa . . . *mi hermana.*" The words came. She could not stop them. Her body convulsed. A deep sob followed. Her body seemed to cave in on itself as she sank into the chair.

Carlos reached out, drawing her close. He murmured to her in words that barely reached across the room to Virgil and Dave. For an instant, the scene became a still life, interrupted only by Connie's low sobs and Carlos's words. Virgil and Dave looked at each other, neither happy with his role.

A cry from another room came as a welcome relief. Consuella, responding to a deeper instinct, rose so quickly the movement startled Virgil. In an instant she left Carlos's embrace and left the room. Carlos sat down heavily in the chair she had just left.

"Her sister," he said. "Her brother."

"We can't be sure," Virgil said. "Not until we have conclusive identification, visual or dental."

"No . . . No, the dress." He nodded toward the piece of cloth on the table. "She made it for her sister."

"I thought the girl at Hayward Ranch was your sister or cousin."

"No, I don't have anybody in Mexico," Carlos said. "My family has been here for over two hundred years."

"Geez," Dave said, "my family hasn't been here for even half that time." It was the first time he had said anything since they had entered the house. "I thought you were . . ."

"Just another illegal wetback," Carlos said, half smiling. "My wife's family is Mexican. She became American once we married. I met her in Mexico when I took a college semester there. Her much younger brother and sister came to Hayward Ranch on temporary work visas. They wanted to experience life here. Tisa met Buddy through me, and then biology took over."

"So when Buddy was murdered . . ."

"I'm not sure. They called right after. It was obvious they were worried. There was someone at Hayward Ranch they were afraid of and they wanted to leave. I told them that it might look suspicious if they left too soon, because I knew you would find out about the relationship eventually. I guess that wasn't good advice."

Carlos paused. He looked at Virgil, his eyes glistening. "I guess my advice got them killed."

"I don't think that got them killed. I think what got them killed has to do with why they ended up twenty-some-odd miles from Hayward Ranch. Down here."

"That's probably also my fault."

"How do you mean?"

"I think maybe somebody was sending me a warning."

"Why you?"

"Because I was Buddy's friend, and maybe they think I know why Buddy got killed."

"Do you?"

Before Carlos could answer, Consuella returned from the bedroom, carrying the baby. She was speaking to the baby in soothing tones. Virgil could see she was fighting hard to stay in control.

"Remember when you told me you had to be careful because of your wife and children? Well now's the time to realize how much is at stake here. These people were willing to kill to intimidate you. They won't stop there."

Carlos looked up at Consuella, then reached up and rubbed the back of his hand against the baby's cheek.

"You didn't answer me," Virgil said. "Do you know why Buddy was killed?"

"I'm not sure, but it began a couple of months ago. Buddy noticed a couple of things. He said there was something odd about the deliveries from the plant in Juárez. Usually he just did the deliveries to the plant, but this past year he'd also been picking up the processed product from Juárez and bringing it to Redbud, which functions as the redistribution point. He said the strange thing that first caught his attention was how cursory the inspection was coming from Juárez, but only for the truck he was driving. His schedule became so set, he got to know the inspectors on a first-name basis. Same guys, same time, all the time. It only dawned on him after a couple of months. He chalked it up to routine and the same cargo. Even coincidence. That is, until about two months ago."

Carlos hesitated before continuing.

"That's when his rig broke down on one of his regular trips, before he got to the border. It wasn't a problem with the engine, but the container. He was trying to avoid an accident. The truck flipped and the axle snapped. Wade Travis got right down there and they got the container up and back to Redbud right away."

"Wade Travis . . ."

"You know Wade, don't you, Virgil?"

"Yes, but I had forgotten his connection with the trucking operation."

"Wade handles all the maintenance now. He and his crew do everything. And he's hands-on. Oversees everything."

"I guess Wade's doing okay," Virgil said. "When I stopped by his place, I saw he's opening a car dealership."

"And Hayward Trucking is sponsoring his NASCAR ambitions. I'd say he's doing a little better than okay. Anyhow, they got the rig back to the depot and Buddy just figured they'd transfer the load to another container and he'd be back on the road to Juárez. But it didn't happen."

"What do you mean?"

"Well, Buddy said they told him to take the rest of the day off. He wasn't exactly unhappy about that, but the next day he had to wait till they finished making the repairs to that container."

"I don't understand," Virgil said. "What's so unusual about that? I mean, the repair, isn't that part of the maintenance?"

"Yes, at some point, but Buddy said that didn't make any sense. You've been to the yard. We've got containers sitting around all over the place. Buddy said they could have unloaded that box with a couple of forklifts and reloaded the contents into another container in a couple of hours. There was no reason to lose a day waiting for that particular container to be repaired. He said it just didn't make any sense."

"Okay." Virgil said. "Then the next logical question is, why did they do that?"

"That's what Buddy said."

"Did he go any further with it?"

"He told me he was going to find out why. Ask Wade what was so special about that particular container and why he was the only driver that pulled it."

"Did he? I mean, do you know if he spoke to Wade?"

Carlos sat back in the chair and didn't answer right away. Then he stood up. He gave Connie and the baby a quick hug.

"Honey, why don't you take the baby out to the patio for a couple of minutes? Let him play with some of his toys. I'll be out in a little while and we'll talk about what has to be done."

They looked at each other for a long, quiet moment. Connie finally left and went through the door to the patio without a word.

"I'm sorry we have to be here, Carlos, and for all of this. But like I said earlier, I'm afraid this has gone beyond Buddy's murder. I don't know exactly where this is going to end up, but I've got to follow the trail before it goes cold."

"I understand."

"So did Buddy find out anything?"

"Yes, but he wouldn't tell me what. He said it was better if I didn't know. It would be too dangerous for me. It was the last time we spoke before . . . before he was killed. He told me that he had found out something and he was going to speak to Wade about it, but when I pressed him, all I could get out of him was that it had something to do with that particular container. That's when he said it was better if I didn't know. It was Buddy who told me not to talk to you, or anyone for that matter, about this. That's why after Buddy was found in that stock tank and I saw you at the Black Bull, I didn't want to say any-thing. Virgil, look how my wife's brother and sister ended up. I guess because of them and her connection to Buddy, and his to me . . . Well, that's why they were killed and why they ended up down here. Someone is sending a message and I guess it was to me. So what am I going to do now? They're going to know I've spoken to you. This is my family. How am I going to pro-tect them?"

"With our help, Carlos," Virgil said, looking at Dave. "With our help."

A few minutes later, Virgil and Dave were standing by their vehicles in the driveway.

"How are we going to handle this, Virgil?"

"For the time being, I want you or Alex here all the time. I'll send Jimmy down to help as soon as I can."

Dave leaned against the car, which was parked under the shade of a mimosa standing by the driveway.

"Virgil, we're not really up to this for the long run. I mean we're small-town."

Virgil didn't respond right away. Instead, he looked back at the house, the well-kept yard, and a bike lying on the lawn.

"I know, Dave. And these are some big-city crimes."

24

The ride back to Hayward took longer than usual. Virgil needed the extra time. There was a lot to think about. At one point he just pulled off the road and sat for a while. Dave's words were lingering in his mind. He didn't want this thing to get ahead of him, just because he was small-town. Ego couldn't be a roadblock. At the moment, his immediate concern was the protection of Carlos and his family. He was back on the road and halfway to Hayward when the answer came to him. He slammed on the brakes and did a quick one-eighty on the deserted road.

The turnoff was only a mile or so back. Most would barely notice it. Even if they did, they would probably think of it as a road to nowhere. The land had been baked hard, so he barely slowed as he left the main road. The dust he did kick up had settled before he was a quarter mile farther on. It was only when he started up the butte, toward the tabletop, that he slowed. The cholla and sage had given way to occasional patches of green as he climbed. It wasn't long before he saw a few sheep. Another mile on, he got the first glimpse of his grandfather's place.

The old man was sitting in one of the chairs outside, again facing the western sky, getting an early start waiting and watching for the evening choreography.

"I see the sheep got clipped," Virgil said as he stepped out of the cruiser.

"Billy and his sons," the old man said.

"Sons?"

"Well, the little one is only seven, so Billy brought him along to teach him a few things." He paused for a moment, never taking his eyes from the faraway view of the horizon. "Imagine. Seven. When I was seven, the world was a different place."

"Do you think it was a better place then?"

The old man didn't answer right away. Then he looked at Virgil.

"No. This is better."

Virgil was surprised by his quick answer, but before he could say a word, the old man continued.

"Too many babies died. My mother lost five. Life was hard. There was no pizza. Sometimes it was cornmeal over and over. Just flatbread. Sometimes nothing. There was no fine home like this." He gestured toward the double-wide. "We would be hungry and cold when the north wind came. Many times. Now, I am comfortable and my stomach is full. But it was nice to be young. There were good times. Riding my pony while I was watching the sheep, being with my friends at the mission school. It was not all bad."

He got up from his chair unexpectedly and with a smoothness that contradicted his age. Then he waved his hand over the broad landscape.

"Many things have changed in the world, but this is the same."

Slanting light of the late afternoon crisscrossed the land in broken patterns, highlighting the rough topography. Sloping buttes, softened and worn by centuries of weathering, sharp arroyos cut by torrents of water, and always the desert stretching to meet the distant sky.

"Stay to eat," the old man said.

"I am hungry, but I should have brought something."

"There's plenty. More than I can eat by myself." With one more glance at the sky, he turned to go into the trailer. "A change is coming. Look at those thunderheads. The earth is thirsty. It needs a drink."

"No argument there. A lot of the creeks are running low. Cesar says there's no chance for a second cutting unless we get some serious water soon."

Virgil followed his grandfather into the trailer. For the next twenty minutes he helped with the preparation of their meal.

"Would you like a beer or a glass of wine?"

Virgil had just pulled his chair into the table. A square of lasagna and a bowl of mixed greens sat in front of him.

"Wine . . . I don't remember you having wine."

"I've been trying some new things. Red wine goes good with lasagna."

"Tired of cornbread and frijoles?"

"No, but I'm trying to eat healthier and it's good to try something new. The red wine goes better with the pasta. I like it."

Virgil nodded. "Grandfather, you continue to surprise me.

The lasagna looks good. Are you developing new cooking skills, too?"

"A little, but I didn't make this. Mrs. Hoya did."

Virgil had poured the wine and just put his glass to his lips. "Mrs. Hoya? From the Senior Center?"

His grandfather nodded.

"So, how's that going?"

"It is going well, but we have not slept together yet. We will see."

Virgil choked a little.

"You all right, Virgil?"

"Just went down the wrong pipe. I'm fine."

They ate in silence until they finished the meal. Virgil filled their emptied wineglasses for the second time, then sat back in his chair and looked around the kitchen. It was indeed a nice place for his grandfather. There was very little maintenance and plenty of room. Much more than he needed for himself.

"Grandfather, I have a favor to ask of you."

"I did not think you came so soon after your last visit for no reason. How can I help you?"

For the next twenty minutes, Virgil explained what had happened as the investigation into Buddy's death had progressed.

"Now it's reached a kind of critical point. To go further I've got to make sure Carlos, his wife, and children are safe. I don't want anything to happen to them. They're good people. But I don't have the resources to draw on like a big-city police force. I know I can reach out for state or federal help, but that will take time and I have to do something now. Carlos's family was a thought, but then I realized that if someone was after them that's the first place they'd look. Then I thought of you. You have no connection with them and plenty of room here. You're also pretty hard to find and even harder to get to. It'd be a good safe place for them."

"Bring them here, but tell as few people as you can. Remember what I said to you before, Virgil. The people that left that man in the stock tank will do anything and they have just proved that."

"I know."

An hour later, as he was headed toward the hard-surface road, night was beginning to cover the land. He glanced in the rearview mirror and he saw the light from the double-wide disappear around the edge of a butte. Coming off the plateau, he reached the flatland, then glanced once more back at the tabletop as he turned onto the county road. Night had taken over. He could not see the cutoff to the desert road or anything but prairie and the low-lying ridge in the distance.

By the time he got back to the ranch, it was a little past nine. He'd thought about stopping at the office, but he was drained. Besides, he didn't need any more on his plate just then. He saw the light outside the door on the porch and he was glad. It was nice to have someone remember you. Once inside, he shed his uniform, draped it over the back of a kitchen chair, then in shorts and T-shirt went to the fridge and took out the quart of cold milk. He put it to his lips and with the door still open, he drank his fill. Then he went upstairs. His shorts and tee lay on the floor where he dropped them. He climbed into the bed relishing the smooth feel of the sheets. He closed his eyes and let a deep breath escape his body. Finally, he set about the task of driving the image of two headless bodies from his mind so he could slip into the narcotic sleep he so badly needed.

25

The world felt different when he awoke. There was no sunlight flooding the room, and when he flipped the switch off on the window AC and opened the other window to let in some fresh air, it was oddly still. No hum of insect life, no soft breeze, no morning song.

He came into the kitchen a half hour later, freshly showered and dressed. His other uniform still hung over the back of the chair. It was a little after eight when he finished his coffee. He called the office and was surprised when Dif Taylor answered.

"Rosie not in yet, Dif?"

"No, Virgil. Something about Dave staying down in Redbud throwing her off her schedule."

"You all right? I mean, she spoke to you about coming in more."

"No problem. I been here since midnight. I'll stay till she shows."

"What about Edna?"

"She's visiting her sister over to Alamogordo for the next few days."

"I don't know how long this will be for, Dif, but I really need the coverage."

"I'm good, Virgil, but lotsa luck explaining the extra expense in the budget to the council. They still think Main Street is a dirt road."

"Yeah, that point came up the other day. Guess they're a little reluctant to move into the twenty-first century. Thanks for stepping in, Dif."

He left the house right after his call and walked to the barn. There was no sign of Cesar, but he knew he couldn't wait around to see him. He had to be at the hospital by nine for the formal identifications. The barn was empty except for Star and her foal in the extra-large box stall. As he got closer, the mare gave a soft nicker. He stood with one foot on the bottom rail, looking over the quiet scene. The foal was lying stretched out on the mix of stage dry and straw, the only movement an occasional twitch of an ear to shake a fly. Star stood in a fixed pose, her weight on three feet, the fourth bent at the ankle, resting on a little mound of bedding at her feet. Virgil knew that while the foal rested, she would hold that position, only shifting her weight from time to time to rest the other front foot. He nodded as he took his foot off the rail and, as if in acknowledgement, she dropped her head in a similar movement. It was one of those moments that he had experienced before, when the communication seemed intuitive. Many times with Jack, the course of action was still forming in his brain when the horse had already acted in anticipation. He'd spoken of it once to his mother. He could still see her nodding, her dark eyes smiling.

"The language of intimacy," she had said. At that age, he

had puzzled at her words, but now as he walked the corridor between stalls to the opened barn door he understood their meaning.

He was at the hospital before Dave, so he took the time to make sure the viewing would be as painless as it could be. Ark Kincaid was in another part of the hospital, but Chet the intern met Virgil when he went downstairs.

"Your deputy called to say they were running late. Something about the kids and all the stuff they had to take."

"Okay."

"Sheriff, they're not bringing children here, are they?"

"No. The children will be outside with the deputy. Only the parents will be here. The children are too young to be left home alone, and the parents are too upset to leave them with anyone."

Virgil didn't want to have to offer more explanation. He hadn't even told Dave about Carlos and his family not returning to their home, and when he told Carlos to pack the necessaries for an extended stay, where they were going was still an unformed idea to him. Now that he had it worked out, he knew that it was key to keep it as secret as possible. No one except him knew that they were going directly from the hospital to his grandfather's. Virgil didn't want to indicate a lack of trust to his deputies, but he knew that the less they knew, the safer Carlos and his family would be. His plan was to send Dave back to Redbud after the viewing, then bring them directly up to the mesa.

"Here we are, Sheriff."

Virgil knew they had been making extensive renovations to

the hospital complex over the last year and was pleasantly surprised by the room he entered. The colors were muted and soft. Although he knew what was behind the drape that covered the viewing window on the far wall, he felt much less anxiety than expected.

"Hey, Virgil." Doctor Kincaid had followed them into the room.

"Hey, Ark. I gotta say, considering what this room is used for, you made it as palatable as possible."

"Hats off to Chet here. It was his idea to get away from that institutional green. A lot of the current dialogue about death and healing speaks to the physical environment which initiates the process. He's even carried some of what he's learned into the actual viewing during the identification process. The board didn't object, because the cost factor was minimal. It's more about a supportive atmosphere for those left behind after a tragedy."

"I had to identify my brother after a motorcycle accident in Chicago," the intern said. "It was one of the worst experiences of my life. I still feel the coldness of the room. I understood how in a big city hospital, death almost becomes routine, just a part of the fabric, but I sat in a bare room on a paint-chipped metal chair waiting for the attendant to bring my brother into the other room. There wasn't even a picture on a wall, a plastic flower in a vase . . . nothing. I've never felt so alone in my life. Then, when the curtain was drawn back and I saw my brother, I could barely process it. It was like a bad dream. The only thing I could think of was that my parents weren't there to see him. That would've killed them."

"Sometimes it takes an experience like that to force change," the doctor said. The moment of silence that followed was broken by a soft knock on the door. Virgil opened it. Dave stood in the hallway. Behind him were Carlos and his wife.

"Jimmy's outside with the children," he said.

"Jimmy?"

"I didn't want to leave the office in Redbud unattended. Jimmy said he didn't mind coming in early."

"Okay. Good, Dave. I should've thought of that."

"Like I said, Virgil, we're in deeper water here than we're used to. You can't think of everything. That's why you have deputies." He gave a little wink then turned and walked down the hall. Virgil watched him go then turned and shook Carlos's hand.

"Consuella doesn't have to be here. I only need one confirmation."

Consuella stepped forward, alongside Carlos. "No. I want to see my sister and brother. I will be all right." She looked directly at Virgil when she spoke.

He brought them over to the curtained window and introduced them to the two men standing to one side. Each of them said a few words of consolation, then Dr. Kincaid nodded to Chet and the intern pulled the cord to open the drape.

Consuella had reached out to rest her hand on the sill. Virgil could see her grip it until the veins in her hand stood out. It was the only movement she made. Carlos put his hand on her shoulder and drew her close. The two bodies lay side by side. Only their faces were visible, and there was no indication that they were not intact. Virgil had not spoken to Carlos or Consuella of the mutilation.

They looked so young, he thought, almost like children. He hadn't expected the strength of the emotion he felt.

Carlos and Consuella stood in silence for a long time,

framed by the viewing window. Finally, the silence was broken by Consuella.

"That is my brother and sister."

Then, unexpectedly, she pointed toward the picture hanging on the far wall of the viewing room. "Look, Carlos, the Borda church."

Carlos's eyes followed hers as she pointed. On the wall behind the two still bodies was a watercolor. Virgil saw a softening come into Consuella's eyes as she focused on the image. Carlos turned toward the three men.

"My wife was from Taxco," he said. "The Borda church was her and her family's church for generations. It is very beautiful."

Another moment passed while their eyes lingered on the scene, then the intern drew the drapery closed. A minute or so later, they left the room. Ark walked with them outside to escort them as they left the hospital. Virgil turned toward Ark and Chet, who stood in the doorway. Dave had brought Carlos and Consuella ahead to join the children.

"That was as good as an experience like that could possibly be. Thank you."

"I told you, he brought his ideas into the actual viewing."

"Great job, Chet."

"It wasn't anything special. Anyone from the area around Taxco and for that matter a lot of the people from Mexico know the Borda church. It's been there for more than two hundred and fifty years. I've used the image a few times, but I honestly did not know their connection."

"It was special for those people," Virgil said. "Life and death became one and, unlike your experience, I don't think they feel so alone now."

26

By the time she got within view of the barns, she could see the dust. Probably Micah trying to recapture something, she thought. Sure enough, before she'd taken a dozen steps more, she could hear the grunts and squeals penetrating the dust clouds. It was only a little after ten, but already she could feel the perspiration under her clothes. If you were going to take a walk for cardio in this part of the country, at this time of the year, you did it by ten or you put it off until dusk. At least, that's what her doctor had told her. She listened to his advice about as much as she listened to anyone else's.

Cresting the last rise, just before the worker's dining hall, she could see her son atop the snorting horse, who was clearly trying to throw him. One slip of the reins and he'd land in a swirl of dust on the hardpan of the corral, which had become unforgiving after years of hooves and the occasional pounding of bodies. She bit her lip as she watched. He was all alone. It was just him and the horse. It wasn't the first time he had done this, but it was the first in a long time. Why was he doing it? Why now?

To her right, standing in the hallway of the dining hall, a man showed his face. She did not know him. This bothered her. It was her place, after all. She should know everybody on it, but there were more and more strange faces and she did not like it. When she looked again, he was gone.

The noise from the corral had lessened. Micah was moving the horse in circles around the enclosure, first left, then right. She knew these were neck-reining exercises, meant to reinforce the horse's response to changing leads. Only once or twice did the horse do a halfhearted crow hop. He had given over his will to the man. The battle was over.

She walked on and by the time she got to the corral, Micah had dismounted and was unsaddling the horse. She watched in silence until at last he acknowledged her presence with a nod of his head.

"You planning on going on the rodeo circuit again?" A reference to a long-ago youthful fling. "For the record, you're just a little south of fifty and the ground's not as soft as when you were young."

"Well, I try to stay off the ground. I managed today."

"Why take the risk, Micah? What do you get out of it?"

He didn't answer as he set the saddle on the post that joined the rails at the corner of the corral. The horse stood quietly, nostrils wide, blowing into the morning air. Micah took the saddle blanket and began working on the steam rising from the horse's back. Audrey moved toward the horse's head, reached through the fence, and stroked his muzzle. The gelding lowered his head to her touch, his sides gently heaving as he settled. Finally, Micah took the blanket he'd been using to wipe the horse down and draped it over the rail to air. Then he slipped the bridle over the horse's head and hung it over the saddle horn. Unfettered, the horse walked to the center of the corral while they both watched, lay down, and rolled the memory of the man off his back in the dirt. Then he scrambled to his feet and went to the horse trough at the side of the barn door. He dropped his nose into the water.

"They always used to say," she said, "a good horse drops his muzzle deep into the water." Her son didn't say anything.

"I asked you a question," she said. "What do you get out of it?"

"I guess it's kind of hard to explain. Maybe it has to do with reminding me of a time when I felt free."

"I don't understand."

"I knew you wouldn't."

"Try me. I'd like to know why you come down here, early in the morning alone, to chance breaking your neck."

Micah looked at his mother full on for the first time. "When Caleb was alive, I was able to do pretty much what I liked because he was the focus, the heir apparent. In college, I'd been on the rodeo team six months before you even knew. I wasn't on the radar. All that changed when he didn't come back from Vietnam. Dad went into the bottle and you . . . all you saw was Rusty. Then, when she was gone . . . Well, that was pretty much the end. Dad took the easy way out, left a mess, and I was the only one around to clean it up. You . . . you just got mean. I don't know all the reasons. Maybe you felt cheated, maybe it had to do with Dad's weakness and the fact that someone you thought might be the answer rejected you. Probably a combination of those things, but you just got meaner and meaner and for the most part I didn't exist to you.

I got stuck with this place and all that went with it and lost myself in the process. So, when things go bad, I come down here, find the rankest horse in the barn, and see if I can break my neck, and wonder, if it happens, will anyone even notice?"

She stood alone, long after Micah turned away, took the lead rope, and caught up with the horse, then disappeared into the barn.

She looked around, but did not see the thousands of acres filled with pecan trees or hear the distant lowing of cattle, or even see the towering house on the knoll that still bore the name Crow's Nest. She saw instead the refuse of her life. It was not so much regret that overtook her, but a sense of profound aloneness. Micah's words had hit their mark. More than he could ever know.

In the distance, where the hard county road met the long driveway that led to where she stood, she saw a car. She watched its progress as it made its way toward the house, finally pulling up to the steps that led to the sweeping veranda and the front door. The man who got out of the car stood as a reminder of her past. A rugged handsomeness, piercing, dark eyes, and an easy air of confidence, just like his father. Even after all these years, the memory of him stirred her. She would have walked away from everything she thought she wanted, for him. He had become her addiction. He had wavered because she was beautiful in her youth and in her strength of will, but in the end he rejected her. He could not destroy a family, nor would he allow her to despite the intensity of their attraction for each other.

The loss devastated her. When, in the years to come, he married and had a son, her grief became complete. The final blow came with his death, along with his wife, in the car crash.

That had robbed her of the last of her hope, and she hated him for it.

Now the same man, reborn in his son, stood by his car, looking up at the house.

Virgil had just put his foot on the first step when an intuition made him look to his right. There he saw a lone figure standing in the road by the corral. Even at this distance, he knew who it was. He looked at the house once more, then took his foot from the step and headed down the road.

"Mrs. Hayward . . ." He took off his hat as he offered the greeting. His sunglasses were on the console in the cruiser and he squinted in the eastern sun, which was at her back. He couldn't see her face.

"Good morning, Virgil."

It was the first time he had ever heard her use his given name.

"I was wondering if Mike . . . Micah was here."

"Yes. He's in the barn putting one of the horses away. A little morning exercise. I'm sure you remember from school, when he was on the rodeo team."

"I saw him when he won the Junior Championship and got that trophy. He sure could ride."

"Don't forget the belt buckle. It's the biggest buckle I ever saw. He still wears it regularly. Do you remember?"

"Yes, yes I do." Virgil was standing alongside the corral, mulling over Audrey's words after she left him, when Micah came out of the barn, carrying a saddle over his right shoulder.

"I thought I heard voices," he said. "Exchanging pleasant-ries with my mother?"

Virgil hesitated before answering. "Pleasantries . . . Yes, I guess they were."

"Probably a first for you." He set the saddle so it was balanced on the top rail of the corral.

"That's seen some use," Virgil said.

"Yeah, busted my first horse on that and a few since."

"You were good. Very good."

"Thanks, Virgil. You were pretty decent yourself, as I remember."

"Not as good as you. Besides, I was too anxious to hear that buzzer. I always got the feeling that you never listened for it. You were aboard just for the thrill."

"Can't deny that. Still gets my blood rising."

"There are safer ways. You're not a kid anymore."

"You're sounding just like my mother. Maybe you two will become cordial yet."

Virgil smiled. "Don't know about that. Like I was just saying, after a couple of minutes I'm listening for the buzzer."

It was Micah's turn to smile. "So what's up? You didn't drive all the way out here to exchange pleasantries with my mother and remind me of my lost youth."

"No, no I didn't. I came to tell you that yesterday we found two bodies at the bottom of a wash over in Redbud. Man and a woman. Or a boy and a girl, really. Both were decapitated. They were the brother and sister gone from here right after Buddy was murdered. Thought you should know."

Virgil didn't miss the slight tautness in Micah's face, or the way his hand tightened on the pommel of the saddle he was steadying on the rail.

"I . . . I don't know what to say. I just thought they lit out, headed back south of the river."

"Nope. My guess is they were scared. The girl was seeing Buddy. Maybe she knew something and somebody wanted to make sure she kept it to herself. Figured by leaving them alongside the road in Redbud they'd maybe send a message to somebody else. Maybe somebody who also knows what she knew. By the way, they were the brother and sister of Carlos Castillo's wife. Carlos works in your office in Redbud, doesn't he?"

"Yes. For years. He's a good worker."

"Strange, isn't it?"

"What?"

"The coincidence. All these people work for you. And you know what? I've always had the hardest time believing in coincidences when it comes to things like this."

Ten minutes later, while he was driving back to town on the county road, Virgil was still trying to figure out the look in Micah's eyes when he delivered that punch line.

The gray skies of the previous day were grayer. The clouds were full. There was a hint of heaviness in the air that Virgil had not felt for a long time. There was no dry breeze blowing across the land, almost as if the earth were holding its breath in anticipation of a change. The diagnosis was confirmed by Cesar when he stepped out of the car.

"Something's coming, pretty soon."

"Maybe I'm ready for a change."

"The cattle and horses are a little restless," Cesar said. "Could be a big one."

"You know what they say about a feast or a famine," Virgil said as he headed for the house.

"By the way, you might want to check your messages. Phone was ringing. Heard Billy's voice."

"You know the phone won't bite you. You could pick it up. Maybe even have a conversation."

Virgil knew his words were wasted. It was a peculiarity of Cesar's that he would only answer the phone in the barn. The fight to get him a cell phone had been going on for almost a year. Virgil figured it was some kind of domain thing and there was little doubt that he spent more time in the barn than in the house. He hit the button on the receiver as soon as he walked into the house, but it wasn't Billy's voice he heard.

"Let's see, it's been three days, so you've either been awfully busy or your sex drive is a lot lower than I thought. Oops, hope I called the right number. If not, have a nice day, whoever you are, and just ignore that sex-drive comment. On the other hand, if I got it right about that sex-drive thing, give me a call."

It was good to hear her voice and for just an instant Virgil felt the hint of a physical need. Then he heard Billy's voice telling him how he was looking out for grandfather and his new guests. He went on to say there would always be a pair of eyes on them and not to worry. Billy's message immediately brought him back to reality. He pressed the delete button then left the kitchen. Upstairs in his bedroom, he sifted through the tie and belt rack until he found a belt that he figured he'd probably have to notch on the last hole, it had been so long since he wore it. He wrapped it up in a coil and brought it with him when he went downstairs.

When he left the house, Cesar was sitting on the front porch. He sat down alongside him.

"Back on the road?"

"Yep, I'll be back late tonight. Don't bother leaving me anything. I'll grab something while I'm out. Sorry I haven't been around much. Been real busy."

"I heard about them young people."

Virgil didn't ask how he knew about something that he had bent over backward trying to keep secret.

"Don't worry," Cesar said. "Everything here is under control. You do what you got to do."

Then, as an afterthought, as if reading Virgil's mind: "What I know, what Billy is doing, ends with us. It's not out there and it won't be."

"Okay. I reckoned as much." Virgil stood up. "Gotta get going." He stepped off the porch.

"Virgil."

Virgil stopped and looked back. Cesar had gotten out of his chair.

"About that other thing . . . that low sex drive. Can't make that same promise about not going public, but if you want to avoid the town talk, there's this blue pill."

A wide smile broke out on Cesar's face.

"Often wondered what kept you going, old man." Virgil waved, then walked to the cruiser, carrying the belt in his hand. At the last minute, with his hand on the door handle, he stopped. He looked around at the only home he'd ever known. The air had a different taste and there was an unusual midday breeze. That, coupled with some big thunderheads blocking the sun, had stifled the record-breaking temperatures. The wind that stirred the leaves on the cottonwood seemed to suggest the promise of growing strength.

He caught the movement of Star in the corral with her foal. The foal had thrived. Cesar said it was as if the mare had gained a new hold on life. Even now as he watched, the two ran around the corral, the foal bucking and wheeling as it chased after its mom, Star's ears forward, eyes wide, and tail up, proud in her newfound motherhood.

Virgil opened the door, threw the belt onto the seat on the passenger side, then walked to the corral.

"What are you thinking?" He hadn't heard Cesar come up In back of him.

"I think it's time the little one got to see more of the world."

Virgil climbed to the top rail, sat there a moment, then jumped down into the corral. Immediately, the mare came to him. As he stroked her neck, the foal came alongside. He reached out with his free hand and stroked the foal in the same way. After a minute or two, he walked to the opposite side of the corral to the gate that led to the great expanse that went beyond the horizon. He unlatched the gate and threw it wide. The mare let out a loud call, then leaped through the opening. The foal, calling after her, raced to close the gap that had so quickly separated them. Star never slowed her stride, bucking a couple of times in the joy of the moment. Virgil and Cesar stood in silence as the two became smaller and smaller in the distance, leaving only a dust cloud as evidence of their passing.

"*Muy bueno,*" Cesar said.

Virgil nodded his head in agreement. "Doesn't get any better than that."

It was a little before three when he pulled into the office parking lot. His was not the only car there. Rosie was at her desk. Facing her sat a man with his back toward Virgil.

"Hello, Ears."

The man stood up immediately, with a slight frown on his face.

"Sorry about that, Bob," Virgil said. "I mean, Mayor. It just slipped out."

Virgil had known Bob Jamison his whole life and just like 99 percent of the town had always called him by the nickname given to him by his own father who once said, "That boy better stay inside on a windy day, because with them ears sticking out at right angles to his head, he's liable to end up in the next county."

It became a nickname that took on a life of its own. So much so that when he ran for mayor, he had been advised to put his nickname in quotations on all his posters. His most famous reelection quote after his first term was, "Remember, when you come to me with your problem, I'm all ears."

"Don't worry, Virgil. I'm past caring. Besides, they got me elected four times so far. Last two without an opponent."

"That's 'cause you're doing a great job, Bob."

"You can put down that shovel, Virgil. You're not in the barn now. Anyway, can't linger too long. Shoulda given a holler first, but just took a chance you might be here. Visiting with Rosie without Dave around has been a pure pleasure. I told her if he ever gets in the way of a stray bullet or she needs some other comfort, I'd be happy to get the call."

"Best offer I've had this week," Rosie said. "I'll pass that on to Dave. I'm sure he'll be relieved to know that I'll be well taken care of if anything unfortunate happens."

"Maybe you better keep that under your hat, Rosita, till Dave's too feeble to pull a trigger."

Rosie smiled then got up from her desk. "Well I'll let you boys talk. Virgil, I'm going to run down to Margie's for a quick bite since you're here. Ain't had anything since breakfast. Want me to bring you back something?"

"No. I'll be here till Dif comes in. Take your time."

"Dif is why I stopped by," Bob said, as Rosie went out the door.

"Figured it was something like that. What's up?"

"The council heard you got Dif on the payroll full-time. They're concerned about the budget. They asked me to look into it. They were wondering if it was a necessary expense."

"A necessary expense . . ." A small vein in Virgil's temple became more prominent. "A necessary expense . . . Let's see, we've had three killings in the last five weeks, more than we've had in the last two years. I got two deputies, in a substation trailer, twenty-five miles away, clear on the other side of the county. It's me and Jimmy on second shift with Rosie as backup here. While I'm working on this, because it's kind of a priority, that Russell kid with his wannabes are still dropping rocks off the overpass on that new interstate spur, Charlie Grissom is still getting drunk and beating on his wife, and Ma Sampson is still calling regularly because she's sure a Peeping Tom is outside her window trying to catch her in a state of undress. That's only the beginning of the list. So I called in Dif, who'd rather spend his golden years with a fishing rod and a cold beer, to help me out because I'm on a thin line here. And you want to know if it's a necessary expense. Ears, you go back and tell the council, I get any more dead people, I'll just space them out on Main Street and we can use them as speed bumps. Then we can save money by removing the stoplights."

"Virgil, take it easy. You know if it was up to me . . . Hell, I'd tell you to go right out and hire as many full-time deputies as you need. You know that. It's just politics. Same old story."

"I know, Bob. It's just been a little stressful lately. Like Dave said, we're dealing with big-city problems and we're small-town. But that's changing. Case you haven't noticed, that old yellow dog hasn't been sleeping in the middle of Main Street lately."

"Don't worry, Virgil. I'll take care of the council. After this thing is done, ask Dif if he can stay on awhile, until we get a new full-time guy. I also want you to plan on taking some time for yourself. By the way, where do you think you are with this situation? Just curious."

Virgil didn't answer right away, but walked to his desk and sat down heavily in his chair.

"Well, I'd say that if this were a play we were watching, I think we're somewhere in the middle of the third act."

27

Dif Taylor walked through the door just before five. Virgil was alone in the office.

"Where's Rosie?"

"I gave her the afternoon off. Had to be here for a couple of hours to get caught up with a pile of paperwork. Figured she could use a break. You okay with the extra time?"

"I'm good, Virgil. Most of the time it's pretty quiet when I first come in, doesn't get crazy till later, especially on Friday and Saturday nights. But you know that. Edna's happy spending the extra money."

"She still in Alamogordo, visiting with her sister?"

"No, she's back. Figures to put any extra income into plans for a cruise this winter."

"Well, you like the water."

"Yeah, when it's mixed with scotch or I got a hook in it. Don't know about being out in the middle of the ocean. I guess I saw that *Poseidon* movie too many times."

"The mayor was in earlier. He's good with you being here. This way, Jimmy can be out on patrol. You here with Rosie, most of the time, Dave and Alex down in Redbud. Should work out."

"Being here is fine with me. No more patrol. I'm done with chasing kids down at the dump shooting rats or getting between Charlie Grissom and his wife every Saturday night. Jimmy's legs are in much better shape than mine. Besides, he's better at it than I was."

Virgil raised his eyebrows.

"No, it's the truth," Dif said. "Jimmy's got nice quiet ways, never loses his temper, and he's got patience Job would envy. He's a lot like you, Virgil. You make a good team."

Virgil put the separate stacks of papers he had just processed onto Rosie's desk. Then he sat with Dif over a cup of coffee. The only sound was the clock ticking on the far wall and a couple of flies buzzing at the window in the late-afternoon sun, which was intermittently peeking through building clouds. Finally, Virgil got up from his desk and grabbed his hat.

"I'll be back later tonight."

"You know," Dif said, "Sam and I made a pretty good team, too."

Virgil paused at the mention of his father.

"But it was a different world fifty years ago. No computers, not a lot of TLC or political correctness, but we got the job done. Sam put the fear of God in the people who needed it. Before they acted up, they'd think twice. He didn't hold with certain behavior, especially a guy beating on some girl. Sam would invite them out back for a little private talk. That pretty much solved the problem. Not too many wanted to have that conversation twice. Can't do that today. Course, there were tumbleweeds still rolling down Main Street back then, chasing after drunk cowboys on horseback. Now you only see a horse on Main Street if there's a parade."

Dif walked to the door with Virgil and opened it.

"Not a day goes by I don't think about Sam," Dif said. "Course, we hardly ever had to deal with the kind of crime that's keeping you up nights."

"Guess nothing ever stays the same," Virgil said as he stepped out into the parking lot. "We each get our own personal slice of time and we have to figure out how to get through it best we can."

"You're right, Virgil, and for me staying put in this office is better. I'll let you young guys deal with this new world."

Virgil gave a wave and got into his cruiser.

Virgil kept thinking about his father as he drove out of town. He wondered how the old man would have dealt with this situation, then was sobered by the fact that Dif was right. In all the years he was sheriff, his father probably never had to deal with anything like this. Not even close. The violence had always been there, but it was different. A bank robbery. An assault. Violent crimes that could end in death, but were never really long on planning or premeditation, much more of the moment and as such they were dealt with in that way. In a sense, he envied that world, where problems could be dealt with up front, maybe even with a one-on-one in the backyard, or in the parking lot outside the jail. He was still locked in his reflection when he reached his destination.

She was standing with her back to him at the end of the bar, speaking in Spanish to someone in the kitchen. The flow of the conversation was so fast, Virgil couldn't keep up. He slid quietly onto a vacant seat and watched her. Her long hair almost reached her waist. He remembered feeling it between his fingers as he pushed it aside to brush the nape of her neck with his lips. When the conversation ended, she became engrossed in tallying up a bunch of credit card receipts at the cash register. She was oblivious to anything else. He sat in his reverie, tracing the curves of her body and feeling her quiver in response to his touch. A waitress dropped a glass at the end of the bar and it shattered in a million pieces.

"Easy, Jody, they're not made of rubber. Careful you don't cut yourself." He liked that she dismissed the accident without raising her voice and with just a hint of a rebuke.

"Say, is there a chance I could get a little service over here? A guy could starve to death. Or die of thirst."

Ruby turned quickly and he saw the flash of white in her smile.

"Sorry about that, mister. I thought you were one of our regulars and wouldn't mind sitting a spell."

"You know, I think I could become a regular. If I could always see what I was admiring just now, I could almost forget that I hadn't eaten all day."

"Well, let's see what we can do about that hunger of yours. Just let me run upstairs and put those receipts in my desk."

She stuffed two handfuls in the front pocket of her apron, then walked to the end of the bar and disappeared through the door that led upstairs, untying the apron as she went. Virgil followed her. As soon as they were both in her office, he put his arms around her. His lips sought hers and she yielded completely. They stumbled through the office, into the living quarters, never letting go of each other. Within seconds, clothes were strewn across the floor in a random fashion, ending at the bed. The rhythm of their bodies was so in sync, the act of passion so intense and outside of time that when it finally abated, they had yet to speak a word. He looked at their bodies still locked together, her long hair falling over her shoulder until it brushed his chest. She spoke first.

"I guess we weren't really just talking about food."

Virgil didn't say anything, but drew her close, burying his lips in her neck, breathing in her scent.

"Here we go again," he whispered in her ear.

Much later, when she was sitting on the side of the bed separating his clothes from hers, she began to laugh.

"What's so funny?"

"I was just thinking," she said. "I've never gotten such an immediate response to a phone message before."

"You've got to love technology."

Virgil glanced out the window at the sliver of a moon hanging in the night sky. It quickly disappeared behind a cloud.

"What are you thinking?" Ruby asked. He turned to face her over his empty plate and the remnants of the meal they had just finished. They were sitting in a corner booth downstairs in the restaurant.

"I'm thinking, I was never so hungry in my life."

She sat back as she put a cup of coffee to her lips. "Are we still talking about food?"

He didn't answer, just smiled and then looked out the window at the parking lot.

"What's the fascination with the parking lot?"

"Wondering if it's dark enough."

"This sounds interesting. What did you have in mind? A little romance under the stars, or some kind of cowboy fetish? I should have told you sooner, I'm not into leather or ropes."

"I want you to do something for me."

For the next couple of minutes they talked, then he got up from the booth, leaned down, whispered in her ear, and teasingly bit her neck. Remembering where he was, he looked around a little self-consciously to see if they had been observed. Outside of one or two late-nighters at the bar, the place was empty. He glanced at a wall clock over the black bull in the other room as he moved toward the door. It was almost midnight. The crunch of the gravel was the only sound as he made his way to his car.

Jimmy had just finished his first tour of the night. Everything was pretty much as it should be. He only came upon two cars, one a pickup, down in a spot by the river locally known as Quiet Cove. He guessed they were watching the submarine races. He got a kick out of the term when Virgil first used it. As he drove by, he didn't stop, just flashed his lights to let them know he was there. They knew he'd be back. He'd watched the submarines a time or two himself. When he got back to the office, he was kind of surprised to see Virgil's car in the lot. Even more surprised to see Dif and Virgil sitting in the semidark looking at the TV. On the screen, he saw an image of a dark figure standing at a distance, barely a shadow. The only break in the dark, like a star in a black sky, was the shine of a large belt buckle.

"Come over here, Jimmy. I want you to look at something."

"I've seen this movie already, Virgil."

"Yeah, well this is a little different and I want your take on something."

He reset the disc and the three of them sat watching the shadowy moments at the Black Bull parking lot on Buddy's last night. When the disc ended, Virgil popped it out and replaced it with a different one.

"If this one's as interesting as the last, maybe we should get popcorn," Dif said.

Virgil hit the fast-forward button. A couple of minutes from the end, he hit the play button and the figure cloaked in darkness could again be seen standing on the edge of the parking lot, just short of the video's range. Virgil froze the image. The figure seemed just as it appeared the first time around. The only brightness in the frame came from the man's belt.

"Anybody notice anything?" Virgil said.

"What are we looking for?" Jimmy said.

"I've shown you two different versions of approximately the same thing and I'm asking you if you noticed anything different."

"Run them both again," Dif said. "Just the last couple of frames."

Jimmy nodded in agreement and Virgil repeated the process. When he was finished, he asked the question again.

"There was something different," Jimmy said. "But I'm not sure what it was."

Virgil looked at Dif, who nodded in agreement. Then Dif sat up in his chair.

"Wait a minute. The light . . ."

"What light?" Virgil said.

"The reflection of light from the belt buckle. It was different."

"That's it," Jimmy said. "There was more of a gleam in the first one than there was here."

"You've both confirmed it," Virgil said.

"But what's it mean?" Jimmy asked.

"That second image was me tonight wearing this belt."

He reached over to his desk and grabbed the curled-up belt that lay there, displaying the belt buckle.

"I think this is a fairly standard buckle for a wide belt. Most of the pickup cowboys wear them. It caught the light from the parking light and reflected, but not as much as that first image. The belt buckle in that first image had to have been larger, not like an ordinary buckle off the rack. It was special."

"How do you mean special?" Dif asked.

"Well, maybe it was commemorative. Like an award for doing something."

"An award for what?" Jimmy asked.

Virgil looked down, fingering the buckle that lay in his lap. Then he rolled the belt up, reached over, opened the drawer of his desk, put it in, and closed the drawer.

"Like winning an event in a championship rodeo."

The thought nagged at him all the way back to the ranch. He knew where the evidence was pointing. It was as clear to him as the road ahead of him, lit up by the headlights. But he didn't want to accept it.

A flash of heat lightning outlined the dark clouds. They were the kind of predictors of a storm to come that he had seen many times before. After over a month-long stretch of dry, searing heat, they could be as welcome as they could be dangerous. They mirrored exactly how he felt.

28

Audrey Hayward had been taking stock of her life. The inventory wasn't pretty, but in the vernacular of the day, it was what it was. She thought back to the time long past when she had made the decision to not leave Hayward. She almost allowed herself the luxury of wondering where life would have led her if she had not made that choice. She could be mean and hard and often manipulative, but she knew that about herself. Whatever quarter she gave to others, she gave none to herself. From the day she chose to become a Hayward, to this very night, every choice was made with a clear head.

She didn't blame her husband for his lack of ambition, any more than she blamed him for his drunkenness. But she did blame herself for his failings. Her lack of will allowed him to become what he was. Now she had to come to grips with the reality that her life was coming full circle. It was no more deniable than the life choices she had made which had brought her to where she was now. That sterile specialist in Houston she had seen the month before only confirmed what she already knew.

Standing at the window with a half-filled glass in her hand, looking out at the black night broken only by the flashes of heat lightning, she thought about her personal finality. The son that had not come back from the war, the daughter she had lost, and the husband who had withdrawn from life had left her embittered, to the point where that very bitterness had become her life force. It had taken a death sentence to make her realize this.

The clink of the ice in the glass was the only sound to be heard. She placed the glass on the end table, then left the room and walked out the front door to the porch. The warm night air layered over her, displacing the coolness of the air-conditioned house. It felt good, a confirmation of life. Her exhaustion blew away on a light breeze. She stood there a long time, alone in the night, until at last she saw a car turn into the drive. She watched its progress all the way to the steps that led up to the porch. The soft hum of the engine ceased as the car rolled to a stop on the side of the driveway, and a beautiful girl emerged from the car. An immediate smile crossed Audrey's lips.

"Oh, Gran, I didn't see you standing there. Were you waiting up for me?"

"No. I just wanted to feel the night air. Your timing was impeccable."

She looked at the girl coming to greet her and saw the daughter she had lost. A stab of pain in her heart made her grip the railing at the top of the stairs.

"Why didn't you turn on the outside lights?" the girl asked.

"The lights on the driveway were enough. Besides, I didn't want to attract the bugs. Where are you coming from?"

"I was out with Cal and a couple of friends. We took in a movie, then met up with some people at the local watering hole."

"Did you have fun?"

"Yeah, it was okay. Always good to be with Cal, but I sometimes feel like an outsider."

"What do you mean?"

"Well, this is where I'm from, but I've spent so much time in boarding schools and away at college that I really don't know anyone here. These are Cal's friends. My friends are scattered in other parts of the country."

"You could make new friends here."

"I don't know if my future is here. Every time I come home, I feel like a visitor. I'm unconnected. Maybe if my mother . . ."

Audrey looked at the silhouette of her granddaughter in the dim light and again saw the girl she had lost.

"It would be nice if we could change things, but it's beyond our reach. Maybe . . ." Audrey's words trailed off into the night.

"Guess we've only got the here and now," the girl said.

"Let's go inside," Audrey said. "Maybe have a little treat before we go to bed. I think there's a piece of that dark chocolate cake left over from dinner."

"Chocolate cake and ice cold milk, a perfect combo." Arm in arm, they turned and walked into the house.

The girl's words kept echoing in Audrey's mind. We've only got the here and now.

A roll of thunder followed by a sharp crack of lightning managed to drag Virgil out of a fitful sleep. He sat on the side of his bed like a somnambulist, barely aware of the world. He stared dully at the rivers of rain running down the window, a fulfillment of the promise of the last two days. Unrefreshed by a night of tossing and turning, he got to his feet and walked to the window. The rain was intense, at times coming sideways, driven by a persistent wind. He could see that the creek was full. Only yesterday, it was a bare whisper of itself, struggling to maintain a trickle.

He stood by the window a long time, almost in a trance. At last, in the distance, he heard a ring, followed by a voice which at first he had some trouble placing. A few minutes later, when he got downstairs, he hit the play button again to confirm his suspicions. He heard Audrey Hayward's voice asking him to come to the ranch.

It was almost eleven when he stepped out into the rain, but the gray day gave no indication of time. There was no sun or trace of clouds, just a sameness that hung over the landscape like a wet blanket. Cesar had not yet come to the house, so he had taken care of the barn chores. Star and her foal were secure. He'd even collected eggs from the coop that was attached to the barn. There wasn't much in the way of production lately. The enduring heat and the full molt most of the birds were in had taken its toll. The ordinary work always left him feeling good and by the time he was on his way to Hayward Ranch, he was ready to put on his other hat.

Audrey greeted him at the door. Every time he entered this place, it was like a step back into his past, but there was a slightly different feel about it today. He couldn't put his finger on it, whether it was the tone of Audrey's voice or something even less discernible, but it was definitely there. She led the way to the huge living room.

"Please sit, Virgil." She gestured toward a chair. Virgil glanced about the large room that to him had always seemed, however it reflected the history of the house, incongruous to its surroundings. The carpeted floors, the stylized decor, the overstuffed furniture. Even the walls were covered in the elaborate wallpaper that you would expect to find in a Fifth Avenue apartment in New York. There was nothing of the spare prairie that showed itself in this house.

"Can I offer you something?"

"No, thanks," Virgil said. "I'm good."

The glass sitting on the end table next to her had not escaped his notice.

"I guess it is a little early in the day," she said almost absent-mindedly as she glanced unseeingly at the window.

When she turned back to face him, he thought for a second she might have lost her train of thought. He thought she looked almost vulnerable, a word he'd never associated with Audrey Hayward before. When she spoke again, there was more strength in her voice, almost as if she was making a special effort.

"I know there's something in the wind. Otherwise you or your deputy wouldn't have been coming here. Something to do with Micah, I think. This place and these killings. As a matter of fact, I know this is probably the last place you want to be. The reality is, I've spent a lot of my life embittered by the way my life turned out, but that is my fault alone. I blame no one for my choices but myself. However, the reality of how I've impacted others has started to weigh heavily on me. Before I leave this world, I'd like to change that and I begin with you."

Virgil was completely unprepared for the Audrey that was speaking. This was a person he'd never known.

"You may or may not know what I'm about to tell you," she went on, "but in terms of what I want to say that doesn't really matter. Long ago, in another life, I was in love with your father. My husband had long since given up on life and crawled into a bottle. I'm sure I was more than partly responsible. My son Caleb, as you know, never came back from the war, and out of anger and resentment I turned to your father, and I fell in love. When reality caught up with us, he rejected me. That was part of his strength, because I was married and had children. I hated him for that. Hated him . . . for the very thing that made me want him. When he married your mother, the hate grew to encompass her and then you. When Rusty fell in love with you, it was almost like fate was taunting me. Micah, my surviving son, paid a very heavy price as this played out. His father died and I didn't care because I had become so self-absorbed. He had to take over here, whether he wanted to or not. Then when Rusty died, my bitterness came full circle and I struck back. That's when I made you pay."

She looked at Virgil with a vulnerability he never expected to see in her.

"I don't understand," he said. "How did you make me pay? Rusty was the only reason I ever came anywhere near you. When she was gone . . . I never had any reason to come here, ever again."

Audrey got out of her chair and walked to the mantle of the fireplace. Then she reached up and took down a framed picture. She held it in her two hands and studied it. A smile touched the corners of her mouth. Finally, she came to him and faced him. She held out the picture and he took it. At first glance, he thought it was a picture of Rusty. As he looked closer, he realized it was the girl from the picture he had seen in Caleb's office at Hayward Trucking. He saw the strong facial resemblance to Rusty, along with the almost impish smile that she had taunted him with many times. Her eyes were slightly wider set, her cheekbones more evident.

"My granddaughter," Audrey said. "You've never met her."

"She's beautiful." He handed back the picture.

"She looks a lot like her mother, but her father definitely left his mark. Her name is Virginia." She held the photo so they could both look at it.

"I never met Micah's wife," Virgil said.

"Micah's wife. Yes, she's been gone almost twenty-five years."

"I had heard . . ."

"It's hard to keep a secret in a small town, especially when you hold the name of that town, but it's not impossible."

"It must have been tough, Mike being left with two little ones."

"That wasn't quite the case, Virgil."

Audrey took the picture and returned it to the mantle, angling it so that it faced both of them.

"It was during the time that Micah's wife was pregnant with Caleb that she started to show signs of instability, and it was within months of his birth that she was diagnosed schizophrenic. Before he reached his first birthday, she had already attempted suicide. Eventually, of course, she succeeded. She never had a second child."

"I don't understand," Virgil said. "Then who . . . ?"

"This is why I called you, Virgil, and this is why I begin with you."

Audrey sat heavily into the chair facing him. Then took a drink from the glass.

"Virginia is not Micah's daughter," she said. "She was named after her father. It was her mother's dying wish. She is yours, Virgil. Yours and Rusty's."

She sat back in her chair and reached again for the glass. The loudest noise in the room came from outside as the rain pelted the windows. Finally, Virgil got to his feet and walked to the picture. He studied it with a new intensity. He saw what he had seen earlier, but now his focus was on the nuances of difference. The set of the jaw, the pronounced cheekbones, along with a hint of other things. He knew Audrey had not told him a lie. He saw Rusty in this picture, and he saw himself.

Without turning, he backed up to the chair and sat down. Then he turned to face Audrey. His mouth opened to frame a question, but she robbed him of his words.

"Rusty knew she was pregnant when you went back to college for your last year," she said. "She didn't tell you because, well, she later told me when I found out about the pregnancy . . . She didn't tell you because she was afraid you'd insist on coming home and not finish your final year. When she died giving birth, I hid the truth from you."

"I was told a ruptured appendix."

"If you have money, there are ways. My biggest problem was Micah. He was the only one who knew the truth here in Hayward, and it took all my powers of manipulation to get him to keep the secret. He was so overwhelmed with his wife and son and trying to salvage this place, that he was vulnerable, and I took advantage of that."

"So why now? After all these years?"

"I'm still who I am, Virgil. When I leave this earth, I still want the name Hayward to mean something in this place. And I want you to protect it. You see, I'm still capable of manipulation, and now you're invested here because of your daughter. These killings are coming a little too close to home. I want you to know that if this family is destroyed by whatever is going on, your daughter is likely to be one of its casualties. I'm hoping you won't let that happen. Micah got the short end of the stick from his father and me, but I know now that if it hadn't been for him we wouldn't have survived. I'm trying in my own feeble way to acknowledge that fact, and to help him while I can to hold on to what he has built and accomplished."

Virgil felt like a wrangler who had just survived a stampede. Now he was trying to come to grips with reality while clouds of dust obscured the world he thought he knew.

"Here." Audrey stood in front of him with a glass in her hand. "You might not have wanted a drink before, but you need one now."

He took the glass.

"Drink up."

He raised it to his lips, in almost pure reflex to her command. When he drained the glass, he saw her through its bottom. She was still standing in front of him, strangely distorted by the thickness of the glass.

She filled his glass again. This time he took a sip without prompting. The burn in his throat felt good.

"You know, I thought I'd go to my grave with this secret," she said. "But I'm glad I didn't. I suppose you hate me right now. I understand that, but if it's any comfort to you, know I hate myself even more."

The liquid continued to burn in his throat, displacing the numbness. He felt the velvet texture of the chair he was sitting in, saw the woman who had returned to her seat, and at last found his voice.

"Does she know?" To his ears the words sounded like they had come from someone else.

"She doesn't even know you exist. I'm sorry."

The feebleness of her words came in a voice almost unrecognizable. Thin and reedy, they didn't go with the Audrey Hayward he knew. He looked at her. The knuckles of her hands gripped the arms of the chair so tightly the veins showed blue against her skin. The hair on top of her head was snow white, her face heavily lined, the remnants of youth and past beauty just about gone. Her breathing seemed labored and Virgil realized that their meeting had taken its toll. An unexpected sadness for her overtook him. He rose from his seat and stood looking down on her. She didn't attempt to stand.

"What are you going to do?" Her voice barely a whisper.

"Honestly, I really have no idea, but like you, I will do what I have to do. There has to be an accounting. I'm not going to walk away from that. Now that you've told me about a daughter I never knew I had, well . . . You brought her out like a poker chip when it suited your purpose. Now, I'll have to play the hand you dealt me. When it's all over, I guess the chips will fall where they may."

Micah Hayward watched from an upstairs window as Virgil Dalton left the house. He saw him running, head down, to his car through the driving rain, then watched while he drove the long driveway until he reached the county road. He wondered why he had come to the house on such a day. Then he saw the path of light coming from the door of the picker's dining hall and knew someone else had been watching Virgil leave. In that instant, he knew there was going to be a change in his life.

When he walked into the living room twenty minutes later, his mother was still sitting in her chair, her eyes wide open, staring at a fire she could not see. He saw one hand hanging to the side of the chair and noticed the slight sag to one side of her mouth. Before he crossed the room to her chair, he knew that whatever else he did from here on it would be as the head of Hayward Ranch and that Audrey Hayward would no longer be there to censure or endorse his decisions.

29

Jimmy was making his final loop of the night when he passed by Virgil's ranch. From the county road, even in the darkness, he could see the light on in the ranch house. He turned off the road without hesitation, even though when he glanced at the digital on the dash it read two thirty. He could see Virgil sitting at the kitchen table as he stepped onto the porch. Virgil seemed to be fixed as he sat staring into space. Jimmy saw the empty glass on the table in front of him. He knew Virgil wasn't much of a drinker, so that surprised him. A cold beer at the end of the day, a glass of wine with dinner, especially during the winter, but that was about it. Hard liquor in the middle of the night, that was something else.

Virgil hardly reacted when Jimmy knocked. Then when he knocked a second time, he barely averted his eyes, then raised his hand and waved Jimmy into the house.

"Having trouble sleeping?" Jimmy knew the answer when he asked the question because Virgil was still in his uniform.

His hat was on the table in front of him alongside the phone, an empty bottle, and a glass with maybe a swallow left in the bottom. His gun belt and gun hung on the back of the chair next to him.

"Audrey Hayward is dead."

Jimmy said nothing because he wasn't quite sure how to react. From the talk around town, he knew that there was some history between Audrey and Virgil and Virgil's father, but Virgil himself had never mentioned any of it.

"Sit down, Jimmy." He said it in a voice that Jimmy had not heard before.

"Is there something wrong, Virgil?" Jimmy rarely called him by his first name.

"Wrong? Yeah, I guess. Or maybe right. Maybe right for the first time in a long time."

"Something you want to talk about?"

Virgil turned and looked full on at Jimmy. Then seeing the concern in Jimmy's face, he smiled.

"No. I'm good, Jimmy, but thanks for the offer. Have to sort everything out in my own head before I can talk about it with anyone else. But when that time comes, you'll be at the top of my list. Guess I just need some sleep now."

The moment passed and Jimmy saw that the man he always knew was back. Virgil got up from his chair a little unsteadily and grabbed Jimmy's shoulder. He looked at what remained in his glass, but left it there.

"That's enough damage for one night," he said. "See you later, Jimmy."

Virgil headed toward the stairs. Jimmy watched until he saw him switch on the light. Then he left the house.

A few minutes later, as Jimmy was pulling out onto the hard

surface, he glanced in his rearview mirror and saw the ranch house go dark.

"Well, you look well rested," Rosita said as Virgil came into the office. "I guess you didn't visit your new girlfriend last night."

Virgil stopped in his tracks.

"C'mon now," Rosita said, "did you think that you were gonna keep that a secret?"

"Damn small towns," he said with a wince.

"Heard about Audrey Hayward, too."

"Did you happen to hear who's doing these killings while you were at it?"

"No. That's on you. You gotta justify all that money this town's paying you somehow."

"Yeah, pretty soon I'm going to have to open one of those Swiss bank accounts. By the way, is there anything going on related to what this office should be concerned about?"

"Not much. Hiram Potts is in one of those cells back there, sleeping it off. Guess he heard there was a vacancy for town drunk since Harry died and he's applying for the job. Third time in the last month."

"Anything else?"

"No, it's been quiet. Everybody staying home, enjoying the rain."

"Yeah, thank God," Virgil said as he glanced at the steady rivulets running off the roof and down the window.

"You making any headway on this thing?"

"I think I am. Couple of things I've got to check on. I'll be out of here for a while, but I'll stop back before you're gone." He got up and headed for the door.

"You weren't here long enough to take off your hat. Where are you going?"

"Can't tell you. If I did, I'd have to kill you."

"Nothing I want to know that bad."

Virgil hesitated before he walked out. "Anything on the arrangements for Audrey?"

"Would you believe the service is tomorrow?"

"Tomorrow?"

"Yep. It's what she wanted. Everybody thought she'd want to go out with a bang, not a whimper. Hell, I thought she'd want to lie in state for at least a month. Just goes to show you. Think you know somebody then they go and surprise you. All her life she was leading the parade, now at the end . . ."

"People change, I guess."

"But Audrey Hayward?"

"Yes, even Audrey Hayward."

The roads were slick, the rain relentless. A couple of times he had the windshield wipers on full. The one plus was that the weather was mean enough to keep people indoors. There was no traffic. Rosita, Dif, even the boys down in Redbud maybe caught a break. He thought of Hiram sleeping it off in one of the cells. The night's sleep had been restorative for him, too. He felt better, had woken up with a sense of direction. What Audrey had told him, he was forced to put on the back burner. He knew that there would be a time to sort it out, but that time could not be now. That's why he was headed for his grandfather's. He needed to talk to Carlos. Maybe he was getting a little paranoid but he didn't want to call him. That's why he didn't even tell Rosie where he was going. He wanted that family safe. That's why he kept looking in his rearview mirror even now. His gut had told him last night, when he had left Hayward Ranch, that there were eyes on him. After three bodies, he was pretty sure that a fourth or more was not out of reach for the people responsible, even if it was a sheriff, a mother, a father, three small children, or even his own grandfather.

He hesitated for just a second when he got to the turnoff, then gunned the engine onto the dirt road, sure no one had seen him. The tires spun a little in the wetness, but he made it to the top of the plateau without incident. He took a deep breath as he got out of the cruiser. Everything looked right. For a second, the clouds broke and he saw a figure on the high tabletop, overlooking everything, sitting in the mist with a rifle in his lap. He would have to remember to thank Billy Three Hats.

Virgil could hear the children before he opened the door. The double-wide that had seemed overly spacious for just his grandfather had become a lot smaller. There were toys on the floor, scattered randomly and temporarily abandoned. He could see his grandfather in his favorite chair with a baby in his lap and the two other children on either side of him. They were all looking at a book. The children were jumping up and down pointing at the pages as he turned them. Virgil looked to his left and could see most of the kitchen. Carlos was seated at the table with a cup of coffee, reading a paper. He could hear the voices of two women. One of them came into view, carrying a steaming tray of food which she set on the table in front of Carlos. When she turned, their eyes met.

"You must be Virgil." She was small but ample, with dark eyes and a ready smile. Her mixed gray and black hair hung in a long braid down her back.

"Chato!" she shouted over the noise of the children. "Your grandson is here. I'm Teresita. Teresita Hoya."

"Yes. Grandfather has spoken of you. Good to meet you."

"You're just in time for dinner. Come."

He followed her into the kitchen. Carlos put the paper aside and stood to greet him. Consuella came to the table carrying more food. After she set her burden down, she came to Virgil and wrapped her arms around him.

"Thank you for protecting my family," she said. When she stepped back, he could see the tears in her eyes. Virgil stood mutely until he felt the strong hands of his grandfather.

"I was wondering when you were going to come to see us."

"I was tired of eating alone. Guess that's not a problem here."

"No, but there's always room for one more. Come, sit, have a piece of fry bread. I'll get you a beer." Virgil slid into the chair that was pulled out for him.

"No beer, just a tall glass of ice water."

The rest of the food was placed on the table. The baby was put in a high chair and the other two children were sent to wash up. During the momentary lull, Virgil was mesmerized by the activity. It had been a long time since he had been witness to a busy family getting ready for the regular nightly ritual. He was amazed at how his grandfather seemed to take it all in stride. He had wondered after the fact if it would be too much for him, the children and the noise, but he sat next to him and he saw the smile on his face as he reached out with a gnarled hand to make a little dancing motion with his fingers on the baby's high chair tray.

"You and the children were reading a story when I came in," Virgil said. "Looked like you were having a good time."

"Not really reading. More like looking for someone."

"Looking for someone? Who?"

"Waldo. A man named Waldo who is hidden in the pictures. I'll show you later."

"You are all right? I mean, this is a good thing you are doing and I . . . I'm sure they appreciate it. I don't know how long . . ."

"It has been good. I'm fine. It reminds me of long ago. Mrs. Hoya has been a great help."

"Yes. I can see. That is working out well for you?"

The old man hesitated, looking at her as she was taking milk from the refrigerator. Then he answered.

"I think, when they all go back to their home, she will stay."

For the next half hour, the room was filled with the sounds of eating and the exchange of ordinary conversation. At the end, Carlos and his wife brought the children into the living room while Virgil and Mrs. Hoya cleared the table and loaded the dishwasher. Grandfather sat at the table, his eyes partially closed, a smile on his lips.

"He is really happy to see you," Mrs. Hoya said to Virgil. "I hope you will come more often."

"Yes, I will. Thank you for all . . . all of this."

She nodded. Then she went into the living room with Grandfather. Carlos returned to the kitchen and Virgil joined him at the table.

"I thought maybe you wanted to speak to me about what's going on."

"I do," Virgil said. "I need some information about Hayward Trucking. Carlos, how are the containers for the semis kept track of? I mean, one from another? They all look exactly alike."

"Each is numbered."

"The particular one that Buddy pulled . . . I guess you would have to look that up in some kind of computer list to know which one it was, right?"

"Normally, that would be the case because there are a dozen or more on the lot at any given time, but I know the one that Buddy pulled."

"You do? Why? Is there something different about it?"

"No, it's just the numbers. I've always remembered. 010883. It's the date Connie was born. I don't know any of the others, but I know that one. Besides, that's pretty much the only one Buddy pulled, which is strange. The other drivers pulled different containers all the time. Only Buddy pulled the same one. He told me that after that breakdown he had."

"Is that container in the lot now?"

"Probably. There's no reason why it shouldn't be. I mean it's just a box on wheels. It's not like they need regular servicing. Besides, harvest hasn't even started."

"What do you mean?"

"Well, until harvest starts, only an occasional trailer load goes down to Juárez. As a matter of fact, the plant is in a shutdown for the next two weeks because it's slow at this time of the year. Once it starts up again, we'll pretty much send down the last of the inventory for processing and we'll be ready for the new harvest. Those containers are pretty much sitting there till then."

"What about maintenance?"

"Like I said, they really don't need much of anything. Unless a tire peels or an axle goes, they don't have much more than a sweep-out. That box that Buddy pulled is probably just sitting in that lot."

Hours later, after the kids were in bed and the noise level had dropped considerably, Virgil made his way toward his vehicle. His grandfather had insisted on walking out with him. There was a light rain falling. There was no moon visible and the night was as dark as it could be. If it weren't for the spotlight, a walk outside in this kind of dark, even for just thirty feet, could end in an emergency room visit at the reservation clinic.

"Thanks again for this," Virgil said.

The old man just waved his hand.

"And thank Billy for that." Virgil pointed to the top of the ridge, high over the trailer where he knew there was a man with a rifle that he could no longer see.

"Take care, Virgil. Don't worry about this. If you're getting closer to the end, remember to keep your own rifle handy."

Virgil drove off the mesa, feeling good about where he had placed Carlos and his family. It had been a long day and he was feeling it, but he wanted to make one more stop. He wanted to get a look at that trailer, but he didn't want to do it alone. He picked up the receiver and put a call in to Jimmy.

"You feel like joining me to make a late-night call down to Redbud and Hayward Trucking?" He explained to Jimmy what he wanted to do.

"Maybe we don't have to go to Redbud," Jimmy said. "I'm just making my rounds and I saw one of those box trailers in Wade's place. Maybe it's the one you're looking for."

"We'll see, Jimmy."

Virgil hung up the receiver. "Wouldn't that be nice," he said to the empty car.

Jimmy's cruiser was in the parking lot in back of the office by the time Virgil got there. Jimmy and Dif were sitting over some coffee and doughnuts.

"Well, if that don't fit the stereotype," he said as he walked through the door. "Those things will kill you."

Dif wiped some cream-filled doughnut off his lower lip.

"Something's gotta, Virgil. It might as well be this. I sure miss those days when it was just booze that'd do you in. Then it became smoke, then for a while it became coffee and butter. Just about everything in my past life that I enjoyed was trying to kill me and I never knowed it. And you know what, I made it this far. So now, creeping up on seventy, I kinda feel like if I'm so close to the edge that this here doughnut is going to push me over, then I'm ready to go. Hell, I'll jump if I'm that close."

Virgil couldn't help smiling. "You know, that's a different way of looking at it. What do you think, Jimmy?"

"I don't know, Sheriff. But if everything you like is bad for you, what's the point? And them doughnuts sure are tasty. I don't want to feel guilty every time I eat one. Besides, I read somewheres that stress is a real killer and if you're always feeling guilty after enjoying something you like then all that stress from that guilt sure ain't doing you any good."

"Well, you've convinced me." Virgil sat down at his desk after pouring himself a cup of coffee. He took a sip from the steaming cup. "Dif, pass me that box of doughnuts."

For the next twenty minutes, they sat around Virgil's desk, drinking coffee, eating doughnuts, and telling lies. Virgil swallowed the last of his second cup, put it down, and looked at the wall clock. It was almost one.

"Okay, Jimmy. Let's get 'er done and make some rounds."

When they left the building, the night air was still heavy with the day's rain and a damp fog was rising like steam off the paved surfaces. Jimmy started heading for Virgil's car.

"No, Jimmy. Let's take yours. It'll look more normal. You just making your regular nightly tour."

Virgil got in the backseat while Jimmy slipped behind the

wheel. Virgil stretched across the seat, his head barely visible in the rearview mirror. "Just you alone in the car on patrol, like usual. Follow your usual route."

It took close to a half hour before they came in sight of Wade's place.

"He opened the new car dealership last week," Jimmy said.

"Wade seems to be really coming up in the world. Not bad for a kid they almost had to burn the school down for so he could graduate. Did you have much to do with him, Jimmy?"

"Nah, Wade and Buddy were older than me."

"But you knew Buddy. And you liked him."

"Yeah, Buddy always treated me nice. One time when some kids were getting after me, Buddy stepped in. He'd give me a wave whenever he saw me. One time, when I was down by the river with my little sister, he even stopped and threw us a Frisbee to play with. I heard some things about Wade that made me wonder why Buddy hung out with him. But Buddy always treated me nice. Here we are, Sheriff."

Jimmy had driven around to the back of Wade's dealership, which was enclosed by an eight-foot chain-link fence. Virgil could see a trailer sitting in one far corner by itself.

"Now we get to see how lucky we are, and whether or not we're driving down to Redbud tonight."

Jimmy sprayed the yard with light from the spot mounted on the side of the car, just as he always did when he made his rounds. The shadows held no secrets and the only movement came from a feral cat that was out looking for a late-night snack. The light came at last to rest on the container.

"How are we going to know if this is the right one?"

Virgil explained about the number identification and Jimmy worked the light until it played on the left front of the container and they could see the panel with the identifying information.

"I can't make those numbers out, Sheriff. Not from here anyway."

"Well, if you can't with those twenty-five-year-old eyes, I've got no shot. We've got to get in there."

"No sense in us both going. It might not be the right box."

"Okay, Jimmy, you're elected."

Virgil got out while Jimmy pulled the car into the fence. He got out, climbed onto the front bumper, then scaled the fence as Virgil looked on, envious at how easy he made it seem. Once on the other side, he quickly made it to the container and after a moment he waved to Virgil to join him. Virgil tried to duplicate Jimmy's agility, but quickly realized that a little more caution would get him on the ground in one piece. When he was at Jimmy's side, Jimmy played the light on the identifying numbers.

"Now all we gotta do is find out what's so special about this container."

For the next few minutes, Jimmy and Virgil checked out the external condition of the box on wheels. Virgil double-checked the ID numbers while Jimmy crawled under the trailer to see if there was any kind of anomaly, but came up empty. Then they both went to the rear.

"It's got to be something inside," Virgil said as he swung open the rear door. Jimmy hopped up, then turned and offered Virgil his hand. They played their flashlights across the interior. Not only was the inside completely empty, there wasn't so much as a trace of its last cargo. Not a pecan or even a shell. Nothing. The box was whistle clean.

"I don't know, Sheriff. There ain't a thing here. Not even

dust. I don't see nothing special about this here trailer at all. Looks just like every other one I check out on the road. Newer than that one on the other side of the yard that Wade stores tires in, but nothing special."

"There's got to be. We're just not seeing it."

Virgil continued to play his light on the walls, the floor, over every inch until he finally came to a reluctant agreement with Jimmy. Finally, they both jumped back down onto the blacktop. Jimmy started heading toward the fence. When he glanced back, he saw that Virgil hadn't moved, so he walked back.

"Staring at it ain't going to make it happen. There's nothing there, Sheriff."

"There's got to be. There's got to be." Virgil had crouched down, shining his light on the undercarriage.

"I checked under there, went over every axle, even checked the wheel wells. Nothing. Nada. There's nothing different between this one and that old trailer over yonder."

Virgil stood up, put his finger to his upper lip in a reflective pose Jimmy had seen before.

"Whatcha thinking, Sheriff?"

"Jimmy, you got a tape measure in your vehicle?"

"Yes, sir, I do."

"Do you mind getting it for me?"

Jimmy's answer was to turn and sprint to the chain-link fence. Virgil watched as he scaled the fence easily and just as easily on the way back, the square green casing of the tape measure visible in his hand. He handed it to Virgil. Virgil walked to the rear of the trailer, then with Jimmy's help measured the length, height, and width of the trailer. Then Jimmy followed as they walked away from the trailer they had been inspecting and headed to the old trailer on the other side of the yard. There they repeated the process and took the same measurements. Each trailer was exactly the same length, width, and height.

"They're exactly the same," Virgil said.

"Did you expect them to be different?"

Virgil didn't answer, but instead climbed up into the empty box, gesturing Jimmy to follow him. Once inside, again with Jimmy's help, he measured the interior dimensions.

"Okay, let's go."

He climbed down instead of jumping down like he first had. Jimmy jumped. Then they walked back over to the other trailer.

"Goddamn, it's locked," Virgil said as he shined his light on the trailer's rear door.

"No it isn't," Jimmy said. "It just looks that way. The lock isn't closed. Wade or whoever handles the tires probably doesn't want to be locking and unlocking, so he just closes it over so it looks like it's locked. Besides, he knows the yard is fenced and locked and Wade told me they're going to install security cameras next week."

"He better put in cameras. That fence didn't keep you from going over it with ease. Pretty careless of Wade."

Jimmy nodded.

"Let's check it out."

The trailer was half loaded, so Jimmy took the end of the tape and climbed to the back, over a few rings of stacked tires. They measured the interior length and width twice before Virgil waved to Jimmy to come back. When Jimmy jumped off the end of the box, he could sense that Virgil was struck by the results.

"It must be there. C'mon."

They returned to the other trailer. Virgil actually ran across the yard and sprang into the trailer with an ease that Jimmy hadn't seen before. He was at the front of the trailer when Jimmy climbed in, the tape stretched out on the floor in front of him.

"I want to be sure," Virgil said.

They measured three times. "Yes!" Virgil said, his voice echoing in the empty chamber of the trailer. "This box is one foot shorter than the other one."

"What do you mean? We measured them. They're the exact same size."

"On the outside, Jimmy. On the outside. Inside, this one's a foot shorter."

"What does that mean?"

"It means that wall back there is false. There's maybe eight to ten inches of space from floor to roof and across which can be used to hide anything that's put in there. Visually, inside and out, this container looks just like any other one on the road. But it's not. It carries hidden cargo. Wade knows it, Buddy knew it. Or at least found out about it. My guess is that, when he did find out, he didn't like it. And that's what got him killed."

There was still a soft mist rising from the pavement when Jimmy pulled the cruiser into the lot in back of the jail.

"Are you coming in, Sheriff?"

"No, Jimmy. It's late and I'm beat."

"What are you going to do next? I mean, about the semi?"

"I've been thinking about it since we left the yard. We know what's different about the trailer, but we're still pretty much in the dark about its cargo."

"What about drugs? It can't be . . . can't be illegals. There's not enough room."

"We can speculate all we want, but that's all it is, speculation. Unless we find out what that cargo was, we'll never know why three people died. And who's responsible for their deaths."

"But how are you going to find that out?"

"I think I might have an idea, but I want to think a little more on it. See you tomorrow, Jimmy. Keep Hayward safe."

He got out of the cruiser and walked to his car.

Jimmy watched as the fog in the filtered light from the solitary lamp pole in the parking lot swallowed Virgil until he was nothing more than a dark figure blurred and indistinct. It was a strange moment and left him with a funny feeling.

30

The sky was leaden, with no hint of sun. There weren't more than fifty people, Micah guessed, a small gathering for someone who had loomed so large. He was struck by the irony, but these had been his mother's wishes. For practically all her life in this town, she'd been the visible center. Now she was slipping away almost unnoticed.

He glanced around at the bowed heads as the minister intoned the familiar liturgy. A sob came from Virginia and he saw his son, Caleb, wrap a comforting arm around her. These two, he thought, were the best thing to come out of this family in a long time. Bright, eager, and smart. A new generation, a new hope for the future, one he had worked hard to secure and one that now was at great risk.

He watched as the minister stepped back at the conclusion of his words and the pallbearers came forward to fulfill their duty. Twenty minutes later at the cemetery, he watched again as they picked up the straps that overlapped the grave and drew them taut. Then in a well-choreographed movement, they stepped to the edge of the waiting hole and slowly loosened their grip. Micah watched as the last trace of his mother disappeared from view. He couldn't help but think it was the quietest exit she had ever made.

The undertaker passed among the group and handed each mourner a rose. In unison, most of the group looked at Micah, and he hesitantly assumed his new role as head of the family. While they looked on, he stepped forward and dropped his rose. He watched as it fluttered down and came to rest on top of the metallic coffin. There was no sound. Then the undertaker handed him a clod of dirt from the loose pile next to the hole. He looked at it in his hand, then wadded it into a clump and dropped it as he had done with the rose. It hit the same area on the coffin as the rose, but with such a loud thud that it startled him. A sudden surge of emotion gripped him as if he heard again one of the thousand rebukes from his mother. He turned quickly and went back to his place, hoping no one had noticed the glisten that had come into his eyes. The tears, he knew, were not so much for her as they were for himself. All those years of feeling like second best had caught up with him in this moment. Looking away from the group, now copying the ritual he had performed, he glanced toward a distant rise where he saw a solitary figure, hat in hand, standing silently. He knew who it was and why he was here and why the future of the Hayward family truly rested in his hands.

Virgil had turned away shortly after Micah saw him. He was on the road long before the family had left the burial ground. Going to Audrey's burial had been an impulsive act. He hadn't planned on stopping, but somehow as he was driving after leaving the service, he felt impelled to stop. He couldn't say why. But as he stood on the knoll next to his mother and father's resting place, he realized that he had come not as a bystander, but as a family member. In a way, what Audrey had told him in that final conversation had become an invitation to this day. The Haywards had always been part of his past, but now as he looked down at them, as they put Audrey into the ground, he knew they would also always be part of his future. Virgil did not feel Micah's eyes staring up at him. His focus had been completely on the slight figure standing at some distance to his left, head down, softly sobbing, her auburn hair stirred occasionally by a breeze.

Audrey Hayward was many things to many people, but to the daughter of Virgil and Rusty she was a beloved grandmother. Virgil could see that now, and he ached for her and that is why he had come.

There was still no trace of sun. Clouds hung so low that when Virgil was on the dirt road climbing the butte to his grandfather's, he could not see the top of the mesa. It bothered him to think it was the same thing in reverse for any rifleman who might be standing guard up there. Carlos and his oldest were throwing a Frisbee in the yard area outside the trailer when he pulled in alongside. The young boy waved to Virgil, then clutching the Frisbee, ran to the front door. Virgil saw his grandfather, who had obviously been watching them standing in the front doorway. He waved to Virgil.

"Any news, Sheriff?"

Virgil waited by the car until Carlos walked over to him. He wanted this to be a private conversation.

He told Carlos about Audrey Hayward's funeral. Carlos responded by asking about his brother and sister-in-law's.

"Their bodies are being sent to Taxco, and I'm in the process of arranging transport for your family to follow them. It'll probably be another day or two. On another point, I remember you saying that the last shipment to Juárez was after the two-week company shutdown."

"That's right. Everyone goes back to work next Monday and the first thing to do is ship the last of this year's inventory. Loading and shipping is necessary to make way for the new harvest. Before the new harvest comes in, the plant is given a thorough makeover and once the last shipment is processed down in Juárez, the same thing happens down there."

"Do you have any idea which trailers will be used to take down the last of the inventory?"

"Not really."

"We found the box that Buddy pulled at Wade's. My deputy Jimmy and I saw it there. The numbers you gave me helped us to identify it."

"If it's there after this week, it's probably not going to be used. Maybe there's some problem with it and that's why Wade has it there."

"I hope that's not the case," Virgil said.

Within an hour, Virgil was on his way back to the office. He went out of his way to pass by Wade's. He circled the dealership and the service yards twice. The trailer was not there. He was sure of it. Because it was a Saturday, it was pretty quiet, but the size of the operation and the new car dealership was impressive. Wade had come a long way from a five-year high school student to where he was now.

Virgil got to the office a little after two. He was surprised to see Rosie's car in the lot.

"What are you doing here on a Saturday afternoon?"

"Helping out the law. You know crime never takes a day off, don't you?"

"Sounds like the title of a movie."

"Yeah, well that's for my next reincarnation. I'm going to be a movie star."

"Movie stars seem to have a lot of fun."

"Yeah, but they spend a lot of time on their backs and I've got a bad back."

"But maybe in your next life . . ."

"Speaking of backs is why I'm here today. Dif fell off a ladder and hurt his, so I got a call."

"Well, what the hell was he doing up on a ladder? He's got an artificial knee and he's more than a little past his prime."

Rosie started laughing.

"What's so funny?"

"Men," she said. "I have never met one man who felt he was past his prime. Look at you, Virgil. You're past forty and showing no signs that you'll admit to. Hell, I saw you one night at the Black Bull with that pretty girl. You still think that you're that young stud romping in the pasture. You better wake up and throw a rope over her or some other one soon so you'll have a nurse for your old age."

"I never saw you at the Black Bull."

"That's 'cause your eyes were strictly on the prize. Hell, even that ole Mex, that more than half raised you, is still randy. He's been visiting one of Margie's waitresses for years. So don't you raise your eyebrow at Dif. Someday it'll be your turn to fall off a ladder. I just hope there's somebody there to catch you when it happens. Men."

She said it a little louder this time, a note of dismissal in her voice. Virgil had no comeback.

A minute or so passed. Finally, he told her he'd stay in the office and that she should go home.

"I might as well," she said. "I've done my life coaching for the day. Besides, I'd have more luck talking to a rock."

Virgil shrugged.

"Why don't you give that girl a call, Virgil? Ain't you tired of being alone? There's more to life than just being sheriff."

She walked out the door. Virgil sat for a minute, then picked up the phone. While it was ringing, he was thinking of Carlos and his boy playing with the Frisbee at his grandfather's. On the fifth ring he heard a familiar voice.

"I haven't heard from you in a while. Thought maybe you'd taken up a new hobby."

"Been busy," Virgil said.

"What doing?" she asked.

He paused a moment before answering. "Having a philosophical moment with Rosie."

"I didn't know you had another woman in your life."

There was a moment of silence before he answered. "Oh, I do. I surely do."

31

When Virgil stepped out onto the porch with a cup of steaming coffee in his hand, the morning sun caught the wetness left over from a quickly passing night storm and everything sparkled. The leaves of the cottonwood hung with the added weight. A sun-washed feeling made the earth fresh. He breathed deep.

Cesar was standing by the corral, watching the mare and the foal. The foal was tearing around the corral, only stopping long enough to buck and kick up its heels. His mother stood in the center, patiently watching the display. The smile that drew at the corners of Cesar's mouth deepened the weathered creases in his face. Having noticed the movement on the porch, he drew his foot off the bottom rail and went to join Virgil. He was almost at the steps when the kitchen door opened and Ruby stepped out, balancing two steaming cups. Cesar hesitated at the bottom step.

"C'mon, she won't bite you. You can see she was expecting you."

Cesar climbed the stairs, accepting the cup when he reached the top.

"*Gracias,*" he said.

"*De nada,*" she replied.

"Ruby, this is my Mexican father, Cesar."

Ruby smiled and raised her cup. "A pleasure, señor." She sat on the top step and Cesar sat next to her.

"I have known about you and am happy to meet you," he said.

"And I don't bite."

"I might not even mind it if you did."

"Hey, old man, remember I'm listening."

Virgil stood up and excused himself. He went inside. From the kitchen he glanced at them once or twice and could see they were in conversation. He joined them again and for a moment they sat savoring the last of their coffee in silence. When Cesar rose to his feet, Ruby did the same and took his empty cup.

"I'll be right back." She brought the empty cups inside and returned just as Cesar was stepping off the porch.

"Give me ten minutes," Cesar said.

"What was that about?" Ruby asked.

"He's going to saddle a couple of horses for us."

"For us?"

"Yep. Time for your introduction."

"I don't know about this, Virgil. I was on a horse exactly once in my life and that was in a ring. I was numb with fear the whole time."

"Well, let's see if we can get you out of the ring this time. Maybe the numbness will vanish."

A few minutes later, Cesar led two horses out of the barn, fully saddled. He tied the reins to the top rail of the corral. Virgil took Ruby by the hand and led her down the steps. He could feel her reluctance.

"This is Jack. I've had him since he was born. He is the sire of that little guy." While Virgil spoke, the foal had come near the rails, ears forward, until he stood within arm's reach. Virgil extended his hand and the foal hesitantly nibbled at the tips of his extended fingers. Suddenly, the mare, who had not moved from the center of the corral, snorted and stamped her foot. The foal wheeled and ran to his mother's side.

"He's beautiful," Ruby said.

"Yes, and he listens to his mother. Now, this is Sugar."

Still holding her hand, Virgil walked around Jack to the other horse.

"Sugar hasn't got a mean bone in her body. You'll love her."

"Well, just remember, I do. And the ones that aren't mean, break."

"Okay, noted."

For the next half hour, Virgil went over some basics. Hesitant as she was, he was pleased to see how quickly she warmed to the mare, stroking her neck almost continuously throughout his instruction.

"Moment of truth," he said as he put Ruby's left foot into the stirrup and elevated her smoothly into the saddle.

"It seems so high up."

"Everybody says that the first time. Don't worry, I've been told the ground is soft when you're young."

"I don't know if I'm that young, Virgil."

"That's nice."

"What?"

"You don't often use my name," he said as he swung into the saddle on Jack. "Sheriff ain't a name, it's a title. Now, let's go, and remember . . . hold the reins together, in one hand. Sugar's neck reins. She doesn't want to be treated like a plow horse. She has her pride. Just nudge her ribs lightly with your heels. Next time, I'll get you some sure enough boots and you can leave your sneakers on the porch."

He turned Jack away from the fence while Sugar followed, needing barely any encouragement from Ruby.

"Next time?" Ruby said. "You mean, I have to do this again?"

"Only if you want to."

They left the corral area, with Virgil pointing Jack toward the low-lying hills that rose up at a distance from the house and barns. He kept Jack on the wide ranch road so Sugar could come alongside. He held the horse tightly collected, while Jack snorted and threw his head from side to side, in miniature rebellion.

"Why is he doing that?"

"He wants to run. Get some of the kinks out."

"I guess that's what they mean when they say he's feeling his oats."

Virgil nodded.

"Why doesn't Sugar act that way?"

"She's content to let Jack show off."

"Smart girl. She understands how dumb some men can be. Always trying to impress."

Virgil glanced sideways at Ruby and tried to stifle a laugh.

"What's so funny?"

"I'll tell you after you tell me what you're doing."

"I told you, I did this once before. The instructor taught me about posting. I'm trying to post."

"That's English riding, not Western. Sit deep in the saddle so no space shows between your butt and the saddle. Kinda hug Sugar."

"Isn't that going to make me sore?"

"You'll get used to it, and you'll get the feel of the horse's rhythm."

"Oh, kind of become one with the horse. I get it. It's a kind of Zen kind of thing."

"A Zen kind of thing. Yeah, I guess."

For the next few minutes, they walked quietly, then Virgil put Jack into a light trot. Without any encouragement, Sugar picked up the pace. Virgil watched to see Ruby's reaction.

"Don't fight it, sit deep in the saddle, and don't hold the pommel. Use your innate sense of balance."

He was pleased to see her respond to his instruction. After a couple of minutes, he pulled Jack to a stop and waited until Sugar came alongside. They were at the base of a low butte.

"You're doing great," he said, taking note of the color in her face. "Don't forget to breathe. Now we're going to do a light canter up this rise. Remember to balance and hug Sugar. Keep your hand off that horn, hold the reins so there's just a hint of slack and you can feel the bit in Sugar's mouth."

He could see the apprehension in her face.

"You might find this gait easier if you can get into a nice rocking chair kind of motion."

"Rocking chairs don't snort," she said.

"She's just feeling good. Let's go. I'll be right alongside of you."

He leaned forward and Jack stepped into a lope with Sugar right next to him. Virgil watched Ruby and after a tense couple of moments saw her start to relax into the saddle and the rhythm of the pace. They loped along a switchback, as it crisscrossed its way to the top of the ridge. When they got on top, Virgil pulled Jack up while Sugar came to a stop a couple of paces back. Then on her own, Ruby nudged her and she moved forward until they were side by side.

"That was fun," Ruby said. "I really liked that and it was a lot more comfortable than trotting. It didn't even hurt."

Virgil smiled. "We're gonna make a cowgirl outta you yet."

They jogged along the top of the rise, then down the descending slope until they reached the flatland. All the while Virgil kept instructing her about shifting her weight back going downhill, staying on the balls of her feet in the stirrups as much as she could and all the time trying to feel the contact with Sugar's mouth. For the next half hour, they rode at different gaits. Ruby responded with eagerness and a willingness that surprised him. By the time they got within sight of the stock tank, where Virgil had discovered Buddy Hinton's bloated body, she had already passed novice status. A couple of times, he had even seen her squeeze Sugar's sides on her own to encourage her to pick up her pace. A wry smile creased his face.

"What are you smiling at?"

"Oh, nothing. It's just that I was thinking probably your old friends back in New York might be more than a little surprised if they could see you now."

She didn't respond. A look passed over her face, then was gone.

"What's that sticking out at the top of the hill?" she said.

"It's a stock tank. The cattle water there in the dry. Creeks are running pretty good right now because of the rain. That's why they aren't there now."

Before he could say more, she sharply nudged Sugar and started forward. Virgil held back. He hadn't been there since the day of his grim discovery. Ruby glanced back and saw that Virgil hadn't moved. She pulled Sugar to a stop then turned her and came back.

"Is there something wrong?"

"No. It's just that I haven't been here since . . . See, this is where I found Buddy Hinton. Floating in that tank."

"Oh!" she said. "I read about it in the newspaper, but I had no idea this was where . . ."

"It's all right. There's no way you could know exactly where. Besides, I don't want ghosts in my life. It's probably a good thing we ended up here."

Virgil put his heels to Jack before Ruby could respond. By the time she caught up with him, Jack had already lowered his head and was making loud sucking noises as he drank from the tank. Sugar came to stand next to him and lowered her head into the dark water. Virgil and Ruby sat in silence while they drank.

"Are you okay?" she asked.

"I'm fine. If you can stand a little more, there's a nice view from the top of that next ridge."

"Let's go for it."

The ride was a bit longer and a little steeper, but Ruby was determined. When they got to the top, they were rewarded with an unobstructed view in every direction that ended only at the horizon.

The sun was higher, but still the rolling country showed

dark, hidden arroyos at the bottom of long, undulating mesas. There were vast grazing areas between the ridges, and clusters of cattle scattered and moved slowly as they grazed. The cloudless sky hung over it all. A couple of hawks and buzzards soared high overhead on the thermals. Crickets and locusts whispered and buzzed to each other. An occasional distant moo or the bawl of a calf could be heard while closer it was the rhythmic heavy breathing of the now well-lathered horses.

"It's beautiful," she said. "Epic."

"Epic. I never thought of it like that."

"You know what I mean. Beautiful just doesn't seem like enough. It's more than just what you see. It's a feeling, like I don't know, like a religious experience. Don't you feel it?"

She looked at Virgil sitting beside her on Jack. He had taken his right leg out of the stirrup and crossed it over the front of the saddle as he sat back, enjoying the moment. There was a slight dampness in his dark hair, noticeable only because he'd taken off his sweat-stained Stetson and set it on his crossed knee. Ruby looked at the sharp features in his face. His dark eyes were scanning the horizon. For the first time, she realized that what she had taken all along to be a facial crease was instead a long thin scar which showed lighter against his tanned cheek.

"I guess religious," he finally said. "Maybe spiritual."

"You have a problem with religious? Seen too many TV evangelists?"

"Maybe I've just seen too much when the TV's turned off."

"Like a body floating in a stock tank."

Virgil didn't answer at first. When he finally did, he turned away from the panorama that had filled their eyes and looked directly at her.

"Maybe it's hard for me to square all this and the idea of a religious experience with what I know goes on in the world I'm going back to after we leave here."

"But maybe this helps to make that bearable."

"Guess that's what you call looking for the silver lining."

He put his hat on, then swung his leg back over the saddle and slipped his foot into the stirrup.

"Sit deep," he said, "and throw your weight back into the saddle as we head back down the ridge."

"My riding lesson is over?"

"Not till we get back to the barn and we're sitting on the porch with a cold beer and a sandwich."

"Why didn't you tell me? I'm so sore even my eyeballs hurt."

"If I had, I probably never would have gotten you up on the horse in the first place."

"Poor Sugar," Ruby said.

"Sugar?"

"Yes. At least I had a beer and a sandwich, and when I get back home before I go downstairs I'm going to soak in a tub for about three hours."

"Don't worry about Sugar. A little hay, a little grain, a roll in the corral and she'll be ready to go again."

"Are you coming by later tonight?"

"I'll try, but I've got to deal with that other world we talked about first. Besides, maybe you've had enough exercise for one day."

"Yeah, well, it's going to take a lot more than a little grain for me. I'm not about to roll in the corral before I'm ready to go again. So if you're looking for that kind of action, you might want to sleep in your own bed tonight."

Virgil was standing in the driveway watching Ruby's car turn onto the hard road when Cesar came alongside.

"How did it go?"

"Not bad. Not bad at all. She's got game."

"Speaks good Mex, too," Cesar said. "Maybe Nogales?"

"New York."

"No," Cesar said, shaking his head. "Nogales first, then maybe New York. Good-looking and spunky. That's a real dangerous combination."

32

When he walked into the office on Monday morning, he brought with him a certain measure of unease. It had started creeping in over the last few days, but it was full-blown by Monday. He wasn't sure when it had started or where it had come from, but he had spent a restless night because of it. Crazy dreams that seemed to have no connection and made little sense. A couple of times as he struggled for rest, he had that falling-off-the-cliff feeling. Twice he awakened in a sweat, in a grip of apprehension that caused him to fear slipping into sleep again. The women that had been in his life came to him, but their faces had become interchangeable. Once it was his mother who became Rusty, then became Ruby, and then at last a less distinguishable face. He wrestled for the connection, but came up empty.

By the time the first rays filtered through the curtained windows, they had all faded into his subconscious, to be replaced by the bloated body of Buddy Hinton in the stock tank and the two headless bodies from the ravine.

He sat on the side of the bed for a long minute, trying to shake off the images and the stupor from the torturous sleep. Finally, he staggered to his feet and found his way to the shower. He sat on the molded fiberglass seat, letting the water pour down in its relentless rhythm until it drove the images from his brain. By the time he got to his car, all that was left was the unease that he brought to the office.

He was glad that Rosie wasn't there, even if it meant that he had to make his own coffee, which for some reason was never as good as hers. He didn't feel up to a glib interchange with her, which had pretty much become standard practice. After a few minutes sitting at his desk in his semidarkened office, the phone rang.

It was a callback from an occasional acquaintance who worked for the DEA. The conversation lasted less than ten minutes. Virgil apprised the agent of the transport of the last of the inventory from Hayward Trucking to the facility in Juárez for processing. He explained to him, relying on the information from Carlos, that with the last of the inventory down there, the facility in Redbud would be put in readiness for the new harvest while that last shipment down in Juárez would be processed and brought back for the final distribution of the old stock. Virgil called his attention to the particular trailer and what he suspected was a hidden compartment.

The agent responded that over the last couple of years, since the factory in Juárez was opened, there had been regular checks of the trailers and they had found nothing. He said canine units had been used regularly and had been all over them.

When Virgil finally replaced the phone, he was genuinely puzzled. In his own head, with the ongoing drug wars south of the river raging, he had convinced himself that the contraband was there in that compartment. The agent assured him that when the trailer was on its way back across the border with its next shipment, they would check it like it had never been checked before.

Virgil sat back in the chair, a cold mouthful of coffee finally swallowed. He had never wanted to believe that Micah Hayward was involved in the grisly string of murders along with drug smuggling, but the only evidence kept pointing back to Hayward Ranch. He sat staring at the stains on the old tin ceiling until he heard Rosie open the door.

"I don't do ceilings," she said. "Maybe sweep a little, make coffee. That's it."

"Sounds to me like you're overpaid," he said, smiling. "And there wasn't any coffee. I had to make my own."

"How'd that work out for you? Never too late for a learning experience."

"It was awful. Tasted like wet socks."

"Now you know why the county pays me the big bucks. I'll make some fresh. Get rid of that taste in your mouth."

Ten minutes later, Rosie was sitting across from Virgil. Each held a coffee mug in their hand.

"Just the smell was worth the wait," Virgil said.

"What's the matter, Virgil? You look like you need about a week of sleep. What's got you up nights?"

Virgil put his cup on the desk. He knew Rosie wasn't just prying. He had long since recognized that she had good instincts and he had used her as a sounding board more often than anyone.

"I don't know, this whole thing seems to be centered around Hayward Ranch. It just doesn't make sense. I've known Mike . . . Micah all my life. I can't believe he's in back of this."

"Then don't."

Her abruptness caught him off guard. "But everything points . . ."

"Listen, Virgil, you are the most perceptive man I've ever known. The radar for most of you men only activates when something stirs in your pants. That includes the lovable guy I've been married to for over twenty-five years. But you, you have great instincts. If something is keeping you up nights, there's a good reason. About the only time you've gotten off track was when your testosterone got the better of you. Even then, you aimed high. The prettiest girl from the wealthiest and most powerful family. It didn't end good, but at least you passed on those good genes."

Virgil sat up so quickly he bumped the desk and had to grab his mug to keep it from spilling into his lap.

"How do you . . . I mean, what?"

"Calm down, Virgil. I'll explain. Years ago, before I came here I worked for Doc Ramsey. You remember Doc. He was a good man, old school, but solid as a rock and back then the only stork-helper in town. He probably delivered everybody in this town over twenty-one. Anyway, babies were more than a little on my mind because I had just found out I was pregnant with Dave junior. Babies were more than half of Doc's practice. He got called out to Hayward Ranch that year a few times. At first it didn't mean anything to me, because no one from there had come into the office. Then one day he got called out, and I was puzzled because by then Micah's wife was in the institution and I knew he had put a call in to an obstetrician who was a specialist and a friend of his from medical school. When the specialist called back, I told him where Doc was and he said to call him back when he returned. Then he said to bring the patient as soon as he could to Phoenix. This was before Hayward Memorial was built. I told Doc when he returned from Hayward Ranch and that was the end of it. Except that two weeks later, Rusty died. You were away at college. Doc never said anything. Like I said, he was old school. He never discussed his patients or their problems, and by then I was getting bigger by the minute, so I had other things on my mind. Then I saw you and that young girl at Audrey's funeral. I knew in an instant. She's you and Rusty. Rusty's hair and coloring, but your face."

A momentary quiet settled over the room.

"Virgil, why didn't you ever say anything?"

"I never knew myself. Not until just before Audrey died. I don't think I saw the girl three times in her life before the funeral. Who else knows? Dave? Dif?"

"Dif?" Rosie laughed. "God love him, but he doesn't have enough sense to come in out of the rain. He'd never figure it out, nor would Dave, and I haven't told either of them. As far as the other thing is concerned, if you can't believe that Micah is at the root of these killings then he isn't. Because you know it in your gut. We might be on opposite sides of the street, gender-wise, but we're a lot alike and one thing we have in common is good instincts. So begin your search for an answer to this thing by excluding Micah, but don't ignore him. He might be tied into this thing somehow and you'll have to figure out how. You might begin by asking him."

"Thanks, Rosie. I don't think the county is paying you enough. From now on, forget the sweeping, but you still have to make the coffee. As far as that other thing is concerned . . ."

"Don't worry, Virgil. I'd say it's between you and me, but

that's not exactly the case and you and I know it. You're going to have to decide what to do. I can't help you with that."

The phone rang. Rosie got up from her seat and went to her desk to answer it. Virgil sat mulling over her last comment.

"Virgil, it's Jimmy. He wants to speak to you about the arrangements for bringing Carlos and his wife to Taxco."

"Okay." Virgil reached over and picked up his phone. "Listen, Jimmy, before we get into anything here, let me make a couple of calls and make sure everyone is on the same page. I'll get back to you."

After he hung up the phone, he sat for a moment alone. Rosie had gone into the cell block. Then he made a quick call to his counterpart in Taxco. He knew Edgar Quintillo personally. They had attended a cross-border conference years before and they had been in irregular contact since.

"Edgar. ¿Cómo estás?"

"Muy bien."

The rest of the exchange was quick and in a mix of English and Spanish. Each was trying to renew the level of intimacy that had caused them to bond in the first place. Rosie returned as he was ending the conversation.

"Let me guess. You and Edgar are planning your next fishing trip in Acapulco."

"I wish. Edgar's handling protection for Carlos and his family while they are in Taxco. By the way, thanks for taking care of the day-to-day lately."

"It's been pretty quiet. Almost like the regulars know you're frying bigger fish these days. We haven't had a full house since the Fourth."

"Who's back there now?"

"Some guy named Smithers who got drunk in the Lazy Dog and picked a fight with Florence. Said she was watering his drinks. There's two things I know about that man. He's not too bright and he must have a death wish."

"Did she nail him with that field hockey stick?"

"Yep, that lump on his head would be a phrenologist's dream."

"I better have a word with her. One of these times, one of these guys might try to make a case."

"I doubt it. They'd be too embarrassed to stand up in an open courtroom and admit that a five-foot-tall seventy-year-old that'd dress out at maybe a hundred pounds got the better of them."

"Anything else?"

"Two young guys who said they were just passing through when Jimmy pulled them over. DUI. Jimmy said he got high when they rolled down the window. Too late for night court, so they're back there. That's it. Said they liked the food, but then when you've got the munchies I think just about anything works. That's it."

"Are they dealers or just users?"

"They say they're on vacation. Jimmy didn't find anything but a roach and an almost empty baggie. Doing a road trip and on their way back to San Francisco. I think they're a couple, Virgil. Seem pretty harmless."

"Okay. If they're cooperative, tell the judge. I don't need any long-term boarders right now." Virgil stood up. "I'll try to get back this afternoon." He headed for the door.

"Be careful out there, Virgil. Ain't like it used to be."

"I don't know if it ever was," he said as he left the office.

On the road down to his grandfather's he thought over

what Rosie had said about his instincts, and by the time he climbed up onto the mesa, he had made up his mind that after he settled the arrangements for Carlos and his family, his next stop would be Hayward Ranch and a talk with Micah Hayward.

It had been close to a week since the family had moved into the double-wide, and he could see that the kids had adapted when he tripped over a soccer ball just inside the door. The living room was littered with the evidence of their presence. He had to move a couple of stuffed animals to sit down on the sofa next to Carlos. For the next ten minutes, he went over the arrangements for the burial trip to Taxco. He told Carlos that as far as he knew, there had been no one looking for him or his family, nor had there been any unusual activity around their house. The story that had been put out was that because of the plant shutdown for two weeks, the family had gone to visit relatives. It seemed to have satisfied any inquiries. The identity of the two bodies that had been found was not linked to them, and any follow-up in the local paper had been fairly low-key. He went over again what Carlos knew about the specific trailer that Buddy Hinton had pulled, and that he and Jimmy had checked out at Wade's, but was left in the same quandary as when his DEA connection had told him that in the past they had found nothing suspicious about it and no evidence of drugs.

"Tell my grandfather I stopped by," Virgil said as he stood up to leave.

"He and Mrs. Hoya probably won't get back from the Senior Center for another couple of hours," Carlos said. "It's a break from the kids. I asked them to take me, but they said I wasn't old enough."

Virgil smiled. "It seems pretty quiet around here now."

"That's because the baby is in for a nap and my wife took the other two up on the ridge to check on the flock. They like to hold the lambs. Your cousin's boy is up there. He is very good with the children. They've had a great time here. We really appreciate what you and your grandfather have done for us. I wish I could have been more help to you about it, about that trailer, I mean. But I came up with nothing. It looked like all the others. I can see it in my mind right now, parked as it always was at the end of the row, right next to the ice cream truck."

"The ice cream truck?"

"Yeah, the semi that Buddy pulled always seemed to be parked at the end of the row, right next to that ice cream truck."

"What was an ice cream truck doing there?"

Carlos paused before answering. "It seems like it was always there whenever the trailer was. At least that's how I picture it in my mind. I think one of Wade's guys did it as a sideline. It'd show up in the afternoon usually. People from the office or the factory would go out on a break and get ice cream. He did a pretty good business. It would always be parked at the end of the line. Buddy's trailer would be parked alongside. That's how I remember it."

Virgil rehashed what Carlos had told him on his way back to Hayward, trying to make a connection. He had the feeling that he had missed something useful, but was no closer to what it might have been when he pulled into the office parking lot. Jimmy's cruiser was there. Jimmy was sitting behind the wheel, making no attempt to exit the vehicle.

"You might as well stay there. It's time to make that trip down to Taxco. I just came from going over everything with Carlos."

Virgil went through the agenda for the trip with Jimmy. "And don't forget to stay in radio contact all the way there and with the Rurales when you cross the border."

"Got it," Jimmy said as he started his cruiser. "See you tomorrow, Sheriff."

Virgil stepped back from the car.

"By the way," Jimmy said, "did Carlos have anything new for you?"

"Not really. He said there was nothing more he could add except when the trailer was parked, it seemed always to coincide with the days when the ice cream truck was there."

"The ice cream truck . . ."

"Yep. That's about it. If there's any connection, I haven't worked it out."

Jimmy half waved and started to back up. Then he stopped.

"Sheriff, I don't know if it means anything, but when we were in Wade's yard, there was an ice cream truck there. I remember seeing it. I remember thinking it seemed out of place. Maybe that's why it caught my eye. Like I said, I don't know if it means anything."

He waved again then backed up, turned the car, and drove out of the lot.

Virgil stood there as the late-afternoon sun beat down and the swirling eddies of dust kicked up by the departing car coated his shoes, trying to figure out why, with three murders keeping him from a decent night's sleep, all he could think about was that damned ice cream truck.

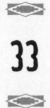

33

Micah Hayward stood on the front porch of his house look-ing at the departing day, waiting for Virgil Dalton. He had always liked Virgil. Growing up, he had always been closer to Rusty than to his brother, and when Virgil came on the scene, Micah and Rusty had become even closer. She shared her feelings for Virgil with him in secret.

He envied what they had. It was something he had hoped for in his own relationship with his wife, but she had already begun slipping away from him, into a world of instability. He realized now these many years later that in reaching out to his wife for what he saw between Rusty and Virgil, he was attempt-ing the impossible. Not because he didn't love his wife or she didn't love him, but because losing her grip on reality shortly after the birth of Caleb meant that any life together for them was doomed. By the time Rusty died, his wife had become a ghost of herself, and in a true sense he lost the two people he had loved the most. By the time she took her own life, she had already been dead for a long time.

The baby that Rusty had left, as well as his own son, had given the only meaning to his life. It was for them that he had stayed when his brother had not returned from Vietnam and his father had died.

Now as he stood waiting for Virgil, he knew that the world he'd tried to secure for them was perched on the edge of an abyss. He had to make Virgil understand.

The last flicker of light had left the sky when Virgil's car turned into the driveway of Hayward Ranch.

Neither Micah nor Virgil was aware of the slight figure looking out of the upstairs window as Virgil exited the cruiser. She thought it odd that a man she barely knew who also happened to be the sheriff should show up at the house at night. She knew that he had been with her grandmother the night she had died, and she knew her grandmother well enough to know that had not been a random visit. Virgil stepped onto the well-lit porch, his face splayed with the light. Their eyes locked for an instant as he glanced up at the window. He blinked and she was gone.

Virgil followed Micah inside to the same room where he had sat with Audrey on her last night. It felt odd, almost like a trespass. Micah motioned to the chair where Audrey had last sat. Virgil instead sat in the chair opposite. Micah walked to the small table next to Audrey's chair and without asking Virgil, half filled two glasses with the same amber liquid that she had offered to Virgil. Virgil took the glass. When Micah slid into Audrey's chair and raised his glass, Virgil did the same. They drank. Virgil felt the sharpness first, then the smoothness. The warmth that followed felt good. It had been a long day. He sat back deeper into the comfort of the chair and took another sip from the glass.

"I think I know why you're here," Micah said. He took another drink. "As soon as you called, I knew."

"If I were just going on what I know as fact, Mike, then we wouldn't be meeting like this with a glass in our hands, like old friends."

"Virgil, I always thought of you as a friend."

"That may be, and whether it's true or you're just trying to play me, I'm here as sheriff, trying to get to the bottom of some pretty grisly stuff. But somebody whose input I value said I should follow my gut instinct. That gut of mine makes it hard for me to wrap my head around you being the guy responsible for Buddy's bloated body floating in one of my stock tanks. Or as a guy who would allow two young people, a brother and a sister trying to get a leg up against great odds, to end up at the bottom of a ravine, with their heads severed from their bodies. But cutting through any bullshit, Mike, everything points toward you, and if you're it, I'll whip your ass into a cell so fast, you'll feel like you were hit by lightning."

The words hung in the air. Virgil was the first to stand. He drained his glass and put it on the table.

"The way I figure, the clock is ticking, Micah. Whether it's in your favor or not, I'll probably know the next time I come here."

Micah didn't respond. He stood silently and nodded as Virgil left the room.

Virgil's hand was on the doorknob when something made him stop and turn around. Virginia was standing at the top of the stairs. It was the first time he had seen her, really *seen* her this close. Her hair fell over her left shoulder, catching the light from the hall chandelier. He saw everything of Rusty that she had passed to her daughter, but at the same time he also saw the face that so much mirrored his own. He thought he heard a slight exclamation escape her lips, but the moment had become too much for him, so he put on his Stetson, turned, and walked out the door.

By the time he reached the ranch, Jimmy had called to say everything had gone uneventfully, and that Carlos and his family were safely under the protection of Mexican authority. He was on his way back to Hayward.

Virgil was still feeling out of sorts when he finally lay back on his bed. Uncharacteristically, his clothes lay in a pile where they had fallen on the floor, and when he closed his eyes he still saw the image of Rusty, standing at the top of the stairs.

34

Virgil was finishing his second cup of Rosie's brew and wondering why he couldn't duplicate it when the phone rang.

"Virgil, it's Kyle." He was surprised to hear from Kyle Harrison, his DEA contact, so soon after reaching out to him.

"Thought I'd try to catch you early before I get caught up. Beginning of the week at the border is always crazy, especially in the summer. That trailer you called me about just went through. No reason to hold it. Dogs got nothing. I checked it myself with two other agents. Nothing but a load of pecans, going to Juárez."

"But what about the fake wall?"

"Virgil, think about it. Nobody would be smuggling stuff *into* Juárez. Wait until the return trip. Even if the dogs don't get a hit then, we'll make sure to check it out."

"Okay, that makes sense. Thanks for the call."

"Virgil, there was one thing."

Virgil sat up in his chair. "Go on, Kyle."

"The truck is idling . . . I mean our look-over takes time and I know the AC in the cab is on, but when he pulled away he left behind a lot of water on the road. We checked it and it was only water, but it seemed like a lot. I know the trailer's not refrigerated, but one of the agents said he remembered this from another time, but he didn't know if it was the same trailer. Could be from a bad water pump, but I just thought I'd mention it, because I know you're friendly with the Haywards. Maybe you'd want to let them know in case it is a bad pump or something up with the AC before they have that truck break down on them, and they have to tow it all the way back to their facility."

"Okay, Kyle, thanks for the effort and the info. I'll look into it." He had just put the phone back into its cradle when Jimmy came through the door.

"You didn't have to come in early, Jimmy, after that trip you made."

"I never went home. Just stopped on the way back once or twice for a catnap. I'm beat and I need a shower. I'm a little ripe."

"Thanks for sharing, but that's more than I needed to know. Go home, get that shower, and catch some z's. I might need you big-time later today."

"What's up?"

Virgil gave Jimmy a quick update.

"I don't get it," Jimmy said when he was through. "Outside of your talk with Mr. Hayward and some water on the road, what's going to bring us any closer to solving this thing?"

Virgil didn't answer right away.

"I think it's going to be the water on the road and an ice cream truck."

Jimmy stopped at the door.

"Go on," Virgil said. "I'll explain later."

Jimmy shook his head and walked out.

Wade's dealership was even more impressive in the daylight. All the construction was done and as Virgil pulled in he could see some landscapers putting finishing touches in place. When he stepped out of the cruiser, Virgil could smell the newness of the asphalt. There must have been fifty brand-new cars of different models and another twenty or so new pickups gleaming in the afternoon sun. He could see another five or six in the showroom.

"Hello, Sheriff."

Virgil recognized the young man, but was fumbling for the name. "Talbot, right?"

"You got it. Me and Jimmy went to school together. Joe Talbot."

"Back of the hardware store. Yes, I remember."

"That's long over and done with. Me and Jimmy are friends now. I've grown up some since then, even learned a thing or two. Hope you don't hold that against me."

"No," Virgil said, giving the young man a level stare. "If it's history to Jimmy, it's history to me. Where's your boss?"

"Inside. Want me to get him?"

"I'll find him if he's there."

Virgil headed for the front door of the showroom, leaving Joe Talbot trying to figure out how, after a dozen years, Virgil could still remember a bunch of kids using Jimmy as a punching bag in back of the family hardware store.

"So you know that old saying," Virgil said when he spotted

the man he was looking for. "You can dress them up, but you can't take them out. Nice suit."

Wade Travis looked up from his desk. It was obvious he was not thrilled to see Virgil.

"Actually, I've got a closetful. I might even have one in your size, Sheriff. I'll check it out."

"Thanks for the offer, Wade. Boy, you've sure come a long way in a couple of years. All this and a closetful of suits. Kind of makes me wonder. I mean, from just automotive repair to Hayward Trucking. Now I hear maybe you're going into the ice cream business."

"Is there some point to this visit, Sheriff?"

"Well, nothing special. I kind of just wanted to stop by and admire your success, but I still can't figure out how you got here so fast. I'm going to keep my eye on you for some helpful hints. Maybe I can learn something. You know on a sheriff's pay I got to buy my suits off the rack, nothing custom like yours, but at least the county picks up the tab for my uniform. Hope the ice cream business works out for you, too, Wade. See you real soon."

The afternoon sun had begun to slide toward the horizon while Virgil sat at his desk trying to get caught up on paperwork. He couldn't ignore the mundane. Rosita took care of the nuts and bolts that went with the day-to-day operations, down to and including washroom supplies, but Virgil's signature had to be at the bottom of every purchase order and every expense had to be validated in a monthly report that went to the county. It had always been the hardest part of the job for him.

This was at the heart of Virgil's nature. He saw life in terms of the least common denominator. Good and evil, life and death, crime and punishment; the rest was all footnote. It had made him hard to know, for some unreachable. Ruby had been the latest to try to break in, but as she said on more than one occasion, he was a tough nut to crack.

"You're really big on small talk," she said sarcastically over coffee on their most recent morning together, as Virgil stared into his cup.

As if in confirmation, Virgil didn't respond.

"I think you've been alone too long. You've forgotten how to share."

Virgil continued in silence, which she would not accept, and for the next twenty minutes she pulled and prodded until he had given up more information about his life and his past than he had to people that he'd known for years.

When he was a teenager, he would often come home from school, throw a saddle on one of the horses, and head out over the rangeland, exploring every gully and wash. He came to know the land and the creatures that lived on it. Time stood still and he never felt alone. Many times his mother would join him. They would often ride in silence, stopping to observe a newborn calf struggling to nurse or a coyote on the prowl. He missed those times, but as the years passed without her, he came to feel that when he went on those solitary jaunts she was riding beside him.

Finally, he signed the last invoice on his desk and placed the overdue stack that had been waiting for his acknowledgement on Rosie's desk so she could enter everything into the computer and file the hard copies. He left a note on her desk and headed out the door.

The sunlight made him squint, but the warm air pushed by

a slight breeze made him feel good, and the dullness of the last few hours of clerical duties faded away. He was still savoring the feeling of a lightened load when Jimmy rolled in.

"You early or am I late?" Virgil said.

"You're late, Sheriff. I just had a hard time getting out of that bed. If it hadn't been for my little sister, I'd still be there."

"Why don't you bring her out to the ranch some day? We'll put her up on Sugar. I bet she'd get a kick out of it. Get to know a little something about horses."

"Well, sure, Sheriff. That'd be nice. Abby would love it."

"Didn't you say something a while back about going fishing with her off the bridge? Well, there's trout in that creek back of the barn. You could try your hand."

"Yes, sir, that'd be nice."

"You know, when I was a kid, I'd skinny-dip in that creek."

It was the first time Jimmy ever heard a reference to Virgil's childhood.

"Well, I guess it's time for me to head down the road," Virgil said. "Any problems, give me a call."

Virgil stepped past Jimmy and opened his car door. A blast of hot air escaped.

"Like an oven in there. Good talking to you, Jimmy."

He gave a wave, got into the car, and left Jimmy standing in the doorway trying to figure out what had come over the sheriff.

Once he was on the road, Virgil's thoughts went quickly to the one thing that had become a constant in his thoughts. There was a basic law of physics he knew: that for every action there is an equal and opposite reaction. Leaning on someone, as he had done with both Micah and Wade, would get a response. He just wished he had a clue what it would be.

The twenty-minute trip to the ranch allowed him time to consider a range of possibilities. He realized as he looked toward the dipping sun that it must have been later than he thought. This part of the country had a reputation for spectacular sunsets. The shades that every artist since the dawn of time had tried to capture. Blends of reds and blues mixed with dust from the earth. The closer he got to the ranch, the more dominant the red in the sky became. He glanced at the clock on the dash. It was 5:40. He glanced at the sky again, then again at the dashboard clock.

This sky was way too red.

As his car climbed the last rise, the ranch came into view. It was then he saw the explanation to the illusion. Swirls of smoke rose into the sky, filtering the light. The ripe orange-red glow that he'd mistook for a departing sun was one of the barns engulfed in flame.

Virgil reacted automatically. He called in the fire as he pressed the accelerator to the floor. Help would be on its way, but it would take time. His eyes fixed, his hands gripped the steering wheel until his knuckles showed white, he barely slowed at the driveway, taking the turn on two wheels.

A dense dust cloud trailed after him all the way up to the house. Flames licked the walls of the barn as they reached for the roof. There was an eerie quiet as he threw open the barn door. The inside was untouched, but dense smoke was rolling down the passageway between the stalls. He knew that he had only moments before the fire would reach the packed hayloft. Virgil had seen barn fires when that happened and he knew what to expect. The intense heat, suddenly fed by all that hay, would blow the barn apart. Anyone or anything inside would become just another combustible.

He threw open the stall doors as he made his way toward the far end of the barn on the outside chance that there was anything within. A couple of chickens squawked as they ran toward the open barn door. The closer he got to the last stalls, the denser the smoke was. It started to gag him and his eyes started to water. He heard the movement in the last stall, followed by a nervous nicker. He couldn't see them through the smoke, but he knew they were there. He knew there was no way he could get the mare and the foal back the way he had come. Before opening the stall, he felt along the wall until he found the double door at the back of the barn. Virgil gave a tremendous push and the doors swung open.

Billowing smoke poured out through the opening as sunlight threaded its way in. He turned to go back to the stall. He threw open the stall door and saw the mare huddled in the back corner with the foal. Grabbing a saddle blanket off a nearby peg, he moved toward her, relieved to see she had her halter on. When he reached her, he threw the blanket over her head, shielding her eyes. Then he grabbed the throatlatch and started to move forward. At first she resisted, then took a few hesitant steps. She called to the foal and it came alongside.

She moved forward more deliberately, following Virgil's lead through the stall door. Virgil became aware of the sudden intense buildup in heat. The mare called again to the foal, then again, even louder. Finally, the foal nickered in response. Virgil was having a hard time controlling her. She was throwing her head left to right and up and down. The blanket slipped from his grasp and off her head and fell to the ground. She let out a scream and reared. Virgil held on and actually felt his feet leave the ground. A shaft of light momentarily showed through the smoke and she bolted. This time Virgil lost his grip and fell.

He saw her plunge through the opening toward the light, the foal at her heels.

He crawled forward, pulling himself to his feet as he ran. He didn't look back, running as fast as he could. The heat was searing his back, but he still ran. Then he heard what he knew he would hear, an explosion of everything inside the barn within the fire's reach. The force of it knocked him to the ground, but didn't stop him. He scrambled to his feet and ran again without looking back. He didn't stop until he reached the creek that ran alongside the far corner of one of the barns. He jumped in and heard the hiss as the water met what was his burning uniform. The sudden relief was followed by a searing pain.

He lay in the shallow water. In the distance, he thought he heard a siren and the wail of a fire engine.

"Over here. Over here."

He didn't respond to the sound of Jimmy's voice. It was too painful to move.

"We'll get you outta there, Sheriff. Just hang on."

"I think we should turn him over to put him on the carrier. Looks like the worst burns are on his back."

Virgil didn't recognize the other voice. He turned his head. Even that hurt. He saw Jimmy and two other men, one in medical white, the other in firefighter gear. Jimmy and the firefighter moved, one to his head and shoulders, the other to his feet.

"Okay," he heard the third man say. "On the count of three. One, two, three, lift. Oh, yeah, it's his back, most of his uniform is in the creek. Let me unstrap his gun belt before you lay him down."

Virgil could barely moan through the pain while tears stung his cheeks.

"I'll give him something for the pain."

Those were the last words Virgil heard before he slipped into unconsciousness.

When he opened his eyes, he didn't know where he was, until he heard one of the nurses who had taken care of him when he had had his operation.

"Just can't get enough of this place, can you? Must be my animal magnetism that keeps drawing you back."

Virgil tried to respond, but the words wouldn't come. He realized he was lying on his stomach when he could only see the lower part of her uniform as she stood next to his bed. "Got some pretty nice burns on your back. Kinda looks like that rare steak my husband likes."

"Thanks for the visual," Virgil finally managed.

"Could've been a lot worse. Skin on the back is tougher than skin on the face. Better you took the blast there. Only damage to that good-looking face is you left your eyebrows and eyelashes in that creek and you won't be needing a haircut for a while. That Brazilian wax job took care of any hair on your back, but that will come back, too."

Virgil felt the coolness as she applied some soothing gel to his back. He thought he saw a small brush in her hand as she continued the application. After she finished, he saw her inject something into the IV he was hooked up to and heard her say something about a nice long sleep as he closed his eyes.

When he opened them next, his back was getting another application from a different nurse.

"What time is it?" His voice sounded strange to his own ears.

"A little after two, Sheriff." It was a male voice.

"Two . . ." He said in the same strange voice.

"Two on Wednesday. You lost a day. That's why you're a little confused."

"My voice . . . ?"

"That's from the smoke you inhaled. The inhalation therapist will be in later. She'll help you with that, but you might be hoarse for a day or two."

"But today is Wednesday."

"All day, Virgil, and you have nothing to do but rest."

The words were as soft as the gel on his back. He smelled her before he saw her. She reached down to him and her lips felt soft on his cheek. The odor of a ripe tangerine just peeled washed over him and obliterated the burnt smell which had persistently lingered.

"How . . ." he said to her. "How . . ."

"Everything is fine. One of the barns is a total loss, but the animals are all safe. Everyone is amazed that you were able to do what you did and escape with only second-degree burns."

That's when Jimmy came into the room.

"Hey, Sheriff." He hesitated before coming to the bed. "I can come back later."

"No, I have to go," she said. "Business as usual."

She bent down and gave Virgil another soft nuzzle. Then she was gone.

"Real nice lady," Jimmy said as he came near the bed. "I see her at the Black Bull all the time. She sure has done a job on that place. Good food, line dancing, and the bull."

"Wish she could have stayed."

"Well, she was here quite a while yesterday. Then here again today. She needs a break."

"I didn't know."

"You've kind of been in Happy Valley. They gave you some serious stuff. Doc says burns are about the worst pain."

"Yes, I remember after the fire, in the water. Did they figure out how it started?"

"Not for sure, but there was one thing practically everyone agreed on."

"What was that?"

"That fire was no accident."

35

The nurse had come in shortly before he got his dinner tray and had moved him in the bed, first on one side then the other. Shortly after she left, a therapist came in and gave him a couple of exercises to do to keep the skin on his back from tightening as it healed, explaining that the discomfort would continue for a while, akin to the kind of feeling people get after a really bad sunburn.

Virgil immediately related to a time in his youth when he had been mowing a field and running the hay through a Haybine for conditioning before baling. He had taken off his sweat-soaked shirt and let the soft breezes dry his body. It didn't seem long and the air currents over his bare skin felt good, but the Southwestern sun was not to be ignored even in the late afternoon. That night and for the next couple of days, he paid the price.

Evening shadows drifted into the room. Another application of the soothing gel had lulled him into a slight drowse. He lay immobile and pain free, enjoying the moment, his eyes barely open. A slight movement caused them to widen. A pair of finely tooled leather boots stood at the side of his bed. Their owner remained unknown, because he didn't want to raise his head yet.

"Sorry about this, Virgil. But I had to come and tell you I had no part in this. I'm no barn-burner. Maybe that's hard for you to believe after our last conversation, but it's the honest-to-God truth. And I'll do anything to convince you. I meant it when I said I always thought of you as a friend. I never saw Rusty happier than when she was with you, and that was enough for me."

"Why didn't you tell me about the baby, Mike?"

There was a long pause. Micah reached over and grabbed the wooden arm of a cushioned chair and pulled it closer, then sat in it and bent over so that Virgil could see him without having to raise his head.

"I guess you'd have to go back some twenty years and step into my shoes to understand, but I'm sorry I didn't. I've regretted it ever since. Guess I was too vulnerable, too easy to manipulate. Maybe just weak. You weren't around. You were away at school. Everything seemed to come apart at once. Rusty . . . the baby, and then my wife. Hell, Virgil, I'm not that much older than you. Five, six years. I had Caleb, and a mentally unstable wife who I finally had to commit to keep her from doing harm to herself or someone else."

His voice trailed off. Virgil could see the pain come into his face, hear it in his voice.

"I could have helped," Virgil said. "I would have left school. I would have come home if I'd known."

Micah shook his head. "My mother wouldn't let me call.

That thing, with your father. That's why when you and Rusty happened, she was so set against it. It was like she somehow felt betrayed. He rejected her, then Rusty rejected her for you. Then when Caleb came home from Nam in a box . . . You can't imagine what it was like. Dad didn't take two sober breaths for the next ten years. She despised his weakness. I was just trying to keep everything afloat. Because Caleb didn't come home to take over, it was left to me. But until Dad died, I had no real authority and it was only after he died that I realized what bad shape we were in. So that's when I shook hands with the devil. Virgil, we were close to losing everything. The banks wouldn't look at us. We were mortgaged to the hilt. Then there were those bad cattle years. You remember."

Virgil nodded.

"Hell, we weren't even breaking even on them and the pecans. Couple of bad years there and selling wholesale was killing us. That's when I thought if we could absorb some of the factors of production, process and retail them ourselves. I got the idea of processing them across the border, then distributing them from the Redbud facility. They'd just built the interchange there. We'd owned that parcel of land for years, and it was ideal for distribution. A facility there would be perfect. But all of this needed money."

Virgil shifted a little in the bed so he could see Micah more fully. "Could you get me a glass of water?"

"Sure."

Micah got to his feet, quickly walked around the bed, got the pitcher off the nightstand, poured a glassful, then returned to Virgil.

"Here, let me help you."

He steadied Virgil by holding his upper arm so Virgil could

raise his head off the pillow. Then he held the glass to Virgil's lips. Virgil almost drained the glass in one swallow.

"Thanks."

Micah laid him gently back on the pillow and returned the glass to the table.

"So let me guess the rest of the story," Virgil said. "Wade hooked you up with some people who bankrolled you. You were able to build the facility at Redbud and the processing plant outside of Juárez. The only hitch was it wasn't strictly a cash deal."

"I thought it was." Micah looked toward the window, which showed the last of the daylight. "I figured because Wade was getting the exclusive contract for all the service work, he set this up as much for him as for us. He was a go-between for the financing, but we would both benefit."

"When did you find out it was more than that?"

"Not until Buddy. I was making regular quarterly payments on the borrowed money. The investment paid off and I was seeing daylight at the end of the tunnel. Then . . ."

"You mean, you never knew until Buddy told you."

"I wasn't sure. I suspected, but . . . Maybe I didn't want to know. Virgil, it was a slippery slope. Wade became more of a factor as time went on. The business grew, so did he. Within a couple of years we were out of the hole. The pressure was gone, we were doing more business and growing even faster than I thought possible. My mother actually backed off. But Buddy wasn't the one. He never told me."

"But that night at the Black Bull . . . the night Buddy went missing . . . You went there. You were there to see him."

Micah sat up in his chair. "How did you know I was there?"

"The technology, Micah. The video of the parking lot."

"But I never went into the lot. He came out to me, and it wasn't Buddy, it was Wade. But how?"

"It's not really important," Virgil said. "But it was the belt buckle. That's how I knew it was you. A lot of guys, ranch hands, guys doing the circuit like you used to, and the wannabes wear big buckles, but damn few of them wear an extra-big commemorative of a PR championship like you. That thing caught the light from the parking lot like a diamond. I knew it was you and I knew you were there. It was actually your mother that reminded me of the belt and your championship win."

"The first recognition from her and it comes from the grave." Micah put his hand to his eyes as if he was trying to wipe away a tear. "You know, Virgil, you're a lot better at your job than people give you credit for, but I tell you, it wasn't Buddy I was there to see. It was Wade. I wanted to tell him that we had gotten into the black enough that I wanted to pay off the debt."

"How did he take the news?"

"Not like I expected. He said the people he had the association with wanted to continue the relationship. When Buddy went missing and then you found him in the stock tank, he told me to take it for a warning. He said Buddy had wanted to quit the relationship, too. That's when I knew that there was something else going on with the business. But honestly, Virgil, I didn't know what it was. I still don't. I tried to figure out what was going on when my mother said something a few days later about not recognizing some of the pickers. I started checking."

"And . . ."

"The foreman told me someone leaned on him. I knew

these guys weren't there for the upcoming harvest as soon as I saw them."

"They still at Hayward Ranch?"

"Yeah. They're still there, watching my every move. I was hoping I could work out something with these people, but then when I heard what happened to those young people and then your barn, I knew I had to come and see you and tell you everything. You've got to believe me, Virgil. I never meant for any of this to happen. I was always just trying to do the right thing for my family. You have to believe me."

Virgil didn't say anything at first. He just looked directly at Micah. Finally, he nodded his head.

They sat in silence for a minute, then Micah got to his feet.

"I'm glad you came," Virgil said.

"Me, too."

Virgil extended his left arm and Micah took his hand.

"I'll take it from here, Mike. Soon as I get out of here. You'll hear from me. As far as those non-pickers are concerned, just go on as usual. I don't want to give them a hint that anything is different."

"Okay, Virgil. Whatever you say." He looked away, toward the window. "Looks like we're losing the light."

Virgil followed his gaze. There was no light coming into the room. The sky was a dark shade of purple, which they both knew was the last gasp of the departing sun.

"Yeah," Virgil said. "It's getting late in the day."

"In more ways than one. You know, life never seems to turn out like you expected it would."

"No. It never does. That's what makes it interesting."

"I guess. Take care, Virgil. And when you get out of here, watch your back."

He looked at Virgil lying on his stomach and gave a little smile.

"No pun intended." Then he left the room.

Virgil lay in the quiet, still looking out the window until the last hint of purple had been swallowed by the night.

A new night nurse came into the room. "Well, it's time for us to get ready for bed."

"If you say so, but if we're going to sleep together, I'd like to know your name."

36

The burnt smell hung heavy in the air, even five days after the fire. The visual was even worse. All that was left of the two barns were a couple of mainframe beams charred black by the fire. Now they stood as a skeletal reminder of what was. Cesar had strung wire to secure the field that had previously been closed off by the barn walls. Amidst the wreckage were a thousand bales of hay that, along with the labor that had made them, were now wasted.

"Not a pretty picture." Cesar had joined Virgil as he stood looking over the wreckage. "Insurance man was here a couple of days ago. Says he'll have a check cut by the end of the week. Can't prove what started it, but says you're covered. He said maybe spontaneous combustion. I didn't say anything back. He was a nice young feller, probably thought I'd never heard the term before. I didn't point out that if that was the case the fire would've come from the top down, not the bottom up. No sense confusing the issue."

Virgil didn't answer.

"I called Rosario," Cesar went on. "He says he'll have it cleaned up in a couple of days now that the insurance man has been here. The cleanup is covered also."

Cesar saw Virgil's shoulders sag as he looked over the scene.

"Coulda been worse. Coulda been a lot worse."

"I know, I know. I see you ran wire to close up the hole."

"Just temporary. I know you don't like it, but it's quick and does the job."

"Okay," Virgil said, touching the pencil-thin scar that ran along his jawbone. He turned and headed toward the house. He was surprised at how tired he was. When he stepped into the kitchen, the stored afternoon heat hit him like a wave. He had told Cesar to stay in the house since he had lost his two rooms in the barn, but the dishes in the sink from his last meal and the blast of hot air told him that no one had been inside since the fire. He opened a couple of windows to let the heat escape, immediately feeling the pull of his skin as he did so. Then he headed upstairs. As soon as he got into the bedroom he hit the AC. By the time he came out of the bathroom, the room had cooled. He stood naked with his back to the air conditioner for a couple of minutes, letting the fan finish the drying process from the shower he'd just taken. A soft towel would feel like sandpaper on his slowly healing skin, while the blow from the AC was like a soothing caress. Then he lay down on the bed with the sheet covering him to his waist. He slept like a dead man for the next six hours.

He was not sure whether he was asleep or in that in-between world where reality and unconscious meet, or if he was just in the grip of an erotic dream. He felt the touch of a hand smoothing the gel. It moved across his shoulders and the back of his neck so lightly, it was almost a whisper. Then, it traced his spine up and down on either side, until his new skin was covered. His eyes were half open, staring into the dark, when he felt her lips brush his ear.

"I let myself in after I spoke to Cesar. I saw the lotion on your nightstand."

"I'm really glad you did. I didn't really want to ask Cesar to put it on my back. He doesn't quite have your touch. What time is it?"

"A little after nine."

"How come you're not at the Black Bull?"

"Things were quiet after dinner so I figured I could steal a little time. Besides, I wanted to practice my massage technique. It might come in handy if I ever need a part-time job."

"If you ever need a reference . . . On the other hand, why don't I just hire you as your only client?"

"Well, you haven't experienced all I have to offer."

"You say you have some time now. I'm ready for a complete treatment."

Virgil slid over in the bed and Ruby slipped in next to him.

"Are you sure you're up for this?"

"Good choice of words. One part of me is. We'll just have to chance the rest. I have a feeling the destination is going to be worth the journey, even if a little discomfort is involved."

Virgil reached out and drew her close.

When he woke the next morning, she was gone. He went downstairs and stood on the porch, trying to visualize what he would do after the mess he was looking at got cleaned up, and what he would replace it with, when he heard the phone. He got it on the third ring.

"Virgil, how are you? I heard . . ."

"I'm fine, Kyle. Really. Just a little tender."

"I can imagine. Listen, I knew you'd want to hear this. We got that semi back from Juárez. I double-checked the ID numbers you gave me, because it seems like a pretty quick turnaround. It's only about a week since it crossed the river. We pulled it out and are getting ready to check it, but you know, as I told you when we went over it last week, the dogs never got a hit."

"I got a feeling they're going to come up just as empty today," Virgil said. "I think we might be dealing with something different here, something they're not trained to pick up."

"What are you saying, Virgil?"

"Listen, Kyle. I hate to ask, but I think you've got to empty that trailer."

There was a moment of silence.

"Are you serious, Virgil?"

"I am, Kyle."

"That box is loaded. I mean, we are talking about a big job here. If we come up empty, there will be hell to pay."

"I get that. I understand, but there is a false wall at the back of that trailer. I told you that. It's got to be concealing something. Something worth killing people over."

"A few inches," Kyle said. "You want me to have that whole trailer unloaded for a couple of inches? Virgil, that's crazy. That so-called false wall might just be a structural reinforcement and have nothing to do with contraband. Remember, the dogs got nothing. What could possibly be hidden in that small a space?"

"I know it sounds crazy, but trust me on this. Three people have gotten killed, my barns are in ashes, and it all in some way is connected to that trailer. It might sound crazy, like you said, but I'm sure there's something worth killing people over in back of that wall."

"Okay, Virgil, you got it. Where will you be later? This is going to take some time."

"I should be in the office. If I have to leave, Rosie can patch you through."

"Lately you've been gone more than you're here," Rosie said.

"Thanks, good to see you, too. I keep hitting these little snags. Dead bodies, barns burning down . . . But I know you're here, so I don't worry."

"With that vote of confidence, you earned a cup of coffee."

Virgil walked to his desk, sat down, and gingerly leaned back in his chair.

"Guess you gotta look on the bright side," she said. "Those burns a little lower, you'd be drinking this coffee standing up."

"Thanks for the coffee and the perspective," he said as he took the coffee from Rosie's outstretched hand. Over the course of the next couple of hours, he looked over and signed some purchase orders, went online to catch up with county events, and generally got up to speed.

A little after two, Jimmy showed up with a bruise under his left eye.

"Somebody forgot to duck," Rosie said to him.

"No. The bull got me."

"I don't believe it. You actually got on that thing."

"Rode him on my second try."

"Great line for your headstone. I'll try to remember it."

Virgil sat back, happy to see Rosie working on a new target.

"You still sparking that Jessup girl?" she said.

"How do you know about that?"

"Well, if you're trying to keep it a secret I wouldn't be hanging out in the Black Bull. Was she impressed with your riding ability?"

"She said I was nuts. When I tripped getting off and hit that chair, she said she knew that bull would get me one way or the other."

"That girl's smarter than I thought. I dated her uncle back in the day. He was a caution. A lot of fun, but he didn't have enough sense to turn on a light in the dark."

"I bet he found you," Virgil said, unable to resist, "even without the light."

"Let's not get personal unless you're ready to talk about that lady that runs that place."

"I told the sheriff," Jimmy said, "she's putting that place on the map. We even met a couple there that came over from way on the other side of Las Cruces. Yessir, I sure wish old Bob could see it now."

"Who's old Bob?" Rosie asked.

"He was the feller who started doing the work to bring it back, till that beam knocked the sense out of him. Didn't you know him?"

"Not really," Rosie said. "I knew someone was trying to reconstruct the place. My granddaddy told me a lot of history was connected with that old building. Used to be a stage stop. Seemed like that guy was working on it forever."

"That's 'cause he was doing it all himself. Wanted it to be exact. He was doing it, up until the accident. He lived there another two years. My mother used to take care of him till Mr. Talbot put him in the home. I used to help her with him sometimes. Mr. Talbot said it didn't look like he was ever going to get any better, so he put him in the home. They were distantly related and since he didn't have anybody . . . Well, I guess he figured that was best."

Virgil was still working on the last of his paperwork when Rosie looked over at him.

"What's the matter?" she said. "You look like Dave when he hands me the crossword because he can't go any further."

Before Virgil could reply, the phones on both their desks started ringing.

"You going to take that?"

Virgil said nothing.

"Virgil?"

Still nothing.

"Virgil!" She started to reach for her phone when Virgil finally put down his paperwork and picked up his phone.

"How did you know, Virgil?"

"I didn't for sure, Kyle. I had to have you prove me right or wrong."

"Do you know what we found?"

"I got an idea it's something that had to be kept on ice."

"You got that right, but it's a first for us. I'm guessing you want to move on this right away."

"Does that work for you?"

"Absolutely. My next call is to bring the people in Juárez up to speed so we can coordinate our moves. I'll see you in a couple of hours. Other federal agencies will be involved."

"I figured as much. See you later."

"Virgil, this was good police work."

"Well, we've still got a ways to go."

"What's up, Sheriff?"

Virgil had gotten to his feet as he finished his conversation with Kyle Harrison.

"Rosie, get ahold of Dave and Alex and get both of them up here from Redbud. This is going to be a busy day. Jimmy, you're coming with me out to Hayward Ranch."

Virgil was heading for the door as he spoke. Ten minutes later, he and Jimmy were flying down the road in the direction of the ranch.

"Jimmy, there's a good chance I'll be leaving you there, and I'll tell Dave. There's at least two felons there. I want you to bring them in, but I want you to wait for the backup from Redbud. Don't take any chances. These guys are hard cases. You make a mistake, you are not going to get a second chance. And if you have to use your sidearm, don't hesitate, because they won't. I'll make sure Micah Hayward is there to identify your targets for you."

Virgil could see the concern on Jimmy's face.

"Jimmy, I know you're ready for this. That's why you're here and why I'm leaving you in charge."

"Where are you going, Sheriff?"

"I'm going to see a man about an ice cream truck."

37

Jimmy was anxious. There was no denying it. But more than that he was aware of a sea change in Virgil. He had seen him in all kinds of confrontations, from breaking up barroom brawls, stepping in the middle of outrageous domestic situations, and getting loaded guns away from felons who wouldn't hesitate to use them. Yet there was a difference here. There was a darkness that had come into Virgil's eyes that he had not seen before.

"Why are we both going to Hayward Ranch, Sheriff? I could have taken my car and waited there for Dave and his partner. I mean, if you have to be somewhere else . . ."

Jimmy felt a little uncomfortable questioning Virgil. Virgil looked back at him in a way that did little to relieve his discomfort.

"I need to ask Micah Hayward something," Virgil said.

Then he stopped talking. They rode the rest of the way in silence. When they turned into the driveway that led to the house, before they passed the second row of pecan trees, Virgil veered to the left so they were riding on the ground, between two of the rows.

"Gets a little rough," Virgil said, "but it will get us to the house unseen."

Jimmy saw that the trees were heavy with pecans, but he knew it would be another few weeks before they would begin the harvest. At the end of the long row, Virgil turned right onto a slightly wider tractor road which started a vertical climb toward the house. A few minutes later, they came out of the orchard on the side of the house. He stopped the car and turned off the engine.

"Real quiet now. We're going around back."

They closed the doors quietly. Then Virgil made his way around the side of the house to the back patio, with Jimmy following. The patio ran the entire length of the rear of the house and offered an astounding view, an endless vision of pecan trees covering the rolling hills. The patio was divided into two sections, with the far end enclosed by screens while the open half nearest them surrounded a large free-form inground swimming pool with a waterfall in a far corner. The perimeter of the entire area was a border of vivid, lush flowering trees and bushes.

"Wow!" Jimmy said, unable to help himself.

"Can I help you?"

The girl rose from a chaise facing away from them. She was wearing a two-piece dark blue bathing suit, randomly covered with small white flowers. Her rust-red hair fell to her shoulders as she stood.

"Yes," Virgil said. "I need to speak to Micah."

"I'll see if he's inside. Do you want to come with me?"

"No, we'll wait here. Just tell him the sheriff wants to see him."

"I know who you are," she said, looking directly at Virgil.

"Wow!" Jimmy said again, as Virginia walked away. "This place is out of sight. And that girl . . ."

"You've been here before."

"Only from the front of the house. On the driveway."

Virgil thought back to his first time. Here in this house, with a different girl. Long before the pool and the patio were put in, sitting with Rusty at the end of a long trail ride in this very same spot. The horses breathing a little harder while they watched the slanting light creeping over the hills.

"Virgil." Micah's voice brought him back.

He introduced Jimmy to Micah and told him of his plan, emphasizing that nothing would happen until Dave and Alex got there from Redbud.

"This thing has more than a few moving parts. Some federal officers will be in the area shortly. If everything happens in sync, it will all be over tonight. Are they on the ranch now?"

"Yes. I saw two of them earlier, but a third one has recently joined them. I'm sure the third one is around. I'll point them out to your deputies and any agents with them."

"Good. Then I want you to get out of the way. I'm hoping they can be taken by surprise, but I don't want any innocents in the line of fire. Keep Virginia in the house."

"Should we leave?"

"No, because if you do, they might also. I want to get these guys. If there's going to be any kind of confrontation, I'd rather it be here than in a populated area. Get in touch with the rest of the ranch crew. Send them off to areas on the ranch, ostensibly for work-related jobs so there are as few people around as possible."

"I'll call down to the foreman as soon as I can to take care of that. You're not going to be here, Virgil?"

"No. Like I said, this thing has other moving parts. I'll probably get back here later. In any event, I'll be in constant contact with my guys or the other agents. Do these guys leave the ranch often?"

"Not often. I'm pretty sure I'm their priority, especially since Buddy Hinton. The only place I've seen them off the ranch, before they started focusing on me, was at the Black Bull."

"That brings me to another question. That night that you met Wade, did he refuse your offer to pay back the money?"

"No. It wasn't his money. He was only a go-between. He had to check with the people who put up the money."

"How did he do that? I mean, how long did that take? To get an answer?"

"I don't think I understand. What do you mean?"

"It was the night Buddy went missing. You met Wade at the Black Bull. You told him you could pay everything back, pay off the loan because business had gotten so much better than you expected . . . Right? Well, when did you find out you couldn't get out of your deal with the devil?"

"That night. A short time later."

"Did Wade call someone? How did he find out? Think, Micah. How exactly did that play out?"

"I don't know. I mean he left us, me and Buddy. I was standing out there on the road. He stopped by the truck, said something to Buddy, who stayed in the truck, then he went inside, into the Black Bull. He was in there awhile, maybe twenty, twenty-five minutes, then he came back out. He told me it wasn't over. I remember his exact words. 'They'll tell you when you're done.'"

"Okay," Virgil said.

Jimmy saw Virgil's jaw tighten. He saw that same darkness come into the man's eyes.

Wade was seated at his desk, visible through the large glass window that looked out on the showroom. Virgil didn't knock. He blew right past the salespeople in the showroom like they were made of stone.

"You sleeping good these nights, are you, Wade?"

Wade looked up from the papers on his desk.

"Why shouldn't I?"

"Well, I was thinking . . . Since you pretty much built this place on the dead body of your so-called best friend, that maybe that'd gnaw at you. Just a little. I mean, what does that feel like?"

Wade rose to his feet, his face flushed, his knuckles whitening as they gripped the arms of the chair he'd been sitting in.

"You son of a bitch half-breed. Who the hell do you think you are?"

"I'm the son of a bitch half-breed who's going to take you out of here in handcuffs. And enjoy every minute of it."

"Fuck you, Virgil."

Wade pulled out the drawer of his desk. Virgil saw the shine of metal come into his hand as he leaped across. A roar exploded in his ears. He felt blood streaming down his left cheek. Everything on the desk flew in all directions. They both crashed into the wall behind Wade's desk. Framed pictures fell to the floor, their glass shattering. They fought for the gun. Virgil broke two of Wade's fingers and the gun fell from his grasp, sliding out of reach. Virgil bashed Wade's head against the wall, then started to pull himself to his feet by gripping the edge of his desk. Wade tried to rise with him, but Virgil punched him in the mouth with such force that his knuckles were ripped open from the contact with Wade's teeth.

Virgil stood up. He saw the audience of salespeople looking through the gaping hole in the huge window which had exploded as Wade's bullet went through. Beyond them, he could see Kyle Harrison and a couple of agents running into the dealership.

"You could have waited, Virgil."

Virgil sucked in a couple of long-overdue breaths as he wiped the blood dripping down his cheek with his sleeve. He looked at the swirl of debris, then at Wade being picked up and handcuffed by two other agents. Then at Kyle.

"I know," Virgil said, "but I didn't want it to be clean. I owed Buddy and those two kids that much, at least."

Virgil followed Wade as he was led out of the building. While he stood outside, Kyle came over with a first aid kit.

"You're damned lucky. An inch to the left and you would have lost half your face. As it is, you'll probably end up with a crease to match the one on the other cheek. By the way, I just checked with your deputy. Sounds like a good guy. They got those three thugs, so we're just about done."

Virgil winced as an astringent was lightly dabbed over his wound.

"This will tighten the skin and slow the bleeding. Before you head home tonight, stop at the ER in Hayward."

Virgil nodded. Then he left.

It was a little after six when he pulled into the parking lot of the Black Bull. The gravel in the lot sounded loud as it crunched beneath his feet. The soreness in his body, the ache in his head, they were all displaced by something else crowding his mind. He was only dimly aware of anything else now. The thud of his feet on the steps leading up to the porch, the noises that engulfed him as he went through the door. The people lined up at the bar, those dining at the tables in the restaurant areas, the servers bustling back and forth . . . It was all a tableau, but he was not part of it. He was detached. Invisible.

"Hello, Sheriff," a waitress said. "Can I help you?"

He saw her reaction when she looked at his face. That's all the answer the woman needed, as she nodded in the direction of the stairs. "She's in the office."

He climbed the stairs, feeling a burden that grew heavier and heavier, until at last he reached the landing and stood before the office door. She was sitting at her desk. Even in the midst of her work, she was desirable. Without a word, he sat heavily into the chair opposite her. She looked up at that exact moment.

"You look like you've had a really rough day."

"Yeah, and I don't think it's going to get any easier."

He laid his hat on the corner of her desk. She drew in a deep breath as she saw the left side of his face.

"What happened to you?"

"Wade Travis tried to shoot most of it off, but I spoiled his aim. The ER people at Hayward Memorial put it back together with a bunch of staples. They said it won't be as noticeable when it heals as this other scar from the barbed wire fence."

"I always wondered about that, but never asked."

"You could have. A pissed-off bull threw me headfirst into some barb I'd just strung when I was about fourteen. I've hated wire ever since. But then, I guess we never spent a lot of time talking about our past. If it even matters . . ."

Ruby pushed back a little from the desk. "What do you mean, if it even matters?"

Virgil crossed his leg, took his Stetson off the desk, and laid it on his knee.

"The other night when you came by," he said, "I had just a moment when I wondered if what was happening was real or part of a dream. Then on the way here I remembered something Micah Hayward said to me, about life never turning out like you expected. I realized he was right. It wasn't real, was it . . . this thing between you and me."

"What are you talking about, Virgil?"

"You don't have to say anything else. I think I pretty much got it figured out."

"Where . . . When . . ." Her voice was barely a whisper.

"When? Is that what you're asking? Guess I'm not the brightest bulb in the pack, but all along there was a constant itch in the back of my mind. So now let's start with Wade Travis, who I figured as the front man for some kind of south-of-the-border drug cartel. Until I came to find out it wasn't drugs at all. It took a while for me to wrap my head around that notion, until everything finally came together. But still, that was all I had. Wade Travis."

Virgil shook his head, uncrossed his legs, winced a little, then set his hat in his lap while he fingered the brim.

"I guess it all began to come together when Jimmy happened to mention old Bob and that beam that knocked him senseless, and how he put most of this place together before you came along. Then all of the pieces of the puzzle started to fit. You know how it is. You got a bunch of little parts, but you need that one thing to see how everything is related. How it all fits together. Well, Jimmy did that for me when he reminded me about how old Bob was distantly related to the Talbots. How he had no close kin and was sitting in some nursing home somewhere, trying to figure out how he got there. That got me thinking. Again, you know how it goes. One thought leads to another. Even though I didn't want to go down that road."

Virgil stopped fingering the brim of his hat, once again crossed his legs, and perched the Stetson on his knee.

"You don't have to go there, Virgil."

He looked at her. She was as beautiful as ever, and he could reach across and touch her like he had so many times. Smell her sweet smell. Feel her soft skin.

"Yeah, I've got to," he said. "For both of us. When something dies, you can't move forward until you bury it. I came to realize that whoever gave Micah the money to build that factory was going to keep an eye on that investment. That wasn't Wade. I knew that. It all came together when Micah told me the night he tried to end his connection, Wade went into the Black Bull and came back later with the refusal. The Black Bull. The centerpiece of this whole puzzle. Everything came together. Old Bob, who was nobody's father, Cesar telling me that your Mex was more fluent than your English. I heard it myself when you talked to the workers in the kitchen, but denied what my own ears heard."

He stopped. Their eyes locked.

"It was you," he said.

"You don't understand, Virgil. You don't understand."

He shook his head, then put his hat on the edge of the desk and stood up. He walked around the edge of her desk, reached down, and pulled Ruby to her feet. He could feel her stiffen in his grasp. The ache to crush his lips into hers was overwhelming. He took a step back, but still held her.

"You're right. I don't understand. Probably never will. Are you two different people? I mean, you oversaw, hell, maybe even okayed murder, traded in body parts. What kind of a person does that?"

Ruby wrenched herself out of his hold. She stepped back to the opposite end of the desk.

"Two people. Yes, I guess that could describe me. You want to know? I'll tell you. My mother was a picker coming across the river with all the others. She ended up outside of Las Cruces in the arms of a rancher's son who kicked her to the curb when she became pregnant. I was born there. She had no support, no way of making it on her own with me, so she went back. An uncle took her in, but she was broken. Broken at seventeen. Her dreams of a better life were shattered. Before I was five, she was dead of an overdose, and my uncle did the best he could with me. He saw that I got an education, but as I grew I came to realize I wasn't like the other kids. My mixed race made me an object of contempt for some people. Racism doesn't stop at the river, you know. But for other people it made me stand out. When he died, I got caught up in the life. I felt desired. Special. I didn't realize I was looked on as just a commodity. When I finally did . . . Well, this was the only way out. They needed somebody over here, and I had something they could use. I was an American by birth and looked more like a gringo. I was intelligent and educated. They even had an English tutor for me. They told me they would set me up here. So I became a kind of broker between them and what Wade did. They said they would even let me stay here and eventually buy the Black Bull. That was probably all lies, but I wanted to believe it."

"Wait, go back. What Wade did? He was part of a system

that harvested kidneys. Body parts that were sold to the highest bidder."

"When was the last time you walked across the bridge into Juárez, Virgil? It's the third world over there. In some parts worse. These people that gave up a kidney got more for that than they'd earn in a year. So don't get moralistic on me."

"That may be, but where does the morality come in when it comes to killing? Buddy Hinton and the two young kids who came here, just like your mother . . . They didn't deserve to end up like they did. They had dreams, too. You sacrificed their lives for yours. Which you didn't have to do. You could have come to me, but then, like I said, we never were real to begin with."

Ruby slumped back down into her chair. When she tried to speak, nothing came. Virgil finally turned and walked away. Before he reached the door, he heard her.

"I had no choice. No choice."

He opened the door. Then he turned to face her.

"There's always a choice, Ruby. There are a couple of agents outside waiting for you. This is out of my hands now."

"Virgil, you have to believe me. This started off as one thing, me keeping tabs on you, but it became something else. We weren't a dream. I swear. It was real."

Her words lingered long after he left the office and walked to his car.

Jimmy was waiting for him when he got to Hayward Ranch. Virgil could see how juiced he was from his experience, and he related it blow by blow. When he started to tell him the third time, Virgil said it was time to get back to the office. Micah asked if he should go with them, but Virgil said it wasn't necessary. He would be questioned by federal agents to determine if there was any complicity on his part, or if any federal or state laws governing transit or money laundering had been broken.

As Virgil turned away, a voice stopped him in his tracks.

"Try to take better care of yourself, Sheriff. After all, we have a lot of catching up to do."

Virgil looked at the girl who had come to stand alongside Micah. He wanted to respond, but the words would not come to him. So he just nodded to Virginia, touched the brim of his Stetson, then got into his car.

They rode in silence for a while.

"Sorry, Sheriff," Jimmy finally said.

"No need to be."

"It's just that I've never felt like this before. This was the first real serious police work I've actually been in the middle of and I . . . I mean . . ."

"It's okay. It's the adrenaline flowing. It's something you can talk about, but until you actually experience it . . . Well, let's just say it's nothing you can prepare for."

"Do you get used to it?"

"Not really."

"Virgil, how did you know they weren't smuggling drugs?"

"Well, first, the dogs. They didn't pick up on anything and they hardly ever miss. But the clincher was the ice cream truck. I knew the semis weren't refrigerated, so whatever was in that small space had to be kept on ice. Maybe a combination of ice and dry ice. When it was unloaded, whatever it was had to go into refrigeration right away. Kinda sad to think that giving up a kidney can make the kind of money that tops drug running, but I guess if you're desperate enough you'll pay a lot for something that's going to give you a second chance at life."

The rest of the trip into Hayward was pretty quiet. Virgil pulled into the parking lot. All of the lights were on. When they stepped inside, Virgil saw that all the deputies, some of the agents, and Rosie were there. There was a shout of greeting and then they were engulfed. Kyle Harrison pulled Virgil aside.

"Good day's work, Virgil. Your instincts made it happen. I think you can expect some federal job offers coming your way. This was big. Real big."

Virgil watched for a few minutes as people intermingled, telling war stories to one another. He was trying to make his way to the door when Jimmy waylaid him with one more question.

"Virgil, that girl Virginia . . . When you walked in and she saw what had happened to your face, and she said you'd better take better care of yourself because you have a lot of catching up to do. What did she mean by that?"

A slight hint of a smile showed at the corners of Virgil's mouth.

"You know, Jimmy, I've been wondering the same thing."

The early-evening sky was already showing a few stars, blinking in and out between the thunderheads. There was a sliver of light on the horizon. A lone figure sat on the tail end of an old pickup, silhouetted against the barely visible landscape. An errant breeze brushed the hair that escaped the Stetson on his head. He shifted his weight and crossed his legs, inadvertently hitting the tailgate. The metallic clank was followed by the sound of an owl hooting.

"Glad to know you're still here. Kinda nice to know some things don't change."

Virgil looked down at a darkening world that had always been his anchor point. Some things *had* changed. The house still needed paint, the cottonwood that stood just off the front porch still caught the air currents, but there was a gaping space where the barns no longer stood. At least Virgil didn't have to look at the burnt and twisted wreckage. It had been nice to see the cleared footprint when he returned, and to begin to imagine what would go in that space. The horses were moving in the field that ran along the road. They were slow shadows until their rhythm was broken by the sprint and buck of one shadow a third the size of the rest, but with twice the energy. Virgil smiled when he heard the squeal of the foal as it ran.

Beyond the field, the ribbon of road was broken by the headlights of an oncoming car. Virgil had a sudden sinking feeling as the car slowed at the entrance to the ranch.

"No, not tonight," he said to the owl. "I don't need any more trouble."

Then he breathed a sigh of relief as the engine caught and the car continued down the road.